"You are under arrest,"

he muttered as he grabbed her elbow and frog-marched her ashore. "What's your name, woman?"

She tilted her chin defiantly, clamped her mouth shut and glowered at him as he dragged her alongside him.

"Where did you learn to fight like that?" he asked.

"In places I'm sure *you've* never been, General," she said impudently.

"Obviously. Where I come from ladies don't brawl. I have already determined—the hard way—that you're no lady. Furthermore, I'm not a general. I'm the commandant at Fort Reno. *Major* Rafe Hunter."

She twisted to flash him a smirk. "You're from back East, right? Uppity accent. Imperious demeanor. Wealth and pedigree, no doubt. Don't you have better things to do than sneak around, assaulting defenseless women?"

"Defenseless?" he hooted. "I can think of a dozen adjectives to describe you, but defenseless isn't on the list!"

* * *

Oklahoma Bride
Harlequin Historical #686—December 2003

Praise for Carol Finch

"Carol Finch is known for her lightning-fast,
roller-coaster-ride adventure romances that are
brimming over with a large cast of characters
and dozens of perilous escapades."
—*Romantic Times*

Praise for previous titles

Bounty Hunter's Bride
"Longtime Carol Finch fans…
will be more than satisfied."
—*Romantic Times*

Call of the White Wolf
"The wholesome goodness of the characters…
will touch your heart and soul."
—*Rendezvous*

"A love story that aims straight for the heart
and never misses."
—*Romantic Times*

CAROL FINCH

OKLAHOMA BRIDE

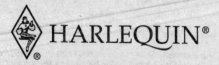

HARLEQUIN®

TORONTO • NEW YORK • LONDON
AMSTERDAM • PARIS • SYDNEY • HAMBURG
STOCKHOLM • ATHENS • TOKYO • MILAN • MADRID
PRAGUE • WARSAW • BUDAPEST • AUCKLAND

ISBN 0-373-29286-4

OKLAHOMA BRIDE

Please address questions and book requests to:
Harlequin Reader Service
U.S.: 3010 Walden Ave., P.O. Box 1325, Buffalo, NY 14269
Canadian: P.O. Box 609, Fort Erie, Ont. L2A 5X3

This book is dedicated to my husband, Ed,
and our children, Jill, Jon, Christie, Jeff, Kurt
and Shawnna. And to our grandchildren, Blake, Livia,
Brooklynn and Kennedy. Hugs and kisses!

A special thank you to my editor, Kim Nadelson.
It is a pleasure to be working with you!

Chapter One

Indian Territory
April, 1889

Rafe Hunter lifted his hand to bring his patrol of soldiers to a halt. His roan gelding, Sergeant, shifted impatiently beneath him, anxious to return to Fort Reno and the anticipated bucket of grain in his stall. Rafe panned the rolling plains that stood knee-high in waving grass then glanced toward the tree-lined creek that meandered southeast.

It was hard to imagine that in a couple of weeks this peaceful countryside would be the site of the nation's first Land Run. He had the unenviable task of guarding the western boundary to the two million acres of free land. It was his responsibility to insure would-be settlers didn't jump the gun and sneak in to stake their claims prematurely.

In addition, it was his duty to keep a watchful eye on the Cheyenne-Arapaho reservation near the garrison. The extra obligation of gathering up trespassers de-

manded long days and stretched his company of soldiers
to the limits.

When Rafe glanced over his shoulder, his longtime
friend—and second in command—lifted a questioning
brow. "A problem, Commander?"

"No, just taking time to appreciate the peaceful moment before all hell breaks loose," Rafe replied.

Micah Whitfield grinned wryly. "By the end of the
month, I wonder if any of us will recall what *peaceful*
feels like."

Rafe stared past Micah to focus on the five prisoners
the patrol had flushed from the nearby creeks. The Sooners—as the army referred to the illegal squatters—had
set up camp inside the territory, hoping to claim prime
property before thousands of anxious settlers could
make the Run. After three weeks of relentless patrolling,
Rafe and his company of men had a stockade crammed
full of Sooners who refused to follow the rules.

To Rafe Hunter a rule was a rule was a rule. Those
who broke the rules paid the consequences.

Rafe's attention shifted southeast when he picked up
a familiar scent in the evening breeze. Micah must have
recognized the scent, too, for he followed Rafe's searching gaze.

"There's more Sooners hunkering down out there,"
Micah said quietly.

Rafe scowled. "There's always more Sooners scut-
tling around out there. You capture five and there's another five waiting to take their place. At the rate we're
going we'll have to build another stockade to house
them all."

"If you want to make another sweep of the area to
determine who started the campfire I'll go with you,"
Micah volunteered.

"No, you take the prisoners back to the fort," Rafe requested. "I'll reconnoiter the area alone."

While Micah led the patrol back to the fort Rafe reined his reluctant mount toward the tree-choked creek. Although he was tired and hungry, he was determined to rout out another nest of Sooners. By damned, this unprecedented Land Run was going to be fair for all participants—at least if he had anything to say about it.

Rafe dismounted and left his gelding to graze. Employing the Indian-warfare skills Micah had taught him, Rafe moved silently along the creek, following the faint scent of smoke that had caught his attention earlier. To his surprise he spotted a young boy dressed in homespun clothes. Rafe scanned the shadows, expecting to see a crowd of Sooners migrating toward the small campfire. He frowned curiously, wondering if the boy's family had sent him into the territory alone to illegally stake a claim.

The smell of brewing coffee and a simmering pot of beans made Rafe's stomach growl. He had been on patrol all day, wolfing down trail rations for lunch and wearing calluses on his backside. And here was this scrawny kid, tucked discreetly beneath a copse of trees, preparing a tasty meal and lounging by the fire.

It just hit Rafe all wrong. He wasn't going to wait until daybreak to come swarming down with his army patrol. He was going to arrest this kid and haul him back to the fort tonight. Then he was going to seek out this boy's parents and chastise them for sending a child out into the wilderness alone.

He wondered if the kid's family expected a soldier to show leniency and look the other way. It wouldn't be the first time some scheming adult had tried that tactic. But it wasn't going to work with Rafe.

This kid was not going to spend the night, nestled up to the heat of the small campfire, Rafe decided. He was going to find himself wedged into the stockade with the other prisoners. That should teach the kid a lesson he wouldn't soon forget.

Filled with purpose, Rafe circled around the trees to sneak up on the young boy's blind side. ''You're trespassing, son, and you're under arrest,'' Rafe growled as he emerged from his hiding place.

The kid shrieked in surprise, bounded to his feet and took off through the trees like a cannonball. There was not the usual moment of paralyzed shock, just immediate flight. In addition, the kid was amazingly agile and swift of foot. He zigzagged around the trees like a gazelle.

Scowling at finding himself in a footrace with a kid half his size, Rafe took off at a dead run. ''Halt!'' he shouted authoritatively.

The boy didn't break stride, just whizzed through the trees and underbrush and never looked back.

Rafe tackled the kid before he could leap over the narrow creek, scramble up the steep incline and disappear in the thick underbrush. He and the boy landed with a splat, and Rafe hooked his arm around his captive's waist.

To his amazement the worming bundle of energy smacked him in the nose with an elbow, squirmed sideways and arched his back. Rafe found himself on the losing end of a mud-wrestling contest before he could blink. The kid was so slippery that he very nearly slithered away before Rafe could grab him by the scruff of his tattered jacket and yank him off balance.

With an enraged squawk the boy fell facedown in the

creek. Rafe bounded to his feet and hoisted the kid upright before he took on too much water and drowned.

To Rafe's amazement the waterlogged kid thrust back his leg—and hit Rafe squarely in the crotch. Rafe's knees buckled beneath him, but he kept a death grip on the squirming kid, determined not to let him escape and have to recapture him again.

"Hold still, damn it!" Rafe growled threateningly, then gave the kid a good shaking. "You—"

Rafe's voice dried up when the boy's scruffy cap fell off and dropped into the creek. A waterfall of flaming red hair tumbled to the kid's shoulders. "You're a girl!" Rafe croaked in disbelief.

He was still trying to digest *that* startling discovery when the female in question ducked her head and plowed into his midsection, causing the air in his lungs to rush out in a pained whoosh.

All those lectures—delivered by his grandfather and father—about treating a lady with the utmost respect and consideration flew right out of his head when the woman shoved him back into the creek and tried to use him as a doormat to make her escape.

In all his thirty-three years he had never encountered a female quite like this one. And *this* one was no lady, Rafe decided as he made a quick grab for her ankle. This was a scrappy, two-legged wildcat who knew how to fight dirty and didn't mind utilizing every trick in the book to make her getaway.

Scrappy female or not, she was an illegal Sooner and it was his job to evict her from the territory, even at the risk of personal injury—which he had already suffered at her hands. His groin was throbbing like a son of a bitch. His ribs were still tender after she had used her head like a battering ram. Plus, the claw marks she had left on his neck, during their most recent struggle for supremacy, were bleeding onto the collar of his mud-soaked shirt.

"Enough!" he roared as he concentrated all his energy on rolling on top of her and pinning her down in the water.

Rafe's conscience tried to deliver a scathing lecture when he straddled her bucking hips, clamped his hand over her face and held her head under water until she stopped resisting. But his noble conscience relented when she practically bit a chunk out of his hand.

Muttering, Rafe shifted the heel of his hand to her forehead and held her underwater until all the fight went out of her. When she sagged beneath him, as if she were about to succumb to drowning, he wondered if this was another of the many dirty tricks in her surprising repertoire. And sure enough, she began to struggle again, lashing out with her arms and fists, trying to do enough physical damage to unseat him.

Only when Rafe was reasonably certain that he had held her underwater so long that her lungs were about to burst did he grab a fistful of her hair and pull her into a sitting position beneath him. She exploded to the surface like a spouting whale, cocked her arm and tried to punch him in the nose.

Rafe hurriedly shifted sideways so the intended blow connected with air. He jerked her up beside him while she raked that mop of red hair from her eyes. As she struggled to get her bearings, Rafe fished into the pocket of his soggy jacket for a length of rope to shackle her wrists. Thankfully, he was able to restrain her before she used those deadly claws on him again.

"You are under arrest," he muttered as he grabbed

her elbow and frog-marched her ashore. "What's your name, woman?"

She tilted her chin defiantly, clamped her mouth shut and glowered at him as he dragged her alongside him to fetch his horse.

Ten minutes later Rafe scooped up the woman and plunked her atop Sergeant. Keeping a firm grip on her leg, he swung up behind her. With her hands secured in the middle of her back, her elbows out so she couldn't clobber him in the midsection, Rafe wrapped one arm around her waist to insure she didn't launch herself off the horse during their jaunt to the fort. Given the battle royal he had just encountered with this female, he wouldn't put another escape attempt past her.

"Where did you learn to fight like that?" he asked five miles later.

"In places I'm sure *you* have never been, General," she sassed.

"Obviously not. Where I come from, ladies don't brawl. I have already determined—the hard way—that you're no lady. Furthermore, I'm not a general. I'm the commandant at Fort Reno. *Major* Rafe Hunter."

She twisted in the saddle to flash him a smirk. "You're from back East, right? Uppity accent. Imperious demeanor. Wealth and pedigree, no doubt. Don't you have better things to do than sneak around, assaulting defenseless women?"

"Defenseless?" he hooted. "I can think of a dozen adjectives to describe you, but defenseless isn't on the list."

She fell silent as they approached the post, and Rafe made no further attempt to pry information from her. It rankled that she poked fun at the privileged background he had spent years trying to overcome. He had prided himself on becoming his own man rather than flitting by on the laurels accorded to him by the illustrious Hunter family name. Rafe had worked damn hard to prove himself capable and responsible to assume command of this military fort. But in one fell swoop, and in a few choice words, this sassy hellion implied that his personal accomplishments were the result of his family pulling strings to land him this position.

When Rafe halted at the hitching post in front of officers' quarters, Micah was leaning negligently against the doorjamb. Micah's astute gaze drifted over the female captive then focused on Rafe's disheveled appearance. The hint of a smile quirked his lips as he pushed away from the door to assist the captive from the horse.

"Met with trouble, did you?" Micah questioned as he set the woman on her feet then clamped an arm around her elbow.

Rafe watched in amazement as the hellcat—who had tried to claw *him* to shreds—turned a radiant smile on Micah. "If that question was directed to me, sir, then the answer is yes. I would like to press charges against your commanding officer for molestation and assault."

Rafe nearly choked when the woman mimicked his Eastern accent and projected an air of ladylike dignity. When Micah's befuddled gaze bounced back and forth between Rafe and the woman, he had the impulsive urge to spout his denial of her outrageous accusations.

"Well?" the woman prompted haughtily. "Don't I have the right to protest such ill treatment, just because Rafe Hunter is the *commandant* of this fort?"

"I…uh…" Micah stammered, his blue-eyed gaze leaping from one mud-covered face to the other.

"Come along, miss," Rafe muttered as he towed her into the foyer of officers' quarters. "Captain Micah

Whitfield is second in command and he's a longtime friend of mine. Your ploy won't work on him.'' He hoped.

To Micah he said, ''She's the one who set up the campfire that we detected before you led the patrol back to the fort.''

Micah's eyes widened as he reassessed the woman in muddy breeches, faded shirt and patched jacket. ''You were out there alone?'' he asked incredulously.

She turned pleading green eyes on Micah, graced him with that feigned-innocent smile and began her spiel about traveling cross-country to rejoin her family and how she had resorted to wearing men's clothes to protect herself from lecherous men—like the post commander.

Rafe barked a laugh. He didn't believe this feisty little con artist for a minute. He had seen her fight like the very devil and then he had watched her turn on the charm for Micah's benefit.

''That is more than enough,'' Rafe interrupted her long-winded explanation. ''Don't waste your breath. Micah isn't as gullible as he looks.''

Whoever this woman was, it was glaringly apparent that she was adept at living by her wits and she would say anything in an attempt to talk her way out of trouble.

Rafe grabbed the woman's arm, wheeled toward the door, then halted in his tracks. As much as he would like to stuff this feisty female in the stockade that was bulging with men, he couldn't. If she antagonized any of them the way she had smarted off to him they would collectively strangle her. Either that or she would find herself molested repeatedly before the guards could reach her. He really had no choice but to lock her in his quarters for the night and bunk with Micah.

"I'll keep her in my room," he announced as he reversed direction.

Micah's dark brows shot up.

The woman refused to budge from the spot. Her eyes narrowed suspiciously. Well, good, thought Rafe. It was about time this mouthy hellion showed him some wary respect.

Rafe uprooted the woman and herded her into his tidy quarters. He slammed the door shut then positioned a chair under the doorknob to make sure she didn't escape while he wasn't here to stop her. With Micah hot on his heels, Rafe walked back outside to lead his weary mount to the stables.

"You gonna explain what is going on or just leave it to my vivid imagination?" Micah teased as he fell into step beside Rafe.

"That female is a chameleon," Rafe declared. "She might have been charming to you, but she fought like a cornered Apache when I apprehended her. I've encountered less resistance and more respect from the men we've taken into custody. I was kicked, bitten and clawed repeatedly."

"So I see." Micah chuckled in amusement as he appraised Rafe's frazzled appearance. "Makes me wish I had insisted on going with you. I'd like to have witnessed that battle."

"It wasn't a pretty sight." Rafe's stomach growled, reminding him that it was long past supper. "I tried to remind myself that I was brawling with a woman, but it wasn't easy when she fought like a man."

"I like a woman with spunk and spirit," Micah said, blue eyes twinkling.

"You're welcome to her," Rafe shot back. "I'm accustomed to a woman who behaves like a lady."

"Like your fiancée? Ah, yes, the poised and dignified Vanessa Payton. Ask me, that will be a dull marriage indeed."

"Marriage is part of my obligation to my family," Rafe reminded him with a casual shrug. "You know perfectly well that I'm devoted to my position here. The army is my life."

"Which is obviously why you allowed your grandfather, the general, and your father, also a general, to arrange this marriage. As I recall, you've only met the lovely Vanessa twice. How can you possibly know if you'll suit?"

"That's just the way it's done in my family," Rafe replied as he led Sergeant into the stall to remove the saddle.

"Being a half-breed, raised among the Choctaw tribe, I was taught to believe that a man and woman should have a certain affection for each other when they marry. You *have* heard the word *love* before, haven't you, my friend?" Micah taunted.

"Heard of it," Rafe agreed as he grabbed a brush to tend his prize gelding. "Never associated it with marriage, however. My grandparents' marriages were arranged, as were my parents, as mine has been. It's no different than accepting an assignment with the army. You take what you are given and you make the best of it."

"And my parents, though they hailed from drastically different cultures and contrasting civilizations, defied it all because they loved each other," Micah maintained then grinned teasingly. "All I can say is that you whites have a strange way of looking at things. And some say *Indians* are heathens," he added with a smirk. "Ask me, it's the other way around."

"Be that as it may," Rafe said as he rewarded Sergeant with a bucket of grain, "I agreed to marry Vanessa when the Land Run is over and business in this territory is functioning smoothly."

He pivoted to shoulder his way past Micah, who was leaning leisurely against the top rail of the stall. "In the meantime, I have to focus my time and efforts on protecting the Unassigned Lands against settler intrusion and attempt to maintain law and order."

Micah shrugged as he followed Rafe from the stables. "Whatever you say, Major Hunter, but I still contend there is life beyond the military. After I served with the Choctaw light-horsemen to police the territory and guarantee my credentials, I joined the army so I wouldn't be stuck on the reservation like my mother's people. I'm not married to the army. When the right woman comes along, I intend to marry for love, not because her name will sound good when it's linked to mine. That, I assure you, will be my very last consideration."

Honestly, Rafe sometimes wondered how he and Micah had formed such a strong, lasting friendship when they came from such different walks of life. Maybe the truth was that Rafe envied Micah's laid-back manner and his philosophies that were steeped in Indian beliefs.

In the early years of their friendship they had relied on each other's knowledge and backgrounds to broaden their horizons and make them well-rounded soldiers. Now they were as close as brothers and had saved each other's hide several times during harrowing campaigns against the hostile Plains Indians who had escaped from the reservations in New Mexico.

"Let me know if you need help dealing with your latest prisoner," Micah commented as he veered toward his quarters.

Rafe snorted at the reminder of the upcoming encounter with the red-haired firebrand who was occupying his room. Now there was a woman he could never love—if there was such a thing as love.

Indeed, Micah was welcome to the smart-mouthed little witch. Rafe preferred to associate with women who allowed him to behave like the gentleman his family had groomed him to be. It didn't sit well to know that he had tackled a woman, straddled her hips and held her underwater until she practically drowned, just to make her surrender.

Rafe smiled in reluctant admiration when he recalled how that belligerent hellion had refused to accept defeat, despite the odds against her. She had more spunk and spirit than most men he knew.

Exasperated, Karissa Baxter paced Commander Hunter's living quarters. It irked her that the bedroom and sitting room were neat as pins. Everything was in its proper place—lined up like soldiers on parade.

Most of the men she had encountered in her twenty-six years never bothered to pick up after themselves. Her father certainly hadn't and neither did her younger brother, Clint. She had taken care of him since he was six years old and she had tried to become the mother they had lost to typhoid. Because she felt sorry for Clint, she had pampered him.

Karissa halted beside the window when the regimental band stuck up a lively tune. There was no way she could escape through the window, not with so many soldiers milling around the place. She had already tried the door and found it had been secured from outside. The commander had taken extra precautions because she had made the mistake of letting him know she wasn't beneath doing whatever necessary to escape.

Karissa sighed audibly and resumed her pacing, serenaded by the regimental band. How long was she going to be detained at the fort? Probably until His Highness decreed that she could leave. And if Rafe Almighty Hunter thought for one minute that she was going to provide him with sexual satisfaction while she was under arrest then he had another think coming!

She had learned long ago to size up men and situations quickly and she could think of only one reason Rafe insisted that she would stay in *his* private quarters. For all his refined good looks and prestigious position at the fort, he was still a man, she reminded herself cynically.

The thought caused her to break stride. She was a woman who had learned to stand up for herself and depend on no one but herself. She had also learned to take advantage of situations, to survive as best she could. If Rafe Hunter had in mind to take her to bed while she was under arrest then she was damn well going to make it worth her while.

In short, one favor exchanged for another. If she was forced to give up her innocence then, by damned, she was going to profit from it.

She would negotiate with that dignified commander who ruled this roost. One night in his bed for her freedom. That was the deal. He was not getting something *that* intimate and personal from her for nothing!

She was determined to quit this place and return to the new territory to protect the land she wanted to claim. Yet, the prospect of surrendering to the lusty desires of a man unsettled her. Karissa had spent years mastering the art of discouraging men from approaching her with amorous intentions. Never once had she tried to attract a man's attention. Who would have thought that she would be standing here wishing she had the skills of an accomplished courtesan?

Karissa laughed at the absurdity of the thought, but she didn't laugh for long. She had made a pact with herself to do whatever it took for her and her brother to make a fresh new start in the newly created Oklahoma Territory. After being dragged along behind her father from one saloon to another in every cow town in Kansas, she asked for nothing more than to put down roots and have a home.

She was sick to death of the gypsy lifestyle her father had forced on her and Clint. Sick to death of being referred to as the gambler's brats and treated like pariahs by the so-called *respectable* members of local society.

Having been soured by proper society's condescension, it was little wonder that she had felt instant hostility toward the fort commander. In her mind he represented the establishment that had treated her shabbily for years on end. Yet, despite his position of authority, despite his mud-caked eyebrows and eyelashes, despite smudges of slime on his chin and cheeks, he was still the most strikingly attractive man she had ever laid eyes on.

He stood six feet four inches tall and had to weigh more than two hundred pounds—she should know since he had nearly squashed her flat while he sat on her to hold her down in the creek. His eyes were the color of hammered steel. His shoulders were noticeably broad and his long legs were solid muscles—she knew that, too, because she had been pressed flush against him during the ride to the garrison.

Although she definitely disliked Rafe on general principle, there was no denying that he could turn a woman's head. Even Karissa's.

"Obviously, he held you under water so long that it turned your brain to bog," Karissa muttered at herself.

When the doorknob rattled, Karissa spun around and mentally prepared herself. She struck a saucy pose, imitating dozens of dance-hall queens who called attention to themselves to entice drunken cowboys to private rooms, in exchange for cash.

Rafe Hunter whizzed into the room and halted abruptly. He snapped back his raven head, drew himself up to full stature and stared down his patrician nose at her. "If you're thinking what I *think* you're thinking, it won't work," he said stiffly. "Do you really expect to pull off that come-hither look, while standing there in mud-covered men's clothes?"

Despite his unflattering remark, Karissa marshaled her courage and unfastened the top two buttons on her shirt. Sure enough, those steel-gray eyes dropped to her chest. Typical man, she thought bitterly. He might be standing there spouting indignantly, but like the rest of his kind, his brains were located beneath his belt buckle. No matter how aloof and dignified the commander believed himself to be, she suspected that he, too, was a slave to his insatiable passions.

"I plan to be standing here wearing nothing but a smile," she purred as she unfastened another button on her shirt. "You really aren't planning to complain about *that,* are you, General?"

To her amused satisfaction, his Adam's apple bobbed repeatedly and his gaze focused on her bosom. Now, if she could keep him preoccupied with the prospect of taking a tumble in his bed, she might be able to catch him unawares, elude him and make her getaway on the nearest horse.

It was definitely worth a try, she decided as she sauntered provocatively toward him and flashed him an inviting smile.

Chapter Two

"Behave yourself," Rafe demanded, though the flicker in his eyes indicated that he wasn't averse to seeing a bit more feminine skin.

Karissa halted a few feet away from him and struck what she hoped was another irresistible pose. "My dear general, you know perfectly well that I have a penchant for *misbehaving*," she said in the most seductive voice she could muster. "I have a proposition for you."

She slid her hands up and over his massive shoulders and felt him tense beneath her fingertips. It gave her an odd sense of power and satisfaction to realize this distinguished military officer was leery yet exceptionally aware of her as a woman.

Damn, if she didn't like knowing that he wasn't sure what to expect from her next and that he was fascinated, in spite of himself.

"What kind of proposition?" he croaked. His eyes dipped to her bosom then he quickly jerked those rainstorm-colored eyes back to her smudged face.

"I think you know what I'm suggesting." She glided her fingers through his raven hair then inclined her head toward his bed. "You won't have a fight on your hands this time...provided you meet my terms."

His dark brows snapped together as he stared down at her. "Am I to understand that you're offering to sleep with me if I agree to release you in the morning?"

His disapproving frown threatened to rattle her composure. She had been certain that any man, even the commander, would succumb to his lusty desires when opportunity presented itself. Men rarely saw past the moment. She, on the other hand, was prepared to do whatever necessary for her release so she could secure her dream of a home in the newly established territory.

Wasn't it just her luck that she had encountered a man who was apparently the exception to the rules she thought applied to all men?

Chin held high, she stepped back to look down *her* nose at *him*—even if he was a good foot taller than she was. "Oh, come now, General, surely you didn't think I'd let you waltz in here and take me to bed without bartering for my freedom."

He jerked back as if she had slapped him. "I have no intention of taking you to bed," he declared.

"You didn't put me under arrest *in your room* so you could take advantage of me?" Karissa smirked at him. "You really expect me to believe that? Just how stupid do I look?"

"You don't look the least bit stupid. During our brawl in the creek, I discovered that you're as wily as a fox. And I *did* expect you to believe that I was trying to show you a modicum of courtesy and consideration," he snapped as he veered around her to gather fresh clothing from his trunk.

"I couldn't very well put you in a stockade that is teeming with men. Therefore, I brought you here for your own protection. Though why I bothered, after that little performance, I'm sure I don't know.'' He did an abrupt about-face and glared at her. ''I plan to bunk in Micah's quarters for the night.''

Karissa's jaw sagged in amazement. She had totally misinterpreted the commander's intentions and she had come off looking like a trollop. Despite what he thought, she was the farthest thing from a woman who made her living on her back.

''I'm posting a guard outside the window and one outside the door,'' he informed her briskly. ''You'll stay here until you promise me that you will not sneak back into the territory before the Run.''

''I promise,'' she said swiftly. ''May I leave now?''

Rafe halted beside her. A sardonic smile touched the corners of his sensuous mouth. ''You might find this astonishing, but I don't trust you.''

''I *gave* you my promise,'' she sassed him. ''That's *all* you asked for.'' She crossed her arms over her chest and stared at him defiantly. ''Some commander you are, General, if you change your mind every other minute.''

''Well, *this* decision stands,'' he said with brusque finality. ''You'll be here indefinitely. It's the only way to guarantee your safety and I can think of nothing worse than a woman so belligerent and contrary that she refuses to admit to her own vulnerability on the frontier. Furthermore, I want to be certain that you won't break the law I'm sworn to uphold.''

Karissa scowled at him. ''I'm finding that I like honorable men less than I like the dishonorable ones. It's impossible to deal with men in general, General.''

''Stop calling me General and fasten your shirt,'' he muttered at her. ''Maybe when you start behaving like a lady I'll reconsider.'' He opened the door then shot her a stony stare. "If you'll excuse me, I would like to treat the injuries you inflicted on me. Sleep well, spitfire."

"*Karissa.* My name is Karissa," she said, striking a proud, dignified pose—just to prove to him she could be dignified if she felt like it. "Karissa Baxter from Kansas."

"I will see that you have a supper tray delivered, Karissa from Kansas," he replied in that aloof, authoritative tone that made her grit her teeth in annoyance. "Good night."

When the door shut behind him, Karissa pulled a face. She definitely did not like that man. Too much spit and polish. Too much blue blood spurting through his veins. He obviously stuck to rules and regulations like flies stuck in molasses. If he had flown through life by the seat of his breeches, as she had, he would be considerably more sympathetic and understanding of her plight. But there was no sense wasting her breath, explaining her situation. Commander Rafe Hunter wouldn't think of breaking his precious rules, much less bending one because of *her*.

Karissa flounced on the foot of the bed. If she gave a damn what that handsome soldier thought of her she would be depressed right now. But she didn't have the time or inclination to wallow in unproductive emotions. She was on a crusade to insure her brother's future in this new territory and she was spinning her wheels in house arrest.

She glanced speculatively toward the window and decided to make her escape *after* her supper had been delivered. She couldn't plan her next move while her empty stomach was growling so loudly that she couldn't think.

When a quiet rap rattled the door, Karissa pivoted and braced herself for another encounter with the fort commander. To her relief, Micah Whitfield poked his dark head around the door and smiled in greeting. His stunning blue eyes glistened with amusement as he directed her attention to the tray of food he carried in one hand.

"According to Rafe, a man can get his hand bitten off when he wanders too close to you. I brought supper so you will have something to chew on besides me."

Karissa chuckled as Micah made a big production of cautiously circling around her to set the tray on the table. This brawny soldier, who was obviously of mixed heritage, had a knack of putting her at ease, even when she was conditioned to keeping up her guard around all men.

"You can relax, Captain," she assured him as she walked over to pick up the slice of buttered bread. "I only bite and claw when physically attacked. You seem reasonably harmless."

Micah laughed. "I'm sure you meant that as a compliment, but I have the reputation of being a hard-bitten, relentless scout and soldier." He grinned teasingly and said, "Of course, thanks to you, Rafe is the one who's *hard-bitten*."

"Well, he tackled me and knocked me in the mud," Karissa defended between bites. "What was I supposed to do? Thank him kindly for nearly drowning me and squishing me down in the slime?"

Micah ambled over to sit down in the chair—backward. He draped his muscled arms on the back of the chair and regarded her with blatant admiration. "Rafe might find you a bit unconventional, but I like your style. I always did admire a woman with pluck and gumption."

Karissa sank down at the table to devour her meal.

"And I'm cautious of men who are quick with compliments." She eyed him with amused curiosity. "What do you want from me, *Micah?*" she said informally. "And do keep in mind that you won't get it."

He threw back his head and laughed heartily. "No small talk for you, I see. Just cut to the chase." He nodded approvingly. "No wonder Rafe is having a hard time dealing with you. You're nothing like the women he's accustomed to."

"The dainty and dignified types who bat their lashes and compliment his striking good looks and intelligence?" She sniffed in disgust.

"My sentiments exactly," Micah agreed. "I've never trusted a woman who fawns and flatters. It means she wants something and that makes me suspicious. But then, I was raised in an Indian camp, not in the posh drawing rooms of the highest military echelon on the East Coast."

"Like Rafe Hunter," she presumed. "So what's a man like him doing on this outpost of civilization? I suspect that he has the necessary connections to land a plum commission in someplace that's safe, civilized and dignified."

Micah shrugged. "He does and he could. Rafe graduated with high marks and honors from West Point. But he isn't the type who is satisfied with taking the easy way out. We've faced hostile Apaches and Comanches together and he's guarded my back while I guarded his. He likes the rigorous challenges of defending the country and protecting its honest citizens."

A dyed-in-the-wool career army officer, Karissa mused. It was just her luck to be arrested by the gung-ho major.

"He's damn good at his job," Micah added. "He's

earned the respect of most of the soldiers under his command. Except for the lazy few who expend more effort trying to avoid work than carrying their share of the load. Rafe has a low tolerance for that type," he added. "He never asks one of his men to do something he isn't prepared to do himself. Despite his privileged background he isn't afraid of hard work and he doesn't shy away from trouble or tough decisions."

"Enough on that dull topic," she said with a dismissive flick of her wrist. "How long am I to be detained? I'm certain my brother and his wife are concerned about me. I would like to get word to them. Even better if I could reassure them in person." She tossed Micah a meaningful glance.

"Does this imaginary brother know you were trespassing on the unopened territory?" Micah asked.

Karissa set down her fork and stared the ruggedly handsome half-breed squarely in the eye. "My brother and sister-in-law are very real. They are camped along the river, about five miles from this fort. At the very least I would like to relay the message that I'm alive and well. Of course, I would prefer to omit the part about being under arrest. No need to upset them, after all."

Micah inclined his head agreeably. "I'll see what I can do to reassure them, but I'm afraid Rafe has his rules about immediately releasing squatters who jumped the gun before the Land Run. You, my dear lady, have to accept the fact that you will be detained until Rafe decides to release you."

Karissa's shoulders slumped in frustration. While she was stuck at the garrison, someone else might sneak into the territory and stake the property that she had fallen in love with the moment she walked over the rolling hill and saw the lush countryside spread out before her. That wild, untamed land had called out to her as nothing else ever had. She could have sworn she heard *home* whispering in the gentle breeze.

"If I'm to be detained then I need something to occupy my time," she insisted. "I'll be climbing these walls if I have nothing to do. Can you arrange for me to become a laundress? Surely with so many soldiers about, I can earn wages by washing and cleaning."

"I don't see a problem with that," Micah replied. "Rafe might, however. He doesn't trust you not to break and run the first chance you get."

Karissa glanced up when she noticed a shadow hovering outside the window. Ten feet away, the fort commandant loomed over her, watching her like an eagle-eyed predator. The man obviously trusted her so little that he volunteered to stand watch so she didn't make a break for it via the window.

Out of pure spite, Karissa emulated the mannerisms of a gushing female by batting her eyes and waving enthusiastically at Rafe. Sure enough, he frowned skeptically at the sudden contradiction of her feisty temperament.

When Rafe disappeared from sight, Micah snickered. "As much as you seem to delight in antagonizing Rafe, that's no way to gain his favor and respect."

"I couldn't care less about gaining his respect. The less contact we have with each other the better." She glared at the resolute presence beyond the window then turned away to polish off her meal.

When the door swung open a few minutes later, Karissa glanced up to see His Truly towering over her. Instant but unwanted awareness sizzled through her. The mere sight of Rafe Hunter in his dress uniform—which

boasted decorative gold braid and dozens of medals—
was enough to take a woman's breath away. Even a
hopeless cynic's like herself.

His dark hair had been recently washed and combed.
His eyes gleamed like silver in the flickering lamplight.
Standing tall, masculine and distinguished in his pol-
ished black boots, he truly was a sight to behold.

It was easy to understand why gently bred ladies from
his social circle would consider him a prize catch. Yet,
there was something about him that testified to the fact
that the army was his life and that he took his duties
very seriously. A woman could never compete with that
single-minded devotion, she predicted.

However, Karissa thought with wry amusement, this
distinguished officer—who practically radiated authority—chose to approach her while Micah was present.
Karissa found small consolation in the knowledge that
Rafe Hunter wasn't sure how to handle her and was
leery of being alone with her again.

Why was that? she wondered. Didn't he trust *her?* Or
didn't he trust *himself?* Whatever the reason, this man
wasn't going to take her for granted the way she suspected he took other women for granted.

"Miss Baxter," Rafe said in an overly polite tone,
"one of the officers' wives offered you decent clothing." Stiffly, he thrust the dresses at her then shifted
awkwardly. "As for the…um…feminine paraphernalia
that goes beneath it, I won't be able to provide that until
the post trader's store opens in the morning. As for
proper shoes, that might take some time in acquiring.
You'll have to wear your cloddish boots."

Difficult as it was to be gracious, Karissa rose from
her chair to accept the dresses. "Thank you," she murmured, uncomfortable with accepting charity. "I was

just telling Captain Whitfield that I would like to occupy my time and earn wages by becoming a fort laundress."

Rafe's thick brows flattened over his narrowed eyes. "I think not. You'll have to find something to occupy yourself in my room. Perhaps you can sew buttons back on uniforms and darn socks. But you will not be permitted to have the run of this garrison."

Karissa hitched her chin in the air and defiantly strode over to the cot. She proceeded to jerk off the blanket and sheets. Holding Rafe's fuming gaze, she dumped the bedding on the floor then made short shrift of transferring his personal belongings from his trunk to the floor.

Beside her, she heard Micah camouflage a chuckle behind a cough. She glanced over her shoulder to see him battling to keep a straight face—and failing miserably.

Rafe glared sabers at her. "Are you finished making your point, Miss Baxter?" he growled.

"Not quite." Karissa knew she was sliding on the thin edge of his temper, but it was her nature to spit in the face of defeat. She made a beeline for the bookshelf that was lined with military manuals and dumped them, one by one, atop the bedding. "*Now* I'm finished and I'm bored again."

Micah bounded from his chair, his eyes dancing with suppressed laughter. "I think I had better leave before the next skirmish starts. Don't wanna get caught in the crossfire."

"No, you'll stay," Rafe demanded without taking his eyes off Karissa.

"You definitely have to stay, Captain," Karissa chimed in then flashed Rafe an impudent grin. "The General is afraid to be alone with me. Terrified, in fact."

She almost cackled when he puffed up with so much indignation he nearly popped the brass buttons off his uniform.

"Given my position of authority here, there are a lot of people who are afraid to cross me." He stared at her through narrowed eyes. "You should be one of them."

"Really? I didn't know you were God's brother," she sassed him.

Micah snickered, but he schooled his amused expression when Rafe shot him an irritated glance.

"Might I remind you, Miss Baxter," Rafe said through clenched teeth, "that your other option here is to be jailed with the male prisoners in the stockade."

Karissa shrugged carelessly. "I can take care of myself, General. And believe me, I have found myself in more harrowing situations than being thrust into a stockade with male prisoners." Her green eyes sparkled with challenge. "Of course, if you wish to contend with a full-scale riot that voices objections to being crowded into unsanitary conditions that, no doubt, plague your stockade, then lead me to it."

"I don't think she's spouting an empty threat, Rafe. It wouldn't take much to incite the imprisoned settlers. Joan of Arc here looks all too eager to champion a rebellion," Micah interjected. "However, we *are* short on laundresses at the moment and we could use her offered services. You can always put a guard on her so you can keep track of her constantly."

Karissa graced Micah with her best smile. "Ah, a man who shows reason and common sense." She turned back to the stony-faced commander. "I can understand why Captain Whitfield has been chosen as second in command to serve as your advisor, consultant and mentor."

She waited, wondering if Rafe would relent, especially after she had purposely goaded him. He stood there so stiffly for so long that she almost gave up and resorted to taking the rest of his room apart and leaving it in shambles. Finally he blew out his breath and nodded curtly.

"Very well, Miss Baxter, you can begin your duties as laundress and housekeeper in the officers' quarters first thing in the morning." He glared at her again. "And you can start by undoing the damage to my room. I want this place to look exactly the way it did before you performed your whirling dervish act."

She flashed him a mocking smile and noticed his jaw clenched in determined restraint. She suspected he would enjoy strangling her for maneuvering him into agreeing to her request. Well, tough. She would like to choke him for detaining her at the post.

"You are *too* kind, General," she cooed pretentiously.

"For the last time," he gritted out, "stop calling me General!"

When the door swung shut behind Rafe and Micah, Karissa half collapsed on the bed. Squaring off against Rafe Hunter was exhausting. She decided to postpone her escape attempt for a day. Besides, she could use the extra money and she would have the opportunity to familiarize herself with the daily routine at the fort. With money jingling in her pocket she could plan the perfect time to make her escape without drawing too much attention to herself. Then she would return to the property she hoped to claim for her brother and sister-in-law.

But this time, she vowed, she was going to be more watchful and attentive when the army patrol came hunting for illegal squatters. She would dig a hole and pull it in after her, if need be, but she *was* going to stake a claim on the land she had selected to be the Baxter homestead.

"You were a lot of help," Rafe muttered to Micah a few minutes later at headquarters as they prepared the duty roster for the following day.

Micah took a seat beside Rafe to peruse the schedule. "Oh, come on, Rafe, you really can't expect a woman with that much restless energy to sit in a room night and day indefinitely. We lost three laundresses whose husbands intend to participate in the Land Run, and we're shorthanded. Plus, if you put a guard on Karissa she can't get far."

Rafe snorted irritably. "*You* haven't scuffled with her. *I* have. She could be gone before a negligent guard realized it. That woman is too crafty and clever for her own good."

"She gets to you, doesn't she?" Micah asked candidly.

Rafe scowled in frustration. Yes, that hellion was definitely getting under his skin—to the extreme. Never in his life had he been forced to match wits with such a quick-minded female. And to his baffled amazement, he found her extremely attractive, even when she looked like a scruffy ragamuffin in those dowdy men's clothes. In all fairness, she shouldn't ooze sex appeal with her tomboyish appearance and her fiery temperament and that sassy mouth.

It was those green eyes that sparked with so much inner spirit that really got to him, he decided. In addition, he had the outrageous urge to grab a handful of that wild mane of curly red hair, pull her to him and kiss the breath out of her when she challenged him. It was an inappropriate and insane reaction—like nothing he had previously experienced in his association with women.

Before Karissa blew into his life like a tornado, he had never had difficulty controlling his emotions. Ordinarily he reacted with logic and intellect. But he couldn't respond normally when she purposely tormented him.

He told himself he was attracted to her because he had been a long time without a woman. That was what caused his volatile reaction to Karissa. Since his parents had formally announced his betrothal to Vanessa Payton, Rafe had denied himself sexual satisfaction. It had been the honorable thing to do.

When Karissa's image flashed through his mind like a bomb bursting in air, Rafe gnashed his teeth. For God's sake, he was engaged to a woman whose family name carried prestige in military circles. It didn't matter that he didn't love Vanessa. How could he? He barely knew her. But she would make an acceptable wife for a career army officer. Even if this fort on the frontier afforded very little in the way of luxuries Vanessa would honor her family obligations and remain by his side.

So why had Rafe spent most of this evening, harboring all these forbidden thoughts of that red-haired witch who prowled around his room? It was beyond ridiculous. In addition, she obviously was in the habit of using her body to gain favors from men.

Even knowing that, he had been tempted by that siren. The realization that he desired her offended his strong sense of personal pride and honor.

She was a woman he knew he shouldn't—and couldn't—have.

"Hello?" Micah prompted playfully. "Are we going

to fill in the duty roster or do you plan to spend what's left of the evening staring off into space?''

Rafe forced himself to focus on the business at hand and set to work assigning tasks for enlisted men. With practiced precision, he and Micah completed the task in a few minutes.

''I suggest we assign Harlan Billings to guard Karissa,'' Micah commented. ''After you put him on report for being drunk and disorderly, he's been digging latrines for three days. Personally, I would rather not have him back on patrol with us. I'm tired of listening to him whine and complain about scouting the area, day after day, looking for squatters. If nothing else, it will keep Harlan out of our hair.''

Rafe was inclined to agree. Corporal Harlan Billings—who had been demoted from the rank of sergeant already—was a pain in the backside. Yet, Rafe wasn't sure he wanted that particular soldier trailing after Karissa. Then again, he mused, she seemed to possess the ability to deal with men. If anyone could keep Harlan in line he would lay odds on the infuriating woman who had taken apart his room for pure spite.

With a nod, Rafe wrote Harlan's name on the roster. ''We'll give him a trial run tomorrow,'' he agreed. ''If that doesn't work out I think Harlan could best serve his country by mucking out the stables for a few days.''

Micah snickered. ''Very appropriate. Why not send an ass to clean up after the mules and horses?'' He shifted in his chair and sighed tiredly. ''I for one will be glad when this Land Run is over and the territorial boundaries aren't crawling with would-be settlers. The camps in this area are filling up steadily. I've counted nearly five hundred wagons circling the encampments. We also received a telegram that reported nearly ten thousand settlers have gathered on the Kansas border, preparing to move south within the next few days. Hopefully, our job will be easier when these settlers can focus their time on tilling the ground and constructing homes on their claims instead of crowding our space and picking fights with each other.''

"After the Run, I suspect we'll be exchanging one set of headaches for another,'' Rafe prophesied. "Free land brings out greed in people. Not to mention the money-hungry shysters who have been selling falsified maps to these hopeful settlers.''

"All the same, I think I prefer maintaining law and order to scouring the countryside for squatters and baby-sitting all these campsites that have sprung up around us.'' Micah sighed wearily as he stood up. "I'm calling it a night. You can have my cot and I'll make a pallet on the floor.''

"No,'' Rafe insisted. "I'll take the pallet. Just because a wildcat is tearing up my quarters doesn't mean you should have to suffer for it. I'm the one who decided to stuff her in there for safekeeping.''

When Micah strode off, Rafe slouched in his chair and drummed his fingers on the desk. Even though he planned to post a guard to shadow Karissa every hour of the day he still didn't trust her not to escape. When he returned from scouting the area for squatters he would keep an eye on her himself. He predicted she would try to make her escape at night.

And he would be there to pounce.

It was going to be a fair Run, for one and all, to claim free land, Rafe thought determinedly. Just because he was suffering feelings of partiality toward Karissa didn't mean he was going to let it stand in the way of duty.

He was not going to show her special treatment by letting her sneak back into the territory prematurely.

On that determined thought Rafe checked the door to see that Karissa was locked up tightly for the night, then he sprawled out on the floor of Micah's quarters to grab a few hours of sleep.

Chapter Three

The next morning Rafe dragged himself off the floor, worked the kinks from his back and heaved a tired sigh. He was definitely going to need more padding for his pallet, he decided.

Glancing sideways, he noticed Micah was up and gone. The sound of a trumpet splitting the still morning air prompted Rafe to grab his clothes and dress hurriedly. Never once had he been late for assembly, which commenced a little after five in the morning. He was always there to take roll call then lead the way to the stables to groom and care for the horses.

Lickety-split, Rafe burst out the door, fastening the buttons of his shirt as he went. He reached the parade grounds just as his men gathered in front of him.

She had done this to him, Rafe mused sourly. Thoughts of that spitfire had kept him tossing and turning instead of enjoying much-needed rest. He could only hope he didn't look as frazzled as he felt.

Assuming his customary position beside Micah, Rafe drew himself up to dignified stature to begin roll call. A few minutes later he strode toward the stable, with Micah hot on his heels.

"You look like hell," Micah murmured. "I doubt the rest of the men noticed since they're still half-asleep. Bad dreams, my friend?"

"Worst nightmare," Rafe grumbled.

And that's exactly what Karissa Baxter was, Rafe mused as he tended then saddled Sergeant. She had tempted him, tormented him and deprived him of sleep. If he didn't believe it was necessary to adhere to the rules of the Run, he'd set her free just to get her out from underfoot. But she had broken the rules and she would suffer the consequences.

At six o'clock, Rafe ambled into the mess hall and plunked down in his chair at the officers' table. He nearly choked on his coffee when Micah escorted Karissa into the room. All conversation dried up when the men noticed the fetching new arrival.

As for Rafe, he wasn't sure what he expected the first time he saw Karissa dressed as a respectable lady, but the sight of her would have knocked him off his feet if he hadn't been sitting down.

All those shapely feminine curves that had been downplayed by her baggy men's clothes were advantageously displayed in the pale green gown. He, like every other man in the mess hall, became distracted by the scooped-neck dress that showcased the full swells of her breasts.

She had twisted that thick mass of wild red hair atop her head, calling attention to the swanlike column of her neck. The trim-fitting gown accentuated her tiny waist and the seductive flare of her hips. In short, she was breathtakingly attractive, even with that smattering of freckles on her upturned nose.

To make matters worse, Karissa flashed a smile

around the room and a collective sigh of masculine appreciation sent a draft of air rushing past Rafe.

Damn, beauty, brains and irrepressible spirit all rolled into one. Much too pretty a package to be such an aggravating misfit, he found himself thinking. He had never considered a woman dangerous before, but that was the first word that sprang to mind when he thought of Karissa. Men naturally assumed that such a dainty-looking, petite female who barely stood five feet two inches and couldn't have weighed more than a hundred pounds wouldn't be a force to reckon with.

Rafe knew better.

"Good morning, General," Karissa greeted him, all smiles and good humor.

While she gracefully seated herself between Micah and Rafe, he noticed that speculative glances were bouncing across the mess hall. He wasn't sure he wanted to know what his men were thinking, as it pertained to his connection to Karissa.

When Rafe flung Micah a why-in-the-hell-did-you-bring-her-to-breakfast glare, Micah shrugged. "She was getting bored again. I was concerned about your room. I don't want to bunk together indefinitely."

Karissa laid her hand on Rafe's arm and turned such a sticky sweet smile on him that he nearly lost his appetite. "Micah is such a thoughtful and considerate gentleman," she cooed pretentiously. "You should take your cue from him, General. His charm brings out the best in me."

Knowing all eyes were on him, he flashed her a smile he didn't feel. Rafe leaned sideways and whispered, "Do not cross me, woman. You will not win."

She graced the mess hall full of men with another dazzling smile. "You don't frighten me in the least," she murmured confidentially. "Last night we discovered *who* was afraid of *whom.*"

His fists curled on his thighs, wishing he could strangle her. "I have the authority to see you deported. One word from me and you won't be permitted to make the Run. You better remember that."

When her smile faded and her lower lip trembled, as if she was about to burst into tears, Rafe silently scowled. His men stared at him as if he had committed the unpardonable sin of upsetting her. She was staging an act for their benefit and threatening his credibility with his men. Even Micah, and the officers' wives gathered at the table, looked at him as if he had committed a breach of gentlemanly etiquette.

Hell and damnation! Was there no way to gain the upper hand with her? First off, she had cleverly countered his every threat. Secondly, she stuck in his mind like a flaming arrow, even after he had vowed not to give her another thought. Rafe decided, there and then, that as long as Karissa Baxter was running around the garrison, his routine would be turned upside down.

A wise commander knew when to charge and when to retreat. He had little choice but to take a company of his men and spend the day scouting for squatters. The less he saw of Karissa the better.

Bearing that in mind, Rafe wolfed down his meal then left Micah with the task of introducing Karissa to her posted guard.

Rafe swore he heard Karissa laughing triumphantly when he turned tail and all but ran from the mess hall.

Karissa's first impression of Harlan Billings, the corporal who had been assigned to keep watch on her while she tended her laundress chores, was not good. After

Micah had made the introductions then walked off to assume his duties, Harlan had leered at her. It annoyed her that he kept finding excuses to place his hand at the small of her back to guide her through doorways and to grasp her elbow as they ascended steps.

His beady black eyes, pointy nose and thin tuft of brown hair reminded her of a rat dressed in a uniform, and each fleeting touch of his hand made her wince. Having this man following like her shadow was quickly spoiling her mood.

While Harlan propped his thin-bladed shoulder against the wall in the washroom, Karissa set to work scrubbing clothes and tried to ignore his unwanted presence. By the time he escorted her to the mess hall for lunch she decided she preferred matching wits with Rafe rather than being subjected to Harlan's lecherous stares and innuendos. It was obvious this skinny weasel of a man wanted something from her—the same thing that he *presumed* she had given to Rafe.

Judging from the snide comments Harlan made about Rafe, she surmised that her guard suffered from a severe case of professional jealousy. Obviously Harlan coveted Rafe's position of authority and had convinced himself that the commander held a personal grudge against him.

When the two other laundresses carried off their baskets of clean clothes, leaving Karissa alone with Harlan, he stepped closer and devoured her with another of those insulting stares that visually undressed her.

"So, is the commander's mistress also available to enlisted men or is he the only one allowed to sample your charms?" Harlan asked rudely.

Karissa tossed the underwear she was cleaning into the soap-filled tub then rounded on the smirking guard. "I am no man's mistress," she informed him sharply.

"I am under house arrest, same as the men in the stockade."

Harlan smiled sarcastically. "Of course, and that explains why you're staying in Commander Hunter's living quarters and dining beside him in the mess hall. Come now, sweetheart, everyone at this post knows that rank has privileges. But you should know that the commander is betrothed already. If you're scheming to become more than his mistress I suggest you think again. The high-and-mighty commander is marrying into another well-known family of military echelon. You'll never be more to him than the time he's killing before the wedding."

Karissa didn't know why that information sent her stomach on a downward spiral. Rafe Hunter was betrothed to one of his own kind? She shouldn't be the least bit surprised...or hurt by the news.

It wasn't as if she wanted Rafe for herself, for she had vowed years earlier that she would never care so much for a man that he could wield the power to destroy her. She had watched her father reduce himself to gambling and drinking when her mother died unexpectedly. She would never let herself become that dependent on anyone.

Looking out for her younger brother fulfilled her need to be useful and needed, and she had no intention of finding herself at the mercy of any man. She had been independent and self-reliant too many years to sit still for that!

She knew Rafe Hunter was far above her station in life, that he was devoted to his military position, that he would—and should—marry someone of equal social prominence. Yet...

And yet nothing, Karissa scolded herself as she went

back to work. Yes, Rafe Hunter was attractive and his dynamic presence demanded her attention. Yes, he was sharp minded and she enjoyed the challenge of matching wits with him. Yes, he appealed to her physically and he stirred something deep inside her the way no other man ever had.

But nothing would ever come of it, she reminded herself sensibly. She *refused* to let it. She enjoyed playing the role of his antagonist until he released her, because ruffling his military feathers provided mentally stimulating amusement.

Harlan nodded toward the soapy tub where Karissa vigorously scrubbed dirty clothes. "There's an easier and more pleasurable way to earn extra money," he insisted. "Although the soldiers don't mind riding into the nearby community to take a tumble with the prostitutes, I've no doubt that I could make arrangements for you to visit the men in their barracks. For a cut of the profit, of course."

Karissa glared at Harlan. It didn't take long to realize that Harlan was an opportunist who constantly looked for ways to make quick and easy money to supplement his army salary.

"Do you also steal from the post's commissary and turn the goods to would-be settlers for a profit, Harlan?" she asked perceptively.

She could tell by the look on his face that her presumption was right on the mark. He jerked upright and stared her down. "Just because you're the commander's whore doesn't mean you can use the power of your new position to hurl false accusations to get me demoted or court-martialed." He stalked over to wag a bony finger in her face and, when he sneered at her, his thin lips all but disappeared. "If you get me in trouble with Rafe Hunter I swear you will regret it."

Karissa flung wet underwear at his chest before hurriedly brushing past him. "Excuse me, I need to see to my needs, Corporal Billings. No need to follow me to the latrine. I was told that you know exactly where it is since you're the one who dug it."

Leaving Harlan sputtering and swearing, Karissa strode across the compound. If nothing else, she needed a mental break from her annoying guard. She was sure she could have handled that weasel better if he hadn't blindsided her with the announcement that Rafe was betrothed.

The news had caught her off balance, was all. It explained why Rafe was reluctant to come near her, why he had been taken aback by her request to exchange intimate favors for her freedom. He was obviously in love with his fiancée and intended to remain faithful to her.

Damn, she certainly had come off looking and sounding like a trollop, she mused, disgruntled. She had completely misunderstood Rafe's intentions of putting her up in his room, and she had tried to turn the situation to her advantage. All she had accomplished was leaving him with the wrong impression of her.

Yes, she had stretched the limits of the law along the way—in the name of caring and providing for her younger brother. She had relied on her wits to obtain funds to support herself and Clint. Never once had she resorted to offering sexual favors for money. She was *not* about to start now. All she had was her pride. If she ever lost that then she would be poor and pathetic indeed.

Karissa took a deep, cathartic breath to regain her

composure. For certain, she wasn't going to let Harlan Billings rattle her. She was stuck with him—at least until Micah returned and she could request another guard who was less offensive.

When she walked across the parade grounds, she noticed Harlan leaning casually against the washroom wall, smiling that nasty little smile that made her want to double her fist and clobber him. The man was a menace to this army post. She could understand why he had been demoted, why Rafe and Micah chose to leave him behind while they scouted for squatters.

No doubt, Rafe had selected Harlan as her guard to punish her for antagonizing him. Well, it had worked. Karissa couldn't wait to deliver the clothes she had washed and return to her room. Being alone was far better than spending time with the likes of Harlan Billings.

Micah frowned curiously when Rafe led the patrol in the same direction they had taken the previous evening. "We're backtracking?"

Rafe nodded. Although the patrol had reconnoitered a different area during the day he wanted to check that no other squatters had pitched camp on the land that Karissa wanted for her own. For the life of him he didn't know why he was granting her that favor. Nonetheless, he wanted to see to it that this plot of ground remained unclaimed until the day of the Run. She would have a fair chance to obtain the property without some Sooner staking it illegally.

A few moments later he heard Micah chuckling behind him. "Ah, now I understand. Very gallant of you, Rafe. You want the *witch*, as you refer to her, to have an opportunity to acquire a deed to the property she has her heart set on.''

"Clam up," Rafe muttered when Micah snickered again.

His thoughts scattered when he noticed movement in the dense trees that shaded the creek where he had first spotted Karissa. He motioned for the patrol to encircle the area so they could swarm down from all directions at once.

Alarmed shouts followed the thundering hoofbeats as the mounted patrol converged. Rafe cursed sourly when three of the eight men bounded into their saddles and raced down the winding stream, eluding the patrol.

Well, no matter, he consoled himself. He would be back the next day, and the next. He wouldn't allow illegal squatters to return and set up camp on this particular plot of land.

It was nearly dusk by the time the patrol, with ten male prisoners in custody, returned to the fort. As much as he hated to admit it, Rafe found himself looking forward to seeing how Karissa had fared during the day. If nothing else, he kept his wits sharpened by associating with her. Just so long as he didn't get lost in the hypnotic depth of those mesmerizing green eyes and allowed his attention to drift to the lush curve of her lips.

Desire slammed into him and Rafe cursed his lack of self-control. Never had the mere thought of a woman left him aching and aroused. This had to stop! He would *not* fantasize about that intriguing misfit. He was engaged to a perfectly acceptable woman and he would carry through with the arrangements his parents had made.

Until now, the thought of marrying Vanessa hadn't disturbed him in the least. He had planned to honor his family's request and share his life with Vanessa. But he also planned to devote most of his time and energy to serving his command post to the best of his ability.

"You looked pained," Micah observed as they approached the fort. "Something wrong?"

"I'm fine," Rafe mumbled as he nudged his mount into a trot. "Nothing supper won't cure."

"The appetite is a very demanding thing," Micah said wryly. "When a man starts craving something in particular it's difficult to get past it."

Rafe shot Micah a scathing glance. "I asked you to clam up. Now I'm making it an order."

"Yes, sir," Micah said with a snappy salute. "If I had known how easily you could be offended today I would have kept my observations to myself."

"See that you do so in the future," Rafe suggested.

Micah's teasing taunts drifted away like a breeze when Rafe rode into the post and saw Karissa headed for the mess hall with Harlan on her heels. Like some foolish schoolboy, his pulse beat accelerated and he found himself overanxious to unsaddle Sergeant, wash up and race over to the mess hall.

Despite Micah's amused glances, Rafe saw to his mount then scrubbed up without appearing to be in an all-fired rush. Although he hadn't expected his men to avoid Karissa like the plague, he was surprised to see so many of them clustered around her in the mess hall.

Rafe felt left out and deprived when Karissa voiced some witty comment that caused an eruption of laugher among his men. He refused to approach Karissa, even if he felt drawn to the sight of that curly red head in the center of the circle.

When some of the men noticed his presence, they bowed politely to Karissa then went to take their places in the mess line. When Karissa pivoted toward him, awareness slammed into him. Rafe tried very hard not to stare in masculine appreciation as she sauntered toward him, smiling impishly.

"Did you catch a few dozen Sooners today?" she asked as she veered around the table to take her seat.

"Only a short dozen," he reported. Reflexively, he pulled out the chair for her then sank down beside her. "Did you scrub your fingers to the bone while I was gone?"

She shrugged nonchalantly. "Considering the long days I was accustomed to working before venturing south from Kansas, this was a snap." She grinned playfully at him. "I decided to add starch to the military drawers that I washed and dried. I think some of them were yours. At least I can only hope."

Rafe tried not to return her smile, but it was contagious. "I wondered how you would retaliate. Leave it to you to be inventive."

"I do what I can so that you know I'm not taking my captivity sitting down." Her eyes sparkled with deviltry. "I wonder how easy it will be for you to *sit down* in those stiff drawers. But they should suit you perfectly."

He presumed she was referring to his personality, but it wasn't the only thing about him that was stiff at the moment. Rafe sighed. He really should release her, if only to avoid the frustrating attraction he didn't want to deal with and could do nothing about.

"On a more serious note—" Karissa clamped her mouth shut when one of the soldiers reached around her shoulder to place a plate of food on the table.

"You were saying?" Rafe prompted Karissa after the private moved on to serve the officers.

"How was your day?" Micah interjected as he took the empty seat beside Karissa.

Disgusted, Rafe watched her turn a beaming smile on Micah. "I'm sure my day wasn't as eventful as yours. I spent most of my time staring at the inside of a wash-tub and doing battle against dirty floors. The General tells me that you apprehended more squatters."

Micah nodded his thanks when the private served his meal. "I swear they're multiplying overnight." When Karissa frowned glumly, he hastily added, "But not to fret, pretty lady. Rafe circled back to chase down the Sooners who infiltrated the property you picked out."

Karissa turned her astonished gaze on Rafe, who shifted uncomfortably in his chair. "You did? And here I thought you didn't have a single saving grace. My apologies, General. I'm grateful for that, at least. Of course, other squatters are probably making camp on my prospective homestead as we speak."

"That's why we patrol the area continuously," Rafe replied between bites of his meal. "I want this Land Run to be fair for all."

"Being a woman, I'll start the race with a distinct disadvantage," she grumbled.

"I doubt it," Rafe said. "I have yet to see you at a disadvantage, distinct or otherwise."

Karissa wasn't allowed the opportunity to request another guard for the following day. She glanced up to see one of the soldiers, who had introduced himself earlier, standing directly in front of her. He, like many of the men she had met, had been exceptionally respectful and polite to her. It seemed to her that the soldiers were pleased to be in the presence of a single woman and she hadn't felt threatened by any of them. Except, of course, for Corporal Billings.

"I was hoping you might find time to sew new buttons on my dress uniform." The soldier offered her the neatly folded garment then placed a coin on the table. "I'll be back to fetch them in a few days."

The soldier stepped aside and Karissa was greeted by another one, and then another. The stack of coins on the table increased as the men pointed out torn shoulder seams, frayed hems on trousers and holes in their shirts.

Well, one good thing about this, she decided, was that she would earn more money and she'd have something to relieve the boredom of sitting alone in her room all evening.

Karissa excused herself from the table and scooped up the tall stack of garments. Rafe came to his feet beside her.

"I'll walk you back to officers' quarters," he volunteered.

Karissa was so aware of his presence beside her that she forgot to ask for a change of guard. It was all she could do to concentrate on keeping the riot of butterflies in her stomach from bursting loose. Damnation, why she allowed this man to affect her was beyond comprehension. She had no trouble dealing with the other soldiers.

"I thought perhaps I could accompany you on a walk around the garrison after I file my daily reports," Rafe said.

"I'm allowed another breath of fresh air before I bed down for the night?" she asked, striving for a flippant tone of voice that would disguise her nervous flutters.

Rafe halted in front of his private quarters and lifted a dark brow. "Is that a yes or a no?"

"A walk around the post will suit me fine," she replied. What better way to acquaint herself with the layout of the fort after dark? When she made her getaway—

and it was only a matter of time before she did—she needed to know the best place to go over the wall.

He bowed ever so slightly then opened the door. "I trust you will be anxiously awaiting my return then?"

"Oh, absolutely, General," she said breezily. "I think I would even offer to polish your boots if it would get me out of solitary confinement." She knelt down to brush her finger over the toe of his boot. "Good heavens! Is that a speck of dust? Isn't that against regulations? You could go on report!"

"Very funny," he muttered. "Try not to climb the walls before I get back. It would be a pity if you fell and broke your neck."

Karissa arched a brow. "Do I detect a warped sense of humor? Send it over to the washroom and I'll have it starched and pressed in no time at all."

When she turned toward the room, his muscled arm shot out to block her path. "I'm not the stuffed shirt you think I am," he murmured as he leaned toward her.

His face was so close to hers that breathing was next to impossible. Her traitorous gaze focused on the sensuous curve of his mouth and her heart commenced pounding so hard that she swore it was about to beat her to death. He was so large and powerful that she felt dwarfed by his massive presence.

Ordinarily, Karissa balked and rebelled when she felt intimidated by a man. Yet, the feelings Rafe aroused inside her went beyond the norm. This ill-fated and unprecedented attraction made her feel more vulnerable than she ever had before. This was worse than *physical* vulnerability; it was *emotional* suicide. A woman who lived by her wits couldn't afford to permit emotions to influence her ability to reason.

Desperate to put some distance between them, she

ducked under his arm and darted into the room. She stood there, clutching the garments to her chest, as if the uniforms could protect her from these sensations that rippled through her body.

He stared at her for a long moment and she stared back at him. Then, without another word, he closed and locked the door. Karissa half collapsed on the end of the bed and dragged in a shaky breath. The man had an incredibly potent effect on her. She'd tried to alienate him, to irritate him, but she could still feel sparks flying when they were alone.

Flustered and desperate, Karissa snatched up her clean breeches, jacket and shirt. It would be better if she was garbed in men's clothes on her walk with Rafe. She didn't want to risk looking like a woman—for fear she would start behaving like a woman and end up doing something totally inappropriate.

Like kiss him. No, better to behave like the tomboy that life had forced her to become, she decided.

Being detained by the army was trouble enough. Yielding to the temptation of kissing a betrothed man, just to see if he tasted as scrumptious as he looked, would be *more* than trouble. It would be a disaster.

Rafe completed his reports then raked his hand through his hair. Why had he offered to spring Karissa from confinement to take her for a walk? In the dark? Hell!

He dragged in a determined breath. He could do this. He could keep a respectful distance, chitchat for a quarter of an hour then return her to the room. Certainly he had encountered more difficult situations than accompanying a woman for a stroll around the post. And she *was* just a woman, after all.

Resolutely Rafe stood up and exited his office. He crossed the compound in brisk strides. When he reached his quarters he rapped on the door. It opened immediately. To his surprise, he encountered the scruffy urchin, not the curvaceous beauty he had dined with an hour earlier.

"Going somewhere?" he asked. "Like on a fast getaway?"

She sashayed past him to exit the building. "Nope, just slipped into more comfortable and familiar clothing. And by the way, I'd like to shoot the imbecile who decreed that women should wear hampering dresses. It was, no doubt, the inspiration of a man who wanted quick and easy access to a woman when he wanted to appease his lusty craving…what's the purpose of that building?" she asked in the same breath.

Rafe glanced in the direction she indicated. "That's the weapons and ammunition depot. Be careful about shooting off your mouth around it. I wouldn't want you, or it, to blow sky-high."

"Point noted, General," she said. "And what's the purpose of that building?"

"Temporary storage for the mess hall and infirmary. The stockade fence will be dismantled and the post will be expanded after the Run. We are cramped for space."

Rafe answered all of her questions—until she asked how many guards were posted in the two guard towers on opposite corners of the enclosed garrison. "Why do you want to know that?" he asked suspiciously.

She lifted her shoulder in a shrug. "Simple curiosity."

He smirked. "There's nothing simple about you. Without a doubt, you're the most complicated woman I have ever encountered."

''Bothers you, doesn't it?'' She halted to stare impishly at him. ''Well, if it makes you feel better, General, you're the most frustrating man I have ever met.''

The angled light cast by a lantern beamed across her enchanting face, compelling Rafe closer. He couldn't remember wanting to kiss a woman quite as much as he wanted to capture Karissa's lush, sensuous lips. While it was true that her sassy mouth was twice as big as she was, he was still intrigued by it, compelled to taste her thoroughly.

Karissa forgot to breathe when she noticed the flicker of awareness in his pewter-colored eyes. When he leaned toward her, suffocating her with his nearness—without actually touching her—unfamiliar sensations coiled in the pit of her stomach. He looked as if he was contemplating kissing her, and conflicting emotions roiled inside her. She wasn't sure she wanted to know how it felt to be wrapped in his sinewy arms and feel his full lips moving upon hers.

She was afraid she might like it *too* much. Yet, that didn't stop her traitorous body from gravitating ever closer to him, leaving the narrow space between them to crackle with sensual speculation.

''Rafe—?'' Her voice faltered. She wasn't sure if she was asking him to move closer or back away.

''Karissa—?'' Rafe stood there, savoring her unique scent, lost in the fathomless depths of her shimmering green eyes. He was torn between reckless desire and ruthless self-denial, unwillingly drawn to her and helpless in his inability to control the aching need that prowled through him.

Just when he felt himself give in to the overwhelming need to draw her into his arms and taste her, a voice called out, ''Ah, there you are, Major.''

Rafe shook himself from the bedeviling trance and stepped back. He would gladly have promoted Lieutenant Johnson on the spot, for his timely interruption. A few more moments and Rafe would have pulled Karissa into his arms, sampled the sweet nectar of those full lips and abandoned the good sense he'd spent years accumulating.

"What's the problem, Lieutenant?" Rafe asked. His voice sounded as if it had rusted.

"One of our men was suddenly taken ill. The post surgeon wants to speak to you about relieving him of his duties until he's back on his feet," Lieutenant Johnson reported.

"Tell Doc Winston I'll be there in a few minutes." Rafe took Karissa's arm and steered her back to officers' quarters. "I'm sorry to cut your walk short," he said very formally.

"Just as well. I have a stack of mending to tend. But thank you for the grand tour."

She didn't protest when he practically shoveled her into the room then secured the door for the night. Rafe leaned against the wall and inhaled a steadying breath. Willfully he forced all thoughts of Karissa from his mind. It wasn't easy, but he was the commandant of this post and his duties always came first.

He wondered why he'd had so much trouble remembering that the past two days.

Chapter Four

Rafe spent the following day doing exactly the same thing he had done the day before—and the day before that. Tracking down illegal squatters. He and his patrol had been led on a hair-raising chase over hill and dale before capturing four men who resisted arrest and had to be forcefully subdued.

Tired, irritable and hungry, Rafe rode into the fort. The place looked normal, with off-duty soldiers strolling about. But something didn't feel quite right. Rafe glanced suspiciously toward the officers' quarters. Karissa damn well better be where she was supposed to be.

He suspected that she had used their tour the previous night to case the area, looking for a niche in the shadows to hide out before making her getaway.

He had anticipated that she would wait until she thought she'd lulled him into a false sense of control and had him thinking she had accepted captivity before she made her escape. But knowing Karissa, his attempt to second-guess her strategy would work *against* him, not *for* him. Much as he hated to admit it, she was a mental step ahead of him.

The woman was too smart by half.

Rafe shifted uneasily in the saddle as he passed by the officers' quarters. The sixth sense that he'd learned to rely on warned him that something was wrong. It left him with an uneasy tension that prompted him to make fast work of tending his horse. In record time he shut Sergeant in his stall and headed straight for his quarters. He needed to see for himself that Karissa was still in custody.

A growl exploded from his lips when he opened the door to find his room in shambles. The sheets and blankets were in a tangled heap. The table had been up-ended; the bookshelf had toppled over, leaving his military manuals strewn about like casualties of war. The glass globe of the lantern lay in shattered pieces on the floor and oil stained the floorboards.

"Damn her!" Rafe said furiously as he stormed outside.

"She's gone?" Micah hooted. "I presumed—"

Rafe wheeled on his longtime friend. "You *never* presume when it comes to that woman!" he fumed. "The moment I think we have reached a workable truce she rips my quarters to shreds and escapes." He swung his arms in agitated gestures. "This is the thanks I get for guarding the land she wants to claim and keeping it free of other squatters."

"I'll go after her," Micah volunteered hurriedly. "I don't think you're in the right frame of mind to track her down."

"Oh, no, you won't," Rafe countered as he stalked off. "She is my responsibility and this is another act of rebellion against my position of authority."

Rafe didn't add that, although Micah was probably better suited for pursuing Karissa, he was suffering from an absurd feeling of possessiveness and protectiveness.

He wanted to be the one to track her down. *He* wanted to be the one to discover she hadn't put herself in harm's way. *He* wanted to be the one to rake her over live coals for destroying his quarters and thumbing her nose at his orders. And, by damned, he was going to drag her back to the post to serve her time for breaking the laws governing the upcoming Land Run.

"Um…Rafe?" Micah murmured as he followed his friend.

"What?" he growled as he headed back to the stables.

"I know you're furious," Micah called after him, "but outright murder doesn't become you. You are first and always an officer and a gentleman."

"Maybe so, but right now I would gladly resign my command for five minutes of justified fury! When I get that woman back in custody she is not going to see the light of day for a week!" He broke into a run and sprinted into the stables. "Assume command of this post while I'm gone, Micah!"

Karissa brushed her fingertips over the bruise on her cheek that still throbbed hours after her harrowing encounter with Harlan Billings. He had tried to force himself on her after he had escorted her back to Rafe's quarters for the evening. Karissa shook off the repulsive thought of how close she had come to being violated. She had made the mistake of dismissively turning her back on Harlan—a mistake she would never make with any man again.

Considering the fact that she had left Rafe's room in shambles—as a show of defiance that first night—she really didn't expect him to believe that lecherous toad had assaulted her. She, after all, was an escaped prisoner and Harlan was a soldier under Rafe's command.

She clutched the torn neckline of her borrowed dress and waited until the wagon in which she'd hidden had reached a thicket of trees. The driver, who was oblivious to the fact that a stowaway was tucked beneath the tarp in the wagon bed, went merrily on his way. Karissa wormed from concealment and hopped off the wagon. Casting a quick glance to make sure the driver hadn't noticed her, she dashed into the underbrush.

She knew she didn't have much time before Rafe discovered she was missing. She had heard the driver of the supply wagon call out a greeting when he encountered the returning army patrol. By now, Rafe would have seen the destruction in his room and assumed she had spitefully laid the place to ruin and made her escape.

Karissa predicted that Rafe would tear off to the site where he had originally apprehended her. Therefore, she would be asking for more trouble than she had already encountered if she made a beeline for her property.

"Well, what have we here?" came a voice from the shadows of the trees.

Karissa refused to let herself freeze up in fear. She had endured one near brush with disaster today and that was more than enough. She had to lose herself in the underbrush and wait until she could use the gathering darkness to her advantage. She didn't have time to retrieve the bag of men's clothing and supplies she had buried on her claim site. But she felt exposed and vulnerable while wearing a dress, and whoever had sneaked up on her had realized she was a woman.

When she heard two more male voices behind her, panicked desperation spurted through her veins. Karissa grabbed the front of her skirt to keep from tripping and dashed southeast, veering away from the cover of the trees toward more familiar territory. She knew the property she wanted to claim like the back of her hand. If she could elude the men until darkness became her protector she was sure she could find a place to hide for the night.

Terror and outrage threatened to overwhelm her when she heard one of the men breathing down her neck. She let out a bloodcurdling shriek when he clamped hold of her shoulder and jerked her backward. As she stumbled off balance she raised an elbow to bash in her attacker's nose. He yelped in pain and covered his face, giving Karissa time to wrest free. Unfortunately, the other two men overtook her and she found herself shoved face-down in the grass.

She screeched, she kicked and she clawed, but three to one odds overpowered her. Karissa screamed bloody murder when two of the men rolled her onto her back and pinned her shoulders to the ground.

A bearded face loomed above her. "You nearly broke my nose, bitch," the man growled as he yanked up her skirts. "And now you're going to pay for it, thrice over."

When the man dropped to his knees, Karissa thrust out her leg and caught him squarely in the groin. He howled like a coyote then lambasted her with curses. But Karissa kept kicking at him and straining against the two men who held her shoulders to the ground. She felt her strength waning and knew it was only a matter of time before these lusty scoundrels did their worst. But Karissa refused to surrender, refused to make it easy on her assailants. She had fought her way through life and it was second nature to battle even the most difficult odds.

"Let her go!" Rafe's booming voice rumbled in the distance and Karissa slumped in relief.

The men sprang away from her and wheeled toward the mounted soldier, who loomed in the twilight like an avenging angel. When one of the men made a grab for his pistol Rafe's rifle barked viciously. Karissa glanced sideways to see one of her assailants wilt to the ground, clutching his arm.

"I said back off!" Rafe thundered as he took the second man's measure on the sight of his rifle.

While dismounting, Rafe kept his weapon trained on the two men left standing. He had ridden hell-for-leather, itching to strangle Karissa for spitefully destroying his quarters and escaping from the fort. But his anger was nothing compared to the outrage that overwhelmed him when he'd heard Karissa's shriek in the distance and had ridden over the hill to see these three men trying to rape her. He considered himself a fair and just man, but committing cold-blooded murder was starting to appeal to him greatly.

"Sit down in the grass, back to back," he ordered gruffly. Reaching into his saddlebag, he retrieved three lengths of rope. "Karissa, bind them together."

She rolled unsteadily to all fours then staggered to her feet. When she swayed slightly, he realized she was suffering from the aftereffects of the attack. Nevertheless, she gathered her composure and tied the two uninjured men together while Rafe inspected the third ruffian's bullet wound.

When he heard the rending of cloth, he glanced up to see that Karissa had torn the hem off her tattered gown to provide a bandage. "I should let him bleed to death after what he tried to do to me," she said bitterly, "but I'm not quite as heartless as he is."

Rafe noticed her hand was still shaking as she offered the improvised bandage. He knew how it felt to ride an adrenaline high, knew she was barely holding herself together. Sooner or later traumatic shock from the unnerving incident was going to catch up with her. Aggravated though he was with her, he was still going to be there to catch her when she fell apart.

"I'm bleeding to death!" the injured man railed as he stared at his bloodstained jacket.

"You'll live," Rafe diagnosed as he hurriedly bandaged his captive's wound. "Considering what you tried to do, you're lucky I didn't aim for your heart."

Swiftly he bound the man's hands then hoisted him to his feet. With Karissa's assistance, he marched the men toward the nearest tree and tethered them. "I'll send a patrol out to retrieve you," he told the men. "Until then, you can sit here and rot."

To his surprise, Karissa sidled up beside him, clutched his hand and murmured, "Thank you."

"This wouldn't have happened if you had stayed put," he said, and scowled.

She jerked up her head so quickly that the last of her disheveled coiffure came tumbling down her shoulders, catching in the last rays of sunset like dancing flames. When Rafe noticed the discoloration on her cheek and the gaping neckline of her dress, his fist clenched around his rifle. Vicious fury took a bite out of him as he glared at the three men.

"They didn't leave the marks," she told him shakily.

His narrowed gaze swung back to her. "Then who did?"

"You don't want to know and probably couldn't care less," she muttered.

Rafe clutched her arm to shepherd her toward his

horse. "When someone assaults a woman who is under my protection, I care," he assured her gruffly. "Even if said woman probably deserved what she got for her reckless daring."

To Rafe's disbelief she didn't snap back at him. She just sort of crumpled beside him and he reflexively reached out to steady her on her feet. He heard her muffled sob and felt her trembling hands clutch at his arm. In the blink of an eye his frustration evaporated and he gathered her compassionately to him.

"Damn it," she mumbled against his chest. "The very last thing I meant to do was let you see me cry."

"It's all right," he whispered as he impulsively brushed his lips over her bruised cheek. "You're going to be fine now. After a warm meal and hot bath you'll be your sassy self again."

Well, so much for reading her every paragraph of the riot act—forward and backward, twice. When she broke down and soaked the jacket of his uniform with tears, he couldn't work up the anger to chastise her.

Yes, she had it coming for putting herself in harm's way. And yes, he had wanted to be the one to deliver a scathing lecture. But when a woman as strong as Karissa buckled to her emotions Rafe couldn't bring himself to do anything except offer comfort.

And he was not even going to think about how good she felt in his arms or how much satisfaction he derived from being the one who had rescued her from disaster. As hard as he tried, it was impossible not to become emotionally involved with this woman, even if she was all wrong for him. Even if he was betrothed…

The thought prompted Rafe to release her and step back into his own space. He scooped Karissa off the ground, gently settled her on Sergeant's back and then swung up behind her.

When he reined toward the fort, she clutched his hand. "I need to fetch my belongings," she said brokenly. "I buried them near the spring…please?"

Rafe relented and allowed her to take the reins to ride toward her abandoned campsite. He listened to her muffled sobs for as long as he could stand and then said, "I'm truly sorry you met with trouble, Karissa. No woman deserves to be treated so disrespectfully. Rest assured that those three men will be punished severely."

Ten minutes later Karissa halted beside the rock-covered hillside where a spring trickled into a shimmering pool. Rafe dismounted and then set her to her feet. Swaying slightly, Karissa approached the site of her buried cache and used a nearby rock to unearth her carpetbag. And then to Rafe's tormented dismay, she burst into tears all over again. He tried to tell himself that it was a manipulative ruse, aimed at drawing his sympathy, but he doubted that even Karissa was that good an actress.

"Can't you bend your damnable rules and just let me stay here?" she said on a sob and hiccup. "Every soldier at the fort thinks I'm your live-in mistress, even if most of them have been polite and respectful in my presence. I don't want to go back there. I would rather take my chances out here." She clung desperately to the carpetbag in her quaking hands. "At least out here I have a disguise for protection. If I had been dressed like a boy, those men wouldn't have accosted me and your—"

Karissa bit down on her tongue before she blurted out that Harlan Billings had tried to do the very same thing to her. She knew Rafe was loyal to the army and to the men in his command. She had no doubt whatsoever that he would take Harlan's word over hers.

"My *what?*" Rafe grilled her as he strode forward to tower over her. "What were you going to say?"

She shook her head. "Nothing. It's not important. What is important is that I need to stay here so I can claim this property. It's all I want in life. Is that asking so much?"

Rafe squatted down on his haunches and curled his index finger beneath her quivering chin. Steel-gray eyes bored into her and, even in the darkness, she could feel their intensity on her. "Tell me why it's so important that you have this property?" he demanded. "Why should I grant you special privileges when this Run for free land is supposed to be a fair race for all other settlers?"

Karissa didn't know why she wanted to take Rafe into her confidence when she had kept her own counsel for years. She supposed the unnerving experiences of the day had simply broken her spirit and left her with the need to lean on someone until she could gather her composure. She had never begged for anything in her life, but suddenly she found herself blurting out her thoughts like a witless ninny.

"As much as I love this property that calls out to me, I want to claim it for my brother and his new wife," she gushed as she clutched her dirty carpetbag to her chest. "On the way down from Kansas, Clint was thrown from his horse. He suffered a broken leg and concussion. He barely gets around on the crutch I…found…for him and it will be impossible for him to make the Run. His wife is seven months' pregnant and she is in no condition to take Clint's place in the race for land. I've looked after my younger brother since we were kids. Now I want him to have a fresh start, the chance to make a new life.''

To her dismay, she realized tears were dribbling down her cheeks. She managed to reroute them, but she couldn't seem to clamp down on her tongue as she should have. Rafe didn't care what a difficult life she'd had. She wasn't his responsibility. He had a blue-blooded fiancée waiting for him back East. He didn't care that she had somehow gotten attached to him the past few days.

It was ridiculous, but it didn't stop her from pouring out her heart to him. She felt the insane need to make him understand there was good reason she had turned out the way she had. She didn't expect him to *like* her, but she wanted him to understand what motivated her.

''I doubt that you can begin to imagine what it's like to be uprooted and moved from one lawless cow town to the next while your father drowns his woes in whiskey and gambles away every cent he's accumulated. I doubt you know what it's like to be a woman who has to dress as a boy and sweep up in smoke-filled saloons, while calico queens and drunkards paw each other and fling lewd remarks, just so you can acquire enough money to feed yourself and your little brother.''

''Where is your father now?'' he asked gently.

''He got caught cheating at poker and the dispute ended badly for him. I couldn't afford to give him a proper burial.''

''I'm sorry, Rissa.'' Rafe tried to pat her consolingly, but she shrugged him off and rambled on before the tears washed away her voice.

''I never had the chance to make friends, only passing acquaintances. Never had a home to call my own or enough money to buy a gown as fine as this one that you borrowed for me. And now look at it!'' To her horror, Karissa wailed like an abandoned baby when she realized the gown had suffered irreparable damage. ''And how am I going to earn the money to replace this gown? What little money I made from washing, scrubbing and mending will barely cover food and supplies for my brother and his wife!''

Shamelessly Karissa fell into Rafe's arms, knowing perfectly well she didn't belong there, that she wasn't particularly wanted there, but needing to be held and comforted.

Of course, she would never be able to look this man in the eye after she had reduced herself to blubbering tears, but she had to get through the night—somehow— if she was going to marshal her spirits to face another trying day.

''I—I'm s-sorry,'' she whimpered, humiliated. ''I— I—''

To her further mortification she flung her arms around his neck and kissed him squarely on the mouth. It was a reckless mistake, a complete lapse of good judgment. She had no idea why she thought she needed to kiss Rafe Hunter so desperately. He didn't belong to her, would never belong to her and she was only reaffirming his belief that she was nothing more than a trollop.

But suddenly Karissa forgot all the reasons she *shouldn't* be kissing him, because he was kissing her back and the world tilted on its axis and time ceased to exist.

It didn't take long to realize that Rafe Hunter kissed as well as he handled a rifle and sat on a horse. He stole the breath right out of her lungs and ignited a fire in her blood that all the water in the creek couldn't extinguish. Karissa had never felt so wild, reckless and needy, never

knew desire could leave a woman's head spinning so
furiously that she couldn't tell which way was up—and
couldn't care less.

Brawny arms crushed her to him and held her fast.
His mouth was like liquid fire on hers and she could
feel his heart hammering in frantic rhythm with hers.
Every unruly emotion that had hounded her throughout
the evening fueled this newly discovered sensation of
desire and compelled her to kiss him as if there was no
tomorrow.

Karissa lost herself in the unprecedented pleasure, lost
herself in this man who stood squarely between her and
her dream of a home that could support her family and
grant them a new start in life. Yet, at the moment, Rafe
Hunter's incredible kisses seemed to be the only thing
she needed to survive from one instant to the next.

While Karissa's thoughts spun out of control, Rafe
kissed Karissa the way he had never kissed a woman—
without the slightest restraint. As fragile as her emotions
were at the moment he shouldn't have kissed her at all.
But *not* kissing her was like telling himself not to
breathe.

She tasted spicy—so like her temperament. She felt
like every man's forbidden dream in his arms. She held
him as tightly to her as he held her to him—like two
drowning castaways floundering on a storm-tossed sea.
And even knowing he was breaking his impeccable code
of honor he still couldn't stop himself from caressing
the shapely curve of her hips and the swell of her
breasts.

Rafe had never felt so reckless, and he was a man
who prided himself on logic and self-restraint. More
than anything he wanted to peel off that tattered dress
and press his lips and fingertips to every luscious inch

of Karissa's body. He ached to let this obsessive desire run its fiery course and finally allow him to reclaim his sanity.

Yet, a quiet voice whispered they were alone in the middle of nowhere and no one would know if he took his pleasure in Karissa while she overcame her tormenting experiences by losing herself in his eager arms.

No one would know. But *Rafe* would know and Karissa would most likely expect him to grant her request to remain on her claim if he took what she had offered to him that first night at the fort.

Just a few more heart-stopping kisses and tantalizing caresses, he bargained with himself. Then he would step back into his role of responsibility and respectability and clear his befuddled head.

"My God," she wheezed when she came up for a breath of air. "I never knew passion could feel like this."

Those enormous green eyes, so full of hungry wonder, dropped to his lips, and Rafe realized he hadn't had enough of her yet. She was the worst kind of temptress a man could encounter. She was complex and complicated. She was spirit, strength, temptation and vulnerability rolled into one enticing package.

There was an innocence about her, even when she'd confided that life had dealt her a difficult hand. But she had defied her fate and fought back with every ounce of energy she could muster, just as she had battled the three men who'd tried to reduce her to an object of sexual gratification.

Rafe knew he'd never held more woman in his arms. That knowledge was an aphrodisiac that left him plundering her mouth and filling his hands with her shapely body. He simply could not get enough of her fast enough to satisfy himself.

He was sorry to say that it wasn't his own good sense that finally prompted him to remove his wandering hands from her generous curves; it was the sudden hoot of an owl. Guilt and frustration hit him like a fist to the jaw. Damnation, for a man who prided himself on honor, duty and commitment, he was no better than the three men who had pounced on Karissa.

He opened his mouth to apologize, wondering if the astounded look on Karissa's face mirrored his expression. Probably. It seemed neither of them wanted to acknowledge the powerful attraction that exploded between them like blasting powder.

In the aftermath of their reckless surrender to desire, her gaze dropped like a rock and she clutched her discarded carpetbag to her chest as if it were her only salvation.

"I think you should go now," she chirped in a voice he could scarcely associate with her. It sounded small, lacking the defiance and confidence he'd come to expect.

Rafe reached over to pull her upright as he surged to his feet. "You're coming back to the fort with me." His strangled voice testified to the devastating effect she'd had on him. "I admire your determination to help your brother build a home for his new family, but you are still trespassing and it is still my duty to keep this area free of squatters. Next week you will have the same opportunity as everyone else to claim your land in the Run."

"On a plodding old horse that already has one foot in the grave, thanks to the accident that left my brother with a broken leg? I sincerely doubt it," Karissa muttered as she jerked her arm from his grasp and thrust back her shoulders.

She'd spilled her guts to this man, practically threw herself at him to compensate for the churning emotion that was dragging her down after the miserable day she'd had. He'd kissed her, as if the world was coming to an end, touched her in ways she had never allowed another man to touch her. And all he had to say was that she was still his prisoner?

Although she understood that he was a man of honor who took his duty seriously it hurt no less that he couldn't find it in his rock-solid heart to view her plight as an exception to his confounded rules.

Karissa drew herself up to dignified stature—at least as dignified as she could muster after she'd made a complete fool of herself in Rafe's arms. "I'm really beginning to hate you, General," she scowled at him. "I swear, if the day ever comes that you have to break one of your precious, honorable and noble rules it will probably be the death of you."

She gave an unladylike snort as she pulled herself up into his saddle. For a moment she considered digging her heels into the gelding's flanks and leaving Rafe afoot. It would take him at least a day to track her down. But he would track her down eventually because he knew exactly where to find her. Furthermore, he would make it his mission and he was relentless when it came to following the rules.

If she pushed him to the limit he would refuse to allow her to make the Run at all. Then her brother wouldn't have an icicle's chance in Hades of claiming property for his farm.

There was a hint of a smile in Rafe's voice when he

swung up behind her. "You had your chance to escape and you didn't take it. Why?"

She wasn't about to bolster his confidence by admitting that she considered him a force to be reckoned with. "I'll let you know when I figure it out myself." She grabbed the reins and headed for the fort. "Maybe it was your irresistible charm that swayed me," she added sarcastically.

Behind her—*too* close behind her for her own comfort—she could feel Rafe's amusement vibrating through every fiber of her body, reminding her of how tightly she had been pressed up against his muscular body moments earlier.

"Compliments from you, Rissa? Now why does that make me suspicious?"

She stiffened her spine to put some distance between them and elevated her chin another notch. "I did not give you permission to use a shortened version of my name, General. It's *Miss Baxter* to you. And by the way, Harlan Billings informed me that you have a fiancée. If I hadn't been so upset earlier I would never have allowed you so close. Despite what you probably think, that incident was not a ploy to maneuver you into letting me stay on my claim. I simply wasn't myself."

"And now you are?" he asked.

The hint of amusement in his voice annoyed her. "Yes," she said with a brisk nod. "Cynical of men for good reason and determined to do whatever necessary to help my brother. What happened between us didn't really happen. I refuse to allow that moment of insanity to cloud my dealings with you. Now that I'm back on solid mental footing, I can view you for what you are— an aggravating obstacle in my path."

"I see," he said. "Then I feel compelled to inform

you that if you don't clean up my quarters, after you maliciously tore it upside down again, that you *will* be sleeping in the stockade with the other prisoners. I granted you a courtesy and you abused my generosity.''

''I'm not the one who wrecked the place,'' she shot back.

''Right,'' he scoffed. ''As if I wasn't there that first night when you demolished my room for pure sport.''

Karissa twisted in the saddle to confront him face-to-face. ''I was not the one who tore your room apart. Furthermore, I did not self-inflict this bruise on my cheek or damage this borrowed dress. That happened *before* I left the fort. It was the reason I left the post in the first place. And if you assign the same guard to me tomorrow, I demand a pistol or dagger to protect myself!''

Rafe's thick brows jackknifed. ''Corporal Billings attacked you in my room?'' he asked in disbelief.

Karissa swiveled around and stared straight ahead. ''Not according to him, I'm sure. No doubt, he will have concocted his own twisted account of the incident. But since you have made it clear repeatedly that you don't trust me, I don't expect you to believe me. In fact, you probably don't believe that I even have a brother with a broken leg and a sister-in-law with child. Why should you? I'm just a nobody from Kansas who has scratched and clawed to accumulate the bare necessities for staying alive.''

Karissa was sincerely grateful when Rafe fell silent and urged his mount into a gallop. She was more than ready to reach the fort and put some distance between them. Having him so close was a tormenting reminder that she had recklessly succumbed to kissing an engaged man who was still more enemy than friend.

Obviously, she had suffered a severe lapse of good judgment when she had come crashing down from her adrenaline rush and felt the overwhelming need to lean on someone for support and compassion.

She should have leaned on a tree until she pulled herself together.

Chapter Five

Rafe escorted Karissa to his room and helped her begin to restore the place to order. He called to Micah to join them, noting the shocked look on his friend's face when he noticed the quarters were a disheveled disaster.

"What the hell happened in here?" Micah asked as he picked up shards of glass. "It looks as if someone had a knock-down-drag-out fight."

When Karissa flashed Rafe an I-told-you-so glance, Rafe shoved the bookshelf back against the wall and crammed the books into place haphazardly. Although he'd had serious doubts about Karissa's character and scruples when he had first captured her, he had observed her behavior during several telling situations that made him feel as if he had known her much longer than a few days. She was a scrappy fighter who refused to whimper in the face of difficulty or defeat. She acted and reacted quickly and decisively. She didn't get scared; she got *mad* when she encountered frightening situations.

True, she might have used her alluring sexuality as bargaining power in the past, but the moment she tore a strip off her gown to serve as a bandage for the man who had come dangerously close to abusing her, Rafe had discovered something else about her. Karissa Baxter could be compassionate and forgiving. When he learned that Karissa had risked arrest in order to help her injured brother, he realized she was self-sacrificing and attended to the needs of her loved ones before her own.

And, yes, Rafe intended to verify her story about an injured brother, but he was pretty sure there *was* a brother out there on the prairie somewhere, waiting to attempt to stake his claim. She might have mocked Rafe for his unswerving loyalty to duty, but she was guilty of that same single-minded devotion to her family.

"Micah, I have pressing business to attend to," Rafe announced as he headed for the door. "Will you see to it that this place is cleaned up, then draw a bath and send a supper tray for Karissa. She's had a rough night."

"I sure as hell hope you weren't the cause of it," Micah muttered as he stared pointedly at Karissa's bruised cheek and tattered dress. "I knew you were furious with her, but—"

"He didn't lay a hand on me," Karissa cut in, tilting her chin upward. "He's too much the gentleman for that."

Rafe cocked a brow. She was letting him know straightaway that she wasn't going to hold that amorous interlude over his head like an ax on a chopping block. Obviously she had meant what she said. To her, the encounter hadn't happened.

He wished his body would stop screaming reminders at him that it most certainly *had* happened. Staring at her, disheveled though she looked, made him want her all over again. And that left him feeling guilty and frustrated and disappointed in himself.

"So," Micah said, his piercing gaze darting back and

forth between Karissa and Rafe, "who is responsible for abusing you?"

"She can fill you in while I send out a patrol to bring in her assailants and tend to some business at the post," Rafe said as he spun on his boot heel.

Jaw clenched, fists knotted, Rafe whizzed outside and stalked across the parade grounds to the barracks. He found Harlan Billings hunkered over a table, studying his poker hand.

"Corporal Billings, I want a word with you." More than *a* word actually, Rafe thought furiously. He was inclined to rain down foul curses on Harlan's head and then beat him to a senseless pulp. The prospect of one of his men assaulting Karissa—in Rafe's room no less— made him boiling mad.

"Outside," Rafe muttered when Harlan joined him at the door.

"I'm glad you came by, sir, " Harlan said contritely as he fell into step behind Rafe. "I need to report a disconcerting incident that occurred late this afternoon. If you haven't observed the results of the tussle by now, I'm sure you will soon, sir."

Rafe grabbed on to his self-control with slippery fists. As commander, he was obliged to hear Harlan out, to let him tell his side of the story. But it was damn hard to stand still when he really wanted to stuff his fist down the man's throat and yank out his tongue!

"It all started when I refused to let Miss Baxter quit early for the day," Harlan insisted. "She seemed to think she was entitled to special privileges since she was staying in your room." Harlan's eyes dropped and he shifted from one foot to the other. "Granted, I don't know exactly what the situation is with Miss Baxter, but

I was under the impression she was hired for a full day's work at the laundry.''

Rafe gnashed his teeth, refusing to comment until Harlan had said his piece. But it wasn't easy when he was stung by the impulsive need to call the man a liar— right to his face.

"Miss Baxter stalked off to your quarters, sir," Harlan went on. "I followed her, of course. She swore and cursed at me when I insisted she return to finish her duties. Then she threw a royal tantrum and tore your quarters apart."

Harlan lifted his arms in a helpless gesture. "I tried to stop her, of course, but she sank in her claws and shoved me aside. She swore she would claim that I tried to force myself on her and see to it that I was punished. She knocked me against the bookshelf, but I tried to restrain her from doing more damage to your room. Then she smashed the lantern over my head. I had kerosene in my eyes and I couldn't catch up with her when she ran off. I have no idea where she has gotten off to, sir, but I swear that woman is a raging lunatic."

"And you didn't immediately notify the officer of the day after the incident?" Rafe said.

"No, sir, I went to see Doc Winston. He washed out my eyes before I took a bath to rid myself of the smell of kerosene."

"For your information, Corporal, Miss Baxter has returned to the fort, but her version of the incident is in drastic contrast to yours," Rafe snapped.

Harlan nodded grimly. "She warned me that she would twist the truth. That crazed female might have led you to believe she's a lady, but she's the exact opposite. I hope you won't assign me to guarding her again, sir. Two days with her was punishment enough."

Rafe waited a beat then said, "I think you're lying right through your teeth, Corporal."

All pretense of polite respect gone, Harlan jerked up his head and jeered, "And I'm wondering, as the rest of the men are, if you're receiving fringe benefits for taking *her* side against me."

Rafe loomed over the weasely corporal, wishing he could have the man dishonorably discharged, right on the spot. But he didn't have time for an investigation and lengthy military proceedings, especially with the Land Run looming ahead of him.

His cavalry was already stretched to the limits. He barely had enough soldiers to keep watch over the Cheyenne and Arapaho reservation, to protect the would-be settlers who had pitched their camps along the boundaries of the new territory from brutal ruffians and dishonest scoundrels, and patrol the area for squatters. He needed every soldier he could get, even ones like Harlan who would be digging latrines and mucking the barn from now until doomsday.

"You will be put on report and I will look into this matter further," Rafe said sharply. "In the meantime, you will be on stable duty and night guard duty until further notice. Your sergeant will be instructed to keep a close eye on you."

"Yes, sir," Harlan muttered before Rafe wheeled around and left.

Harlan cursed colorfully as the commander disappeared into the officers' quarters. It was fine and dandy for Rafe Hunter to bring his own private harlot to the fort, but the rest of the men were denied such lusty pleasures. Obviously, the commander was placing his own interests above the men under his command.

For months Harlan had resented the commander's position of authority and he swore he was being picked on each time his name was overlooked for promotions. Indeed, he'd been demoted for nothing more than a few charges of drunken and disorderly conduct.

Well, he'd kowtowed to Rafe Hunter for the last time. If that feisty trollop was going to make Harlan's life hell then he'd return the favor by contacting Rafe's fiancée. No doubt, she would be interested in knowing that her betrothed was tumbling in the sheets with a camp follower who sought to better her life by cozying up with the commandant of this military post.

Harlan smiled wickedly as he headed for the post's telegraph office. Rafe Hunter wasn't going to threaten him with discharge without facing the consequences. Harlan would spread the word around the fort that Commander Hunter wasn't fit for command and he'd bring Hunter's harlot face-to-face with his fiancée. That should cause the uppity major more trouble than he'd know what to do with.

Whether Rafe Hunter and his whore knew it or not, they had crossed the wrong man. Harlan grinned in satisfaction. Nothing would make him happier than to see Major Hunter relieved of his command. That would be a crushing blow to him and his highfalutin family.

The prospect of ruining Rafe's career left Harlan chuckling devilishly as he sent off the message urging Vanessa Payton to catch the first train west if she wanted her wedding to Rafe to take place.

A few days later, Vanessa Payton excused herself from her dance partner when a courier arrived with a message. Stepping into the abandoned hall, she read the brief telegram and gasped in outrage. According to Har-

Ian Billings—whoever he was—her betrothed had taken a mistress who had set her cap at Vanessa's intended.

''Blast and be damned,'' Vanessa muttered irritably. Whether she was in love with Rafe Hunter—which, of course, she wasn't since she barely knew him—was not the point. She needed the security of this union and she needed it as quickly as possible.

Rafe had already put her off another few months, using the excuse that his constant duties in Indian Territory demanded so much of his time. But it wouldn't be long before her peers in the palatial ballrooms in Virginia realized the Paytons were suffering serious financial difficulties.

Vanessa's father had taken her aside eight months earlier to confide that he needed to make a match with the Hunters. Although Jonathan Payton had social connections galore, he had made several bad investments. He intended for his one and only daughter to marry well and he had struck a deal with his old friend who had served with him during the Civil War.

Of course, Vanessa had no intention of living in some backward army post during her marriage. With a generous allowance from Rafe, she could continue to enjoy the gala affairs in Virginia society. But none of that was going to happen unless she packed her bag, caught the train and persuaded Rafe to move up the wedding date a few months.

He was dallying with a nameless strumpet, she thought with an outraged huff. At least *her* dalliances included wealthy, respectable men from proper society. Men who could shower her with costly gifts that helped her keep up appearances.

Well, Vanessa mused as she called to her escort to see her home, she would marry Rafe before she returned to Virginia. She knew how to charm and bedazzle men. Charming Rafe shouldn't be too difficult. He had been an honorable man who stood by his commitments—until that little tramp sank her claws into him.

"Is something wrong, my dear?" her escort asked as he assisted her into his carriage. "You look upset."

"I will be out of town for a few weeks," Vanessa said absently. "I need to pay my fiancé a visit."

William Gable sighed in frustration. "I don't know why you think you need to go through with this marriage. I've made it clear that I love you, Nessa. I know I can't compete with the Hunters' wealth and prestige, but I could make you happy—"

"Will you please stop whining, Willy," she fussed at him. "I have too much on my mind at the moment."

"But I don't understand why—"

She kissed him to shut him up. "Nothing between us will change when I return from my trip, but I promised my father I would agree to this match. I see no need to put it off. The sooner I have a ring on my finger the sooner we can resume our affair."

"I wanted you as my wife," he grumbled.

And no doubt, that floozy out in Indian Territory wanted Rafe as her husband, Vanessa silently fumed. Not everyone could have their way, but Vanessa was accustomed to getting hers, and she was not about to lose the monetary funds and social prestige she could acquire by hustling Rafe into a quick marriage.

After all, a woman had to do whatever necessary to preserve her social standing and enjoy the luxuries of wealth. Rafe Hunter would marry her, as promised. She was heading west—immediately—to protect her investment.

*　*　*

Micah inclined his head toward the gaggle of soldiers who had gathered around Karissa in the mess hall. She was handing out the uniforms she had mended. "She's certainly become popular around the fort," he remarked, while Rafe sullenly finished his meal. "I noticed one of our men had purposely ripped off a button just to have an excuse to take Karissa aside and ask her to mend the garment for him."

"Yes," Rafe grumbled, staring at his plate. "I observed the same thing myself on two occasions."

"So…when are you going to release her?" Micah asked.

That was the same question Karissa had asked Rafe for the past three days. In fact, it was the only thing she ever said to him when he came within speaking distance. He had been avoiding her as much as possible. He'd figured that if he kept his distance maybe she wouldn't drive him out of his mind. He'd been wrong. Nothing had prevented him from thinking about her all the live-long day. And half the night. Rafe had never had difficulty focusing on his military duties until that red-haired female disrupted his life.

He looked at Harlan Billings, who was staring bitterly at the crowd of men vying for Karissa's attention. In a way, Rafe understood Harlan's resentment—even if the woman had caused the corporal a different kind of trouble. But it was trouble Harlan deserved, nonetheless.

"Well?" Micah prompted when he didn't receive an immediate response. "When are you releasing Karissa? You've already released the male squatters who were rounded up about the same time you brought her in."

"I'll release her in a few more days." Which is what he told Karissa every night when she asked.

Micah smiled wryly. "And what's the reason you're

detaining her when you've delivered your authoritative lecture to the other illegal squatters and then sent them back to the settlers' encampments? Getting attached to her, Rafe?"

"No," he replied vehemently. He could tell Micah didn't believe him. Of course, Micah had incredible instincts, damn his perceptive hide.

The frustrating truth was that he was so protective of her that he didn't want to drive himself crazy, wondering if other lusty scoundrels had set upon her. He still had nightmares about that unnerving incident. And though he refused to go near her for more than three minutes at a time, he wanted her close at hand.

Observing her from a distance was the only pleasure he allowed himself.

When Karissa glanced in his direction, her smile fading, Rafe felt as if someone had punched him in the gut. How could she do this to him? Why did he let her? And what the hell had happened to his unwavering dedication to duty?

Maybe Micah was right, Rafe mused. It was time to let Karissa go. She was, after all, as scrappy as an alley cat and she had been fending for herself and her brother for more than a dozen years. Obviously she was adept at it.

"Well, I'll be damned."

Rafe followed Micah's gaze to the doorway. He nearly fell out of his chair when none other than Vanessa Payton materialized out of nowhere. All conversation in the mess hall died a quick death and all eyes turned to the striking blonde who was dressed in an expensive gown usually reserved for fashionable social balls.

"I've only seen the chit once," Micah said, "but that

definitely looks like your fiancée. What's she doing here? Did you decide to move up the wedding?''

"No." Stunned, Rafe came to his feet.

"Rafe! There you are at last! I've been looking all over the post for you!'' Vanessa gushed enthusiastically.

Chapter Six

Flashing a dazzling smile, Vanessa made her grand entrance. When she swept across the room like a colorful, velvet-enshrouded butterfly, the soldiers' attention swung from her to Karissa and back again. And so did Rafe's.

It was the damnedest thing—because Rafe *should* have been relieved to see Vanessa—but her arrival felt more like intrusion. When Vanessa sashayed to him, curled her arm around his elbow and smiled brilliantly, there was nothing for Rafe to do but press a kiss to her wrist.

"Vanessa, it's a pleasure to see you again. But what are you doing here? I didn't receive a telegram notifying me that you were coming."

She tossed her blond head and graced him with another radiant smile. "I wanted to surprise you. Besides, we are to be married and it only seemed reasonable that I should visit the post you command. I'm very impressed, by the way."

Rafe cocked a brow at that. He would have expected a woman who was accustomed to every luxury imaginable to be disappointed by the modest accommodations at the army post.

"Micah, isn't it?" Vanessa said as she outstretched her free hand. "It is so good to see you again."

Micah dutifully took her hand and kissed her perfumed wrist. Rafe noticed he looked less than enthused.

"Aren't you going to introduce me to your officers and their wives?" Vanessa prompted. "Really, Rafe, you have been on the frontier so long that you have forgotten your manners."

"Nice of you to point that out," Micah muttered half under his breath.

"Excuse me?" Vanessa said, tossing one of those practiced smiles at Micah.

Micah feigned a polite smile for her benefit. "I said Rafe must've been so surprised by your arrival that he forgot himself." He bowed slightly then backed away. "If you will excuse me, Miss Payton. I'll take Rafe's evening duties so he will have more time to see that you are settled in."

Rafe glanced sideways, startled to note that Karissa had vanished into thin air. He suspected she had ducked out through the kitchen to save them both from any embarrassment.

Dutifully, Rafe introduced Vanessa to the officers and their wives then escorted her outside to listen to the regimental band that performed each evening after mess call. She insisted on seeing every nook and cranny of the fort, while she clung to him like a limpet to a ship. It was with shameful relief that Rafe collected her luggage and saw to it that she was settled in the suite usually reserved for visiting military dignitaries.

Damn, he mused as he headed back to the officers' quarters. Just what he needed right now. More complications. The past few days he had sensed the tension and anticipation of the settlers who were gearing up for the wild race to stake land claims. It was only going to get worse. Adding Vanessa to the mix was going to overload his days.

She had insisted that he show her around the area. She even claimed she wanted to visit the Cheyenne and Arapaho agency at Darlington—the small community that sat a mile northeast of the garrison, just across the river. According to Vanessa, she wanted to see real live Indians in their natural habitat.

Rafe was relieved that Micah hadn't been around to hear *that* comment.

Rafe sighed in frustration. On one hand he should be grateful for the opportunity to get to know the woman he had agreed to take as his wife. On the other hand—

His thoughts trailed off when he veered into the foyer of the officers' quarters to find Karissa awaiting him.

"I think it's time you released me," she said stiffly.

"No, because I know exactly where you'll go and what might happen to you," he countered just as stiffly.

She hitched her chin at him. "I am not your responsibility. Do not force me to leave without permission. I intend to leave, first thing in the morning."

"No," he said with sharp finality.

Karissa glared at him, spun around and stalked into her room. Rafe thrust up the heel of his hand to prevent her from slamming the door in his face.

"You're enjoying this, aren't you?" she fumed when he invited himself inside.

"Enjoying what? Sparring with you? No, not particularly."

Karissa rolled her eyes in exasperation. But then, she had been exasperated since the moment Vanessa Payton fluttered into the mess hall, the very picture of proper breeding and refinement.

The woman, who looked to be about twenty-two—Clint's age—was decked out like a regal princess. There were enough diamonds and rubies encircling her delicate neck to strangle half the horses in the post stable. Karissa had never attended a royal coronation, but it seemed to her that the fetching blonde had arrived to play the role of the queen of the military post to the hilt and she was anxious to accept her jeweled crown.

For reasons she preferred not to dwell on, it hurt to see Rafe bestowing all that gentlemanly politeness on his fiancée. He had never treated Karissa with that much formality and polite respect. In fact, he treated his fiancée as if she was a delicate and fragile flower of aristocracy, and he kept a respectable distance at all times.

But Rafe treated Karissa like…well, she didn't know what. It didn't bother him in the least to toss her a glare, jump down her throat or latch on to her arm, as if he wanted to give her a good shaking when she dared to turn her back on him while he was talking—which she had done on several occasions, just to irritate him.

"She's very attractive," Karissa admitted begrudgingly.

"Yes, she is," Rafe agreed. "She's changed considerably since I saw her while I was on leave last year."

"*Last year?*" Karissa blinked in disbelief. "You are marrying a woman you haven't seen in a year? Surely you correspond with her regularly then."

"She's written twice and I have written once since my father announced our engagement," he informed her. "But that is beside the point. I came in here to discuss your—"

"Beside the point?" Karissa scoffed. "Damn good

thing I'm not the one marrying you. I'm afraid I would have to insist on more than an impersonal letter once a year—''

She clamped her mouth shut so fast she nearly clipped off the end of her tongue. Up to this point she had successfully managed to use her defense mechanism of flinging barbed remarks to disguise deeper feelings for him. The last thing she wanted to do was imply that she had given so much as a passing thought to what it would be like to be married to Rafe. They were as different as paupers and princes and that was never going to change, even if she had developed this ridiculous, ill-fated fascination for Rafe.

He lifted a brow, crossed his arms over his broad chest and smiled in amusement. ''You don't approve of my method of courtship? Why am I not surprised? You disapprove of most everything I do.''

''That's because you're an annoying man who delights in bossing people around. Hence your position as post commandant,'' she sniped. ''You wouldn't make it ten minutes as a flunky around this fort.''

He puffed up with indignation and stared her down. But it didn't stop Karissa. She was on a roll to vent the envious frustration that had welled up inside her when Vanessa had made her spectacular entrance to the mess hall.

''I think you revel in the fact that everyone knows who you are and that they are aware of the power you wield,'' she went on. ''This territory is presently under military rule and *you're* it. You're called upon to settle civil, Indian and military disputes and you like knowing your word is law.''

''If that's true then why do I have such a devil of a time shutting *you* up?'' he questioned with a snort. ''If you continue to harangue me I'll double the time of your captivity and no one will dispute my decision.''

Karissa stamped up to him and tilted up her head to stare him squarely in the eye. She was all set to let him have it with both barrels blazing, but he beat her to the draw.

''And do not offer me your body again in exchange for freedom,'' he said, glaring at her. ''I'm sure you have used that trick before to maneuver other men, but it won't work with me.''

Karissa reared back as if he'd slapped her. She knew she had given him the wrong impression that first night. But then, *she* had completely misunderstood *his* intentions. ''Think what you will, General, I couldn't care less. All I want is to return to the settlers' encampment to check on my brother.''

''Right,'' he said sardonically. ''As if there isn't a hundred and sixty acres of fertile prairie, spring-fed pool and winding creeks that isn't calling *home* to you.''

Impulsively, Karissa cocked her arm to slap him for taking what she'd told him in confidence and using it to antagonize her. Unfortunately, Rafe caught her forearm before her palm could connect with his cheek.

When she stared up into those silver-gray eyes she could see the storm building, could feel the lightning-quick sizzle of attraction when he touched her. God forgive this maddening weakness, but she wanted to kiss him, if only one last time before he married his princess and Karissa raced cross-country to stake land for Clint and Amanda.

''Damn you, Rissa,'' he muttered as his head came deliberately toward hers. ''You make me crazy.''

And then he claimed her mouth and stole the breath right out of her lungs. Before she realized it, she had wrapped her arms around his neck and was kissing him back with all the pent-up torment that had been hounding her since Vanessa stood in the doorway of the mess hall, shining like the brightest star in heaven.

Karissa was ashamed to admit that envy and jealousy had been spurring her to pick a fight with Rafe. And now she was secretly where she wanted to be—tasting him thoroughly, feeling his masculine strength surrounding her, experiencing this phenomenal pleasure that he alone incited in her.

When Rafe glided his hands down her rib cage to pull her against him, she became blatantly aware of his arousal. She told herself that it was a man's natural reaction to any woman, before she foolishly started to believe that *she* had some exclusive effect on him.

And damn him for starting this anyway, she thought as she struggled to regain her common sense. He had a fiancée he could kiss senseless anytime he wanted. He didn't need Karissa. Didn't want her because she wasn't good enough to be anything except the place he came for sexual release.

Karissa somehow found the willpower to press her hands against his chest and push away. She was thoroughly annoyed with herself for letting her forbidden attraction to Rafe control her. Never mind that when he let loose and kissed her, as if he was starving for a taste of her, her knees wobbled to such serious extremes that she had to brace her hip against the nearby table to prevent collapsing at his feet.

She had to say something sassy to break this tormenting spell, she thought frantically. "And what was that, General? A dress rehearsal for the affection you plan to bestow on Vanessa? Go practice on someone else. I have better things to do this evening. Like sort my clean laundry.''

Thankfully, he reared back, as if *she* had slapped *him*. It gave her time to draw in a breath that wasn't thick with his masculine scent and to reconstruct her usual defenses.

''Considering that mouth of yours, hellion, I'll be shocked if any man ever asks for your hand. You'd bite *his* hand off at the wrist.''

She shrugged carelessly, far more comfortable now that they were back to verbal pistols at twenty paces. ''I do not *need* a man in my life,'' she informed him airily. ''I can take care of myself and I've had lots of practice at it. I can darn my own stockings, do my own laundry and cook for myself. I can also earn my own wages.''

''And you can't bear the thought, being as independent as you are, of having any man tell you what to do,'' he added with a smirk.

''Precisely,'' she agreed. ''Which is why we clash so often. You delight in giving orders and I live to thumb my nose at them.'' She emulated Vanessa's sophisticated air and flicked her wrist to shoo him on his way. ''Run along now, General. I've sharpened my tongue well enough on you tonight to hold an edge for tomorrow. Once I file my nails I will be good to go.''

''You still aren't leaving the post, no matter how much you antagonize me,'' he muttered at her. ''You're not as tough as you would like me to think, either.''

Maybe not, but never in a million years would she admit it to him. She gestured toward the door. ''Leave now, before I decide to whittle you down to size. Believe me when I say that you haven't seen anything yet. I've gone a lot easier on you than most men.''

She inclined her head ever so slightly and smiled

wryly. "If not for your prestigious position here I wouldn't have shown as much restraint with my insults."

"This is restraint?" he hooted. Rafe stepped forward to wag a lean finger in her face. "And do not try to sneak away from this fort, Karissa. Are we clear on this?"

"Perfectly clear, General," she said before she scooped up her nail file and ignored him as if he wasn't there.

It was with tremendous relief that she heard the door click shut behind him.

Harlan Billings tapped lightly on the door to VIP quarters. He was treated to an enticing view of cleavage when Vanessa struck a seductive pose in her expensive silk negligee. Her welcoming smile turned upside down when he stepped into clear view and she realized it wasn't her fiancé who had come to call on her.

"What do you want?" she snapped rudely.

Harlan slunk inside and closed the door. "I'm the one who sent you the telegram," he announced. "I suppose you noticed your competition this evening in the mess hall?"

Vanessa clutched her robe around her and sauntered over to grab the wine bottle she had obviously brought with her from Virginia. You couldn't get that kind of fine liquor in a place like this.

"Yes, I think I know which one Rafe is sleeping with," she scowled distastefully. "It is the unattached redhead in that dowdy calico gown who obviously doesn't know that any self-respecting lady would not allow her skin to become tanned and has done nothing to conceal that smattering of freckles on her nose. Am I correct?''

Harlan nodded, waiting for Vanessa to offer him a glass of her fancy wine. She didn't. Neither did her snippy behavior gel with the well-mannered sophisticate he had seen flitting around the mess hall.

Vanessa was a haughty, self-serving bitch—exactly the kind of woman Harlan would have wished on the high-and-mighty Rafe Hunter.

''Just how long has Rafe been carrying on a liaison with that whore?'' Vanessa asked bluntly, then sipped her wine.

''A week. I thought you should know that she intends to land your fiancé.'' Harlan licked his lips, hungering for a taste of wine. He was sure it was sweeter than Vanessa.

Vanessa sniffed in disdain. ''She isn't going to get her hands on him,'' she promised resolutely. ''And you are going to help me insure that she doesn't. Of course, you will be compensated for your services.''

That was what Harlan wanted to hear. He was always eager to acquire enough money to indulge in his two favorite pastimes—guzzling whiskey and paying occasional visits to the red light district in the nearby community that catered to the needs of the soldiers at the fort.

''And just where is that tramp staying? In a tent somewhere outside the fort?'' Vanessa asked.

Harlan shook his head. ''In the commander's room.'' He delighted in watching Vanessa lose all her polished charm.

''With Rafe?'' she howled in exasperation.

''No, he's bunking with Micah Whitfield.'' Harlan

smiled slyly. "Or at least, that's where he starts the evening, before he sneaks in to join his trollop."

Vanessa slammed down her glass, slopping wine on the table, then motioned Harlan toward the door. "Get out of here while I dress. I intend to pay that strumpet a visit straightaway. The sooner she leaves the better."

When Harlan stepped outside, Vanessa hurriedly changed into her velvet gown. Things were worse than she had imagined if Rafe had turned his private quarters over to his harlot.

Everything else around this post was so far below her standards that it had taken all her restraint to prevent snorting in disgust when Rafe took her on a short tour of the garrison. She could not imagine why Rafe had accepted this position in the middle of nowhere, surrounded by a company of men—most of whom were uncultured and probably illiterate—keeping watch over a bunch of savages that had been contained on reservations.

With his wealth and social connections he could be back East, sitting behind a desk during the day and attending sophisticated balls at night. He could be rubbing shoulders with the crème de la crème of society.

The man must have some perverse need for challenge that she had failed to comprehend. But as soon as she had his ring on her finger—provided he could even find a wedding band out here in the outback of civilization—she was heading to Virginia to set up housekeeping with the allowance she would insist upon.

If Rafe Hunter's family wasn't practically made of money she would have canceled the engagement and caught the next train home. But she needed to seal this match as quickly as possible. With his well-respected family name to open any doors that might slam shut when her father's mounting debts became public knowledge, she could avoid embarrassment and disaster.

Her gown gaping, Vanessa whipped open the door and turned her back on the weasely informant who awaited her. "Fasten me up, Harlan."

"With pleasure, miss," he said as he accommodated her.

She endured his repulsive touch until he had completed the task then pushed him ahead of her. "I won't need your services after you show me to that trollop's room. If she isn't gone by tomorrow then you must meet me here after dark so we can plan our strategy."

"For a price," Harlan reminded her. "I've already taken a great risk by summoning you here. I'll definitely need compensation for sticking my neck out."

Vanessa rolled her eyes in disgust. She was short on funds herself. Now she would have to share them with this homely cretin in return for his cooperation. But with any luck, she could confront Rafe's whore and send her packing then turn all her charm on Rafe and persuade him to move up the wedding date.

She could be married within a week and on her way home before the Watham's annual ball. No one who was anyone would think of missing that grand affair. And Vanessa planned to be there, swathed in an outrageously expensive gown, bought and paid for with the Hunter family money.

The quiet tap at the door brought Karissa upright in bed. She had drifted off to sleep after Rafe left and she planned on rising before the crack of dawn. She did not need late-night interruptions when she had a long walk ahead of her in the early morning.

Serenaded by rumbles of thunder and flickering lightning that flashed against the window, Karissa rolled off the edge of the bed to dress hurriedly. Raking her tangled hair away from her face, she padded barefoot to the door. To her surprise, Vanessa Payton stood outside, dressed in her expensive gown, wearing a necklace of jewels and sporting sparkling rings on every finger—except the one where a wedding band was supposed to go.

If the woman intended to make her feel dowdy and outclassed she had succeeded. Seeing the striking, statuesque blonde up close was a vivid reminder that their social classes were worlds apart.

Without requesting an invitation, Vanessa swept past Karissa to pan the modest room with visible distaste. She spun around, the rustle of her gown breaking the stilted silence. "We weren't formally introduced this evening," she said aloofly. "Small wonder why."

Reflexively Karissa raised her chin when the prissy chit looked down her nose. "I beg your pardon?"

Vanessa sniffed distastefully. "I should hope so. Obviously I am not going to tolerate your presence in my fiancé's quarters. And more specifically in his *bed*."

All pretense dropped away as Vanessa strode purposefully toward Karissa. "Let me be brief and to the point. I want you off this post immediately. I will not be humiliated by your presence. With your passable looks I'm sure you can entice someone else to become your meal ticket. Rafe Hunter is mine and I intend to keep him."

Karissa blinked, startled by the abrupt change in Vanessa's demeanor. And Rafe thought Karissa's tongue was a double-edged sword? This woman had fawned and gushed all over Rafe in the mess hall. Apparently that was just a pretentious charade to disguise the real Vanessa Payton's grating personality.

"You have the wrong impression," Karissa declared. "You obviously don't know your fiancé well enough to realize that he is a man of honor."

Vanessa smirked arrogantly. "I certainly do not need a nobody like you to offer advice on men in general or my fiancé in particular." Her blue eyes narrowed threateningly. "If you are not off this post and out of Rafe's life for good, I will make your life miserable. And believe me, *tramp,* I have had plenty of experience in getting what I want."

Karissa met her condemning glare with typical defiance. "I plan to leave because it is *my* wont, not yours, Vanessa. And by the way, you are welcome to the commander. We have nothing in common."

Vanessa flashed her another contemptuous glance. "*That,* of course, is more than obvious." Loftily, she flounced toward the door. "Make certain we don't cross paths again."

When Vanessa exited, Karissa wasted no time dressing in breeches and stuffing her belongings into her carpetbag. After her encounter with Rafe this evening she had intended to go over the wall and disappear into the dark hours before dawn. Then that snippy sophisticate showed up to reaffirm Karissa's belief that she had endured this captivity long enough.

This week, while tending to her laundress duties, Karissa had studied the soldiers' routine of changing guards and surveyed the post so she could utilize the best avenue of escape. After the guard passed by, she sneaked out the window and clung to the shadows to avoid detection.

Most of the guards, she had noted previously, never

glanced upward—which is why she tossed her carpetbag onto the roof then shinnied up the supporting beam and moved swiftly across the top of the barracks. The leap between the barracks and arsenal was a mite unnerving—especially when accompanied by the crack of thunder and streaks of lightning—but she made the jump with six inches to spare.

Rain pounded on her in torrents as she waddled like a duck on the roof. Karissa bypassed the south lookout tower that housed a guard. Reaching out, she clamped a slippery hold of the rough-hewn stockade fence. Slinging one leg sideways, she managed to balance herself momentarily while the wind howled like a coyote and rain hammered at her back. Rolling sideways, she dropped to the ground outside the fort.

She knew the property that she hoped to claim would be the first place Rafe looked for her, so she tramped off to the settlers' encampment to rejoin her brother and sister-in-law.

Karissa hoped that when Rafe didn't find her trespassing in the new territory he would simply leave her be. It was for the best, she reminded herself as she scurried through the stormy darkness. Nothing was ever going to come between them, even if she had developed an unexplainable yearning for him. Now that his fiancée had arrived on the scene Karissa's presence was most awkward and unwelcome.

A rueful smile pursed her lips as she wiped raindrops from her eyes and scuttled toward the encampment that consisted of prairie schooners and tents. Even as aggravated as Rafe made her on occasion she almost felt sorry for him. Vanessa Payton was not the woman he thought he was marrying.

Karissa would bet her last cent that Vanessa was only

interested in the wealth, influence and prestige the Hunter name provided. After all, Vanessa didn't know Rafe well enough to love him—or even to like him, for that matter.

No, Karissa assured herself during her late-night trek through the wind and rain. Money and prominence motivated Vanessa. Of course, Karissa couldn't tell Rafe that without appearing spiteful and jealous. She only hoped that, intelligent man that he was, Rafe would figure it out for himself before it was too late.

Karissa wasn't sure she would wish the haughty Vanessa on her worst enemy. And especially not on the man for whom she had developed this forbidden attraction.

Well, that fascination ended here and now, she told herself resolutely. She would have no further association with Rafe. It was over and done and that was for the best.

Chapter Seven

Rafe knocked on the door to his quarters then swore colorfully when he peered into the room to find Karissa and her belongings gone. Damn it, how had she sneaked past the guards?

"So she's gone, is she?" Micah said from behind him. "I'm not surprised."

Rafe closed the door and glanced suspiciously at his friend. "And I wouldn't be surprised to discover that you aided in her escape."

Micah grinned as he ambled toward the mess hall. "Karissa doesn't need my help. She's developed impressive survival skills of her own. Besides, it's for the best and you damn well know it. You can't keep her underfoot while your fiancée is here."

Rafe scowled as he fell into step beside Micah. What the hell was Vanessa doing here anyway? He had informed her by correspondence that he would return to Virginia after the Land Run, when things had settled down and law and order prevailed.

And damn it all, he had been perfectly satisfied to make the match until he had encountered the tormenting distraction that went by the name Karissa Baxter. Last night he'd lain in bed, comparing his sophisticated and attractive fiancée to Karissa—and wishing Vanessa had stayed home.

Well, she was here, nonetheless, and Rafe was obliged to entertain her. "Vanessa asked me to show her around the area," Rafe commented as they entered the mess hall.

"Not to worry, Rafe," Micah quickly assured him. "I'll handle the patrol."

"If you find Karissa—"

Micah held up his hand and smiled wryly. "I'll take care of everything, my friend. The resourceful young lady included."

Although Rafe had no reason to be jealous or possessive he didn't like the sound of that. He shot Micah a dark look then scowled when his friend snickered.

"It is beyond me how you think you can court one woman when there's another woman on your mind." He inclined his head toward the dazzling blonde who had taken her place at the table and was chatting with the officers' wives. "Enjoy your day, Commander, and I'll enjoy mine."

Rafe took his seat and listened to Vanessa prattle incessantly about the balls she had attended during the social season and updated him on the recent activities of their mutual acquaintances. By the time he returned from taking her on a tour of the Cheyenne and Arapaho reservation at Darlington and strolled the boardwalks of the small community, he was sporting a raging headache. Vanessa's conversation bored him to tears. She batted her long-lashed eyes at him, oozed feminine charm…and he felt oddly disappointed. If he married Vanessa, as planned, this is what he had to look forward to each evening for the rest of his life.

The thought made him grimace.

"I have decided that since I'm here we should make arrangements for our wedding," Vanessa was saying as Rafe escorted her back to the mess hall for their evening meal. "You won't have to bother with the plans. I will take care of everything." She smiled brightly at him. "After all, that is one of the duties of a proper wife. Working behind the scenes to make a man's life run smoothly and efficiently."

"We planned to be married in Virginia with our families in attendance, in a few months," Rafe reminded her. "My time-consuming duties, and the problems in this new territory, will escalate after the Land Run. I'm sorry, Vanessa, but this is a bad time."

It was an excuse and Rafe damn well knew it. Promise or not, he was not inclined to rush into a wedding that was becoming less appealing by the hour. He couldn't look at Vanessa without making another dozen comparisons to Karissa.

While Karissa challenged, defied him and kept his emotions in a tailspin, Vanessa merely bored him with inconsequential chatter. He didn't give a fig how many social affairs she and his former acquaintances had attended. He had obviously been on the frontier too long, because the life Vanessa referred to constantly seemed surreal and meaningless.

And no matter how many times she touched his arm and graced him with her enchanting smile, Rafe couldn't work up enthusiasm to kiss her. Definitely no attraction, he mused as he ate his meal and listened to Vanessa drone on monotonously. There was simply no spark between them.

And yes, damn it, he specifically remembered telling Micah that it didn't matter, because marriage was a distant second to his duty as post commander. Unfortunately, his encounters with the fire-breathing redhead had forced him to rethink his attitude toward this marriage of convenience.

"There is no reason to wait," Vanessa was saying when Rafe finally got around to listening. "The officers' wives have agreed to help me make all the arrangements for the ceremony and reception. Just leave everything to me. I have been trained to host such social affairs. All you have to do is attend the ceremony and everything else will be taken care of."

"Who's taking care of what?" Micah asked as he showed up late to take his place at the table.

"Our wedding," Vanessa said excitedly. "I'm making arrangements to hold the nuptials within two weeks."

"Two w—" Micah choked as his gaze darted to Rafe.

"Two—" Rafe wheezed incredulously.

He barely knew the chit, but he was *trying* to like this woman who was supposed to become his wife. Yet, when he looked past her outward beauty, he found very little substance that endeared her to him.

Maybe it was only because visions of Karissa squaring off against him and challenging his authority kept getting in his way. Maybe the memory of how it felt to hold her in his arms and taste the fire of desire that burst into flame when he kissed her made it impossible for him to give Vanessa a sporting chance.

Whatever the case, he wasn't going to agree to a hasty wedding that he might come to regret. He was a soldier, first and foremost, and he was in no particular hurry to become a husband.

Vanessa chortled lightly as she patted his clenched fist. "You will have time to get used to the idea, Rafe.

Our wedding will be a grand affair, even if I don't have all the resources at my disposal here at this post.''

His appetite spoiled, Rafe pushed aside his plate and came to his feet. ''You'll have to excuse me, Vanessa. I need to attend to tomorrow's duty roster and check that no altercations between settlers have erupted in the nearby camps. Micah has had to serve double duty for me today and he needs his rest.''

''Beating a hasty retreat, Rafe?'' Micah mocked quietly when Vanessa was out of earshot. ''Thanks so much for dumping your fiancée in my lap. I would rather dig latrines.''

Rafe was beginning to feel the same way himself. He needed space and time alone to deal with the frustration that had been hounding him since he found Karissa gone.

A curious thought sprang quickly to mind and Rafe glanced down at Micah. ''Did you come across many trespassers while on patrol?'' he asked.

Micah nodded then sent him a meaningful stare. ''Several of them. I locked the male prisoners in the stockade.''

So he hadn't come upon Karissa, Rafe mused as he headed out the door. Perhaps she had decided to visit her brother. Good. That was safer than camping out alone on her would-be claim. Her injured brother couldn't offer her much protection from trouble, but at least Rafe could rest easier knowing Karissa was in good company.

Karissa helped her sister-in-law tote in their evening meal from the community campfire. It had taken her most of the night to make her way through the heavy thunderstorm and reach camp. She was astounded by

how many tents had been pitched beside the stream
northwest of the fort. The number of hopeful settlers had
mushroomed from several hundred to well over a thousand. More competition for land, she mused as she
glanced at the string of powerful-looking horses that had
been tethered on the south side of the encampment.

She stared miserably at the sorry piece of horseflesh
that she had purchased to make the Run. The old gray
mare that had tripped over its own hooves and caused
Clint to take a spill during their trek from Kansas was
not a quality mode of transportation. She would be lucky
indeed if she didn't break her neck on the back of that
horse when she plunged off the starting line to race for
her claim.

"Why so glum?" Amanda asked as she appraised
Karissa's expression. "You're beginning to look like
Clint. And here I thought nothing ever got you down."

Karissa mustered a smile for her sister-in-law. "I put
in a long evening and a long walk," she insisted. "I'm
sure I'll be my old self again after a good night's rest."

Amanda nodded and glanced down at her protruding
belly. "I can't recall the last time I had a good night's
sleep. I swear this babe is as energetic as you are. I have
been kicked from inside out so much lately that I feel
like a punching bag."

When Amanda lovingly brushed her free hand over
her midsection Karissa's determination to claim a home
for her family increased tenfold. She *had* to sneak back
into the new territory to make her claim. She couldn't
face the disappointment of not providing a new start for
Clint and Amanda. Even if she couldn't realize her very
own dream of owning property and building a home to
call her own, Clint and Amanda would have their name

on the deed to one hundred sixty acres of fertile farmland.

Karissa ducked inside the shabby tent to see her brother ease upright on the cot. He muttered under his breath as he massaged his broken leg.

"Hell and damnation, I hate this." Clint glowered at his leg. "The one time in my life when I wanted to take responsibility for you and Amanda, I can't even stand up for more than ten minutes without getting light-headed."

"We are in this together, all for one and one for all," Amanda insisted, ever the optimist. "Karissa has assured me that she will do her best to stake a claim, but you have to rest while you can, because we have a home to build and crops to plant. Everything will work out, Clint." She handed her scowling husband a tray of food and offered him a cheery smile. "You'll see."

"Amanda?" One of the women from the camp called from outside the tent. "There's a soldier here who is asking to speak to a Miss Baxter."

While Clint and Amanda frowned curiously at her, Karissa set aside her meal and ducked beneath the tent flap. She couldn't say she was surprised to see Rafe sitting atop his roan gelding. But couldn't he have arrived *after* she had eaten supper before he dragged her back into custody?

"Miss Baxter," Rafe said with exaggerated politeness. "I would like to have a private word with you."

"Of course, General." She gestured toward the tent. "Perhaps you would like to meet my brother and sister-in-law first, just to reassure yourself that they aren't fictitious."

"My pleasure," he said as he swung from the saddle. Karissa eyed his muscular steed covetously. She would give her eyeteeth to exchange horses with Rafe during the Land Run. At least then she would have a chance of outrunning the other settlers to reach her promised land.

"Nice of you to leave without saying goodbye," Rafe said dryly as he strolled up beside her, looking all too handsome in his uniform. "I had to inquire at two encampments before I finally located you."

"Sorry," she said, her voice a long way from apologetic, "I was so homesick to see Clint and Amanda that I was compelled to leave in a rush."

"And during a dangerous storm to boot," he remarked as she led him toward the battered tent. "You're lucky you weren't lightning-struck."

"Disappointed?" she asked flippantly.

He gave her an exasperated look before he ducked beneath the tent flap. "I'm not as spiteful and vindictive as you seem to think, Karissa. I was worried about your safety."

And she was worried about the fragile condition of her heart. When he was nice to her, it was difficult to keep up her sassy pretense that protected emotions simmering too close to the surface.

To her further dismay, Rafe's dominating presence seemed to fill the small tent to overflowing and heightened her awareness of him. He took up entirely too much space and stood entirely too close for her to take a breath without breathing him in.

"Clint, Amanda, this is Commander Rafe Hunter from Fort Reno. He was kind enough to let me stay at the post and earn wages as a laundress before I returned to camp."

Rafe arched an amused brow. "Most of my men were sorry to see Karissa go," he said as he walked over to shake hands with Clint then bow politely before Amanda. "We've been shorthanded lately and Karissa took over some of the duties that we haven't had much time to attend to ourselves."

Always the gentleman, Karissa mused. Except when they were on opposing sides of a debate. He never thought twice about chewing her up one side and down the other in private. No doubt, she could expect more of the same when he dragged her out of earshot from her family and the other prospective settlers in camp.

"I won't take much of your sister's time," Rafe said to Clint. "If you will excuse us?"

"It's an honor to meet you, Commander Hunter," Amanda said graciously. She offered her own tray of food to him. "Are you sure you won't stay and take our meal with us?"

"Thank you, but I ate before I left the post. You are very thoughtful, Mrs. Baxter."

When Karissa led the way back outside, Rafe fell into step beside her. "I like your sister-in-law."

"Sorry, but she's taken. Furthermore, you have a fiancée of your own," Karissa said before she could stop herself.

"I came to call a truce," he said as he took her elbow and shepherded her toward the canopy of trees away from the crowded campsite.

"Well then, you should have come waving a white flag over your head, General," Karissa replied. "I presumed you had come to rearrest me."

"No, you have served your time." Rafe braced himself against a tree, crossed his arms over his chest and stared at her for a long moment.

Karissa fidgeted nervously. She couldn't stare into those pewter-colored eyes for too long without forbidden memories torturing her. "Then why are you here?" she demanded impatiently.

"I have a proposition for you."

She cocked her head and smirked. "A concession of some sort from you? I must not have heard you correctly, General."

Rafe glared at her. "I'm trying to be nice, damn it."

"Save it for Vanessa. I'm not accustomed to niceties from you," she shot back.

"That's because your fiery disposition and distrust usually set me off," he muttered. "I came here to make you an offer and I urge you not to refuse, out of that pure contrariness that is so much a part of your temperament."

Karissa regarded him warily. "If you want me to resume my duties as laundress I must decline. I have no wish to return to the post, even if I could use the wages."

"Why not?" he asked reasonably.

"Because—" Karissa shut her mouth before she blurted out that she wanted to bypass further encounters with Vanessa. If Rafe knew Vanessa had demanded that she leave he wouldn't be here asking her to return.

"Because why?" he persisted, watching her all too closely.

"It really doesn't matter," she said with a nonchalant shrug. "I'm needed here with Clint and Amanda. It's either here or at my claim site. You choose, General."

Rafe sighed and shook his head. "When are you going to learn that I can see right through your tough facade? I've come to know you, Karissa. I have seen for myself that you have a brother and sister-in-law depending on you. If you weren't kindhearted by nature your family would be back in Kansas, managing as best they could while you made this Land Run for yourself.''

She wasn't sure she wanted him to look beneath her cast-iron exterior. It made her feel more vulnerable to him than she already did. ''So I'm a tenderhearted softy in disguise. Is there a point to this conversation or are you here to prevent me from eating my supper while it's still warm?''

Although she felt the instinctive impulse to turn tail and run, she stood her ground when he pushed away from the tree and strode up to curl his forefinger beneath her chin. She was forced to meet his mesmerizing gaze and she had to steel herself from flinging herself into his arms and helping herself to another exquisite taste of him.

What was the matter with her? Was she a glutton for punishment? This man was off-limits to her. He had a fiancée—who, despite her witchy disposition, did hail from his lofty social circle. Nevertheless, being near him was pure torment and she had enough problems without her traitorous thoughts centering around him more often than she preferred.

''Just climb down off your high horse for one minute and listen to me, Karissa,'' he murmured, his gaze focused on her lips.

''I don't have a high horse,'' she chirped, her feminine body reacting helplessly to his stimulating presence and his touch. ''If I did I would stand a fighting chance in this race for land.''

''That's why I'm here.''

Karissa frowned, befuddled. ''You've lost me.''

He smiled enigmatically. ''I know, but I do have a high horse for you to climb on.''

When it dawned on her what he implied, she sucked

in a shocked breath. "You're offering to let me ride *your* horse? My God, *why?*" she asked incredulously.

"Because you have earned the chance to stake your claim," he explained, then frowned warningly. "Provided you don't sneak back into the territory and break the rules I'm sworn to uphold. You should also know that I have continued to check your would-be claim daily. No one has squatted on it."

"Oh, Rafe! Thank you!" Karissa couldn't help herself. She was so thrilled that she impulsively leaped into his arms and showered him with grateful kisses.

She didn't even realize she had hooked her legs around his waist until his hands clamped onto her hips, holding her tightly against him.

"It's the least I can do," he murmured before his mouth came down on hers and he kissed her with such desperation that she almost melted on his uniform.

Forbidden... The word haunted her even as she kissed him for all she was worth. She savored this space out of time for as long as it would last, inhaling his unique scent, tasting him, feeling his masculine body molded familiarly to hers.

She knew she would never earn his affection, and probably not his respect, but he had offered his horse so that she could realize her dream. If she couldn't have him then perhaps she could stake the land and live with her family until they were financially stable. Then she would have to make a life of her own, one that was far away from Rafe and his intended bride. Seeing them together would be more than she could bear.

Reluctantly she squirmed for release then stepped a safe distance away. "Forgive me," she apologized, casting him an embarrassed glance. "I got a little carried away with my gratitude."

Rafe didn't look all that pleased that he hadn't re-
strained himself, either. "I'll bring my horse to you the
night before the Run. In the meantime Sergeant will be
well fed and exercised."

Karissa recovered enough to chuckle. "Sergeant?
You named your horse *Sergeant?*" She stared pointedly
at his polished boots. "And these are first and second
lieutenants, I suppose. You do eat, sleep and breathe the
military, don't you?"

"I couldn't very well call my horse General when he
spends most of his time beneath me," he said as he
grasped her arm to escort her back to the tent. "We do
pay strict attention to rank in the army, after all."

Karissa smiled in wry amusement. "Are straitlaced
blue-bloods like yourself allowed to have a sense of humor?"

"Micah taught me to laugh at myself occasionally,"
Rafe informed her as he approached camp. "Between
you and him, I don't have to worry about taking myself
or my duty too seriously."

Her heart squeezed in her chest when Rafe's hand
tangled with hers, giving it a light squeeze. She knew
Rafe would never be her lover. The best she could hope
for was a tenuous friendship. He belonged to someone
else, although that snippy *someone else* didn't deserve
him. But Rafe was granting Karissa the chance to chase
her dream without bending his rules. For that she was
immensely grateful.

Rafe drew her to a halt a stone's throw away from
the hustle and bustle of activity in camp. "Take care of
yourself, Karissa," he murmured as he brushed his lips
against her forehead. "I worry about you because your
daring nature has a way of inviting trouble."

She shrugged carelessly. "I have survived this long,

haven't I?" Karissa flashed him a grateful smile. "I can't thank you enough for your generosity. I will never forget it."

He returned her smile as he playfully tapped his index finger against the tip of her nose. "You're welcome. I'll see you the night before the Run."

Then he became one of the silhouettes moving through the darkness and her heart squeezed with so much regret that it was difficult to draw breath. "I could have loved you, Rafe Hunter," she whispered as man and horse vanished in the night. "I know I'm not the right one for you, but Vanessa isn't either. I pray you will realize that before it's too late."

Vanessa paced impatiently from wall to wall in her room. Where was that weasely little man she had summoned? She needed his assistance and she needed it now. She knew Rafe was slipping away from her. She had tried to bedazzle him and engage him in conversation most of the day, but he had been so distracted that it had taken all her dignified reserve not to club him over his handsome head and screech at him for not fawning over her the way most men usually did.

She spat an unladylike oath as she wheeled around to pace in the opposite direction. Rafe had left the garrison two hours ago and had yet to return. Of course, she didn't buy his lame excuse about patrolling the settlers' camps. No doubt, he had gone to be with his whore. He had stashed her out from underfoot, but she still preyed heavily on his mind.

Damn him! He had balked when she had mentioned moving up their wedding date. Well, just let him try to back out on her. She would make him very sorry indeed if he broke off the engagement.

Although she wanted and needed his family connection as a feather in her cap—and the means to acquire a comfortable monthly stipend—this was also a matter of pride. She would not be cast aside for that scrawny, freckle-nosed little nobody! What could Rafe possibly see in that woman?

Well, he wasn't going to see anything in her from this day forward, Vanessa mused. Karissa Baxter had to be dealt with severely because she was an obstruction that stood directly between Vanessa's goals and aspirations.

The quiet tap at the door sent Vanessa spinning about. She practically yanked Harlan Billings inside to prevent anyone from becoming aware of their clandestine association.

"Where have you been? I expected you a half hour ago."

Harlan opened his hand, palm upward. "If you expect promptness then you will have to pay better than you have thus far," he insisted. "And thus far, I have received nothing in return for the information I provided."

Scowling, Vanessa stalked across the room to retrieve a few coins to pacify him.

"Here," she said, thrusting the coins at him. "Now stop thinking about greasing your palms and pay attention. The only way to prevent Rafe's trollop from spoiling our upcoming wedding is to cast a bad light on her name."

"And how do you propose to do that?" Harlan asked as he pocketed the money.

"We will have to find a way to link her name to some of the less desirable elements of society," Vanessa decided.

Harlan snorted. "There is no *society* hereabout—yet.

That won't happen until communities are established after the Land Run.''

Vanessa muttered sourly. She knew all the tricks of casting aspersions on her rivals in the East, but she was definitely out of her element in the middle of nowhere. "When is this stupid Land Run supposed to take place anyway?" she demanded. "These people have no dignity whatsoever. Racing after free land like a pack of starved wolves. It's disgraceful! No one in my social circle would think of doing such a thing.''

Harlan shrugged his thin-bladed shoulders. "The Run will be held in a week. And most of us common folks do what we must to get ahead in life. Which is why I insist on being paid in advance, if you expect my cooperation.''

Vanessa clamped down on her tongue before she shouted the odious man from her room. She had to be cautious about letting anyone know of her scheme to rout Karissa from Rafe's life without appearing to be involved. She was stuck with Harlan, offensive and distasteful though he was to her.

"Oh, very well, but I expect results for my money," she demanded as she marched over to her reticule to fish out two bank notes. "I expect you to find out where she is and what she's doing. Then find a way to frame her for whatever crime necessary that will get her in trouble and make her lose face in Rafe's eyes.''

Harlan snorted resentfully as he greedily took her money. "I'm on stable duty during the day, lady. I can't wander away from the post on a whim to track down that Baxter bitch. The best I can do is sneak away at night while I'm supposed to be on guard duty.''

"All the better," she insisted. "There will be less chance of you being recognized. You can find out where she is, fleece her most recent benefactor and see to it that she's blamed for the robbery. Whatever money you pocket will be yours to keep.''

Harlan grinned devilishly. ''I do like the way your mind works.''

''And *I* would like to find myself legally wed the moment this Land Run is over,'' she muttered as she showed him the door. ''You have two days.'' She eyed him sternly. ''You better have located that trollop by then.''

''I'll see what I can do,'' Harlan promised.

''No,'' Vanessa said determinedly. ''*Do* it.''

When Harlan left, Vanessa poured herself a tall glass of wine and slouched on her lumpy bed. She couldn't wait to get this marriage over and done and return to the comforts of proper society. There was no cultural entertainment to be found on the frontier—nothing except a few spur-of-the-moment horse races, footraces and horseshoe-pitching contests. She was forced to associate with men and women who were so far beneath her status that it was all she could do to put on a cheery face and pretend to tolerate this mundane existence.

This was all her father's fault, she fumed. If he had the slightest head for business, she wouldn't find herself in such dire straits, forced to wed a man who seemed to prefer the company of a strumpet.

Men, they were such a nuisance. A woman had to maneuver and finagle to get ahead in this world. Well, she would just plunge ahead, manipulate Rafe into a hasty wedding then return home to set up housekeeping on Hunter family funds. Then she could do as she pleased, when she pleased.

She would have financial independence and Rafe could have his crude fort and his silly command over this sorry troop of soldiers. These men might be the salt of the earth, but they didn't hold the least bit of interest or appeal to Vanessa. All she wanted was to see that Baxter woman's reputation ruined and Rafe's ring on her own finger. Then she would quit this place as quickly as possible.

She guzzled more wine to take the edge off her mounting frustration.

Chapter Eight

Dressed in the homespun clothes that he'd swiped from a makeshift clothesline in one of the settlers' camps, Harlan Billings circled the perimeters, looking for Karissa. He had sneaked away from guard duty to follow Vanessa's demand the previous night to make trouble for the redhead. Surely she was here somewhere. Harlan had already checked the other two encampments and hadn't seen a thing of her.

His thoughts scattered when he caught sight of her flaming red hair glinting in the flickering light of the community campfire. He watched Karissa duck into a shabby tent then he appraised the other settlers who ambled around the area.

When he spotted a man on crutches, hobbling toward the river to fill a canteen, Harlan smiled maliciously. Here was his unsuspecting mark.

Wasting no time, Harlan darted through the trees and waited until the crippled man awkwardly knelt down on one knee to fill the canteen from the river. Using a broken branch, Harlan darted forward to club the man over the head. With a muffled groan his victim collapsed on the riverbank.

After checking that there were no witnesses, Harlan crouched down to search the man's pockets. He grinned in satisfaction when he came away with a fistful of coins and banknotes. Tucking the money in his own pocket, Harlan scuttled through the trees. With his stolen cap pulled low on his forehead, he paused beside a settler who was grooming his horse.

"I swore I just saw a red-haired woman take after a crippled man down by the river," he reported, employing a heavy Southern accent. "I would check on him myself, but I've got a sick child in my tent who needs attention."

The settler wheeled around to squint into the distance. "I'll see to it, friend."

Harlan grinned triumphantly as he scurried off to fetch the horse he had tethered on the outskirts of camp. He would return to the fort, scale the fence beside the guard tower and assume his duty before anyone realized he had abandoned his post.

After the changing of the guards he would call on Vanessa, demanding payment for framing Karissa for the robbery and assault. There was considerable profit in helping that snooty lady with her scheme to land Commander Hunter as her husband, he mused. As vindictive as Vanessa appeared to be, Harlan could make a killing off her.

He chuckled as he galloped his horse toward the garrison. Vanessa considered him a lowly soldier, worthy only to carry out her schemes, did she? Well, she would soon discover how clever he was. Ah, he looked forward to springing his upcoming surprise on her and watching her puff up with all sorts of haughty indignation.

Vanessa Payton lunged toward the door when she heard the quiet rap. As expected, Harlan appeared, smiling his hideous little smile that indicated he was well pleased with himself.

Vanessa stepped aside and watched the corporal strut into the room like a high-ranking brigadier general.

"I trust you have been successful, Harlan. Is that gold-digger in custody?"

"No, but I'm sure she will be soon," he replied confidently. "The settlers will take the law into their own hands when she's accused of clubbing a crippled man over the head and stealing his money."

"Preying on a cripple is a nice touch," she complimented him. Perhaps she hadn't given this man full credit for his devious cunning. "That should stack the cards against that uncultured strumpet."

"I expect so." Harlan thrust out his hand. "Now, if you please, I would like to be compensated for the risks I took tonight by abandoning my post."

Vanessa whirled around to fetch her purse. The moment she had discovered that today was payday at the garrison, she had approached Rafe to request cash. She explained—with just the right amount of blushing embarrassment—that she hadn't had the foresight to bring enough funds from Virginia to purchase necessary supplies. She had also confided that she'd had no idea there wasn't a bank nearby to wire her father for money when she needed it.

Rafe had handed over half of his salary without batting an eyelash. Of course, money was no concern to him. She knew he had a sizable trust at his disposal. Rafe would never be short of funds.

To Vanessa this was the ultimate and most satisfying irony. She was using *Rafe's* money to pay for having his harlot set up for a crime and destroying what little respectability she might have acquired.

Pivoting, Vanessa dropped several shiny silver dollars into Harlan's greedy hands. She could afford to be generous since this was the last time she would need the corporal's services. Plus, she had discovered this morning that Rafe didn't bat an eye at providing money when she requested it.

Although she had spent another boring day at this backward fort she would sleep well tonight, knowing that in less than two weeks she would be wed and would have the Hunter family fortune at her disposal. She could play the role of the fawning fiancée until she returned home. Indeed, she could be sweet and charming, if the situation demanded—so long as she was assured of financial security.

"You may leave now, Corporal," she said dismissively. "We have concluded our business. But I shall call upon you in the future if the need arises."

Harlan simply stood there, grinning craftily at her. Impatiently, she thrust her arm toward the door—as if he were too ignorant to see where it was. "Leave at once. I refuse to take the risk of having Rafe find you here."

"That is exactly the person I need to discuss with you," Harlan replied, refusing to budge from the spot. "There is the matter of hush money to discuss."

The color drained from Vanessa's cheeks. Hell and damnation, she never dreamed this backward soldier would try to double-cross her!

"You need to know that I won't think twice about exposing your devious plot to Commander Hunter." He waited a deliberate moment then added, "Unless, of course, you pay me periodically to keep my mouth shut.''

Vanessa glowered furiously at him. Her hands knotted in the folds of her gown and she itched to claw out his beady eyes for backing her into a corner. She found herself in this exasperating situation because of Rafe, she silently fumed. If he hadn't invited that whore to stay in his quarters, right under her nose, she wouldn't have to resort to conspiring with the likes of this offensive little toad. And by damned, she would dream up excuses to bleed Rafe for money. *He* was going to pay to keep her blackmailer's trap shut!

"I'll come by once a week to receive my payment," Harlan announced before he turned toward the door. He tossed her a gloating glance. "It's a pleasure doing business with you."

When left alone in her meager quarters, Vanessa let loose with a string of unladylike curses. She hoped she didn't have to draw someone else into her scheme and hire that *someone* to dispose of Harlan permanently. But she would if she had to. It galled her no end that Harlan held the upper hand. He was a worthless nobody, just like that wench who had used her seductive wiles to bewitch Rafe.

Muttering another string of colorful obscenities, Vanessa poured herself a glass of wine, and then scowled when she realized she had nearly depleted the bottle she had brought along with her.

And where, she wondered, was she going to find quality wine to replenish her supply? She flounced onto her lumpy cot. She was on the godforsaken frontier, surrounded by bumpkin soldiers and their wives, deprived of luxuries. No one from her prestigious circle of society should have to tolerate such deplorable conditions and distasteful companionship.

Vanessa snuffed the lantern. Her new husband would pay dearly for forcing her to humiliate herself by chasing him down in the middle of nowhere and pretending to endure these despicable accommodations.

On the eve of the Land Run, Rafe trotted toward the settlers' encampment. He was mounted on a military issue gelding, leading Sergeant behind him. He could feel anticipation sizzling in the air as he watched the prospective settlers pack their gear and mentally prepare themselves for the race for land in the soon-to-be-established Oklahoma Territory.

Unfortunately, Rafe predicted that he would soon encounter another set of headaches. He wouldn't have to patrol the region to round up squatters. But since the territory was under martial law—and would be, until law enforcement agencies were established and functioning efficiently—he would have to settle land disputes so the undesirables didn't fleece the new settlers.

Rafe's thoughts trailed off when he noticed Amanda Baxter waving her slender arms in expansive gestures to flag him down. Nice woman, he mused as he veered in her direction. He could understand why Karissa was so determined to see her brother and his wife claim a homestead. Rafe was silently cheering for the Baxter family's success.

"Oh, Commander, we are eternally indebted to you," Amanda gushed as Rafe dismounted. "Kari told us of your generous offer." She reached out to stroke Sergeant's soft muzzle. "If not for this week's unpleasant incident, Clint and I would be walking on air in anticipation of tomorrow's race."

"Incident?" Rafe questioned warily as he tethered the two horses to the nearest tree. If Karissa was involved, there always seemed to be an *incident* of one kind or another. "What happened this time?"

Amanda pivoted to lead him toward the tent. "A few days ago Clint limped down to the river to fetch a canteen of water," she reported. "Someone sneaked up behind him and whacked him on the head while he was unaware." Amanda sighed miserably. "The poor man is having the most difficult time adjusting to his broken leg and accepting the fact that his sister will once again become his champion and provider by making the Run on his behalf. Now he feels ten times worse because Kari had given him all the money she has collected the past few months, plus the funds she earned at the fort. All the cash was stolen from Clint's pocket while he was unconscious."

Rafe gnashed his teeth in frustration. He had heard complaints from the prospective settlers about such incidents, but now it seemed personal because it pertained to Karissa and her family. He would like to get his hands on the opportunist who had assailed Clint while he was barely able to walk, and had difficulty defending himself from harm.

"Clint didn't need another knot on his head," Amanda murmured. "The blow caused a setback because he hadn't recovered from the concussion he suffered after his disastrous fall from the horse."

Rafe ducked under the tent flap to see Karissa perched on the edge of the cot, blotting a cloth against Clint's peaked face. Although Clint was muttering and scowling at his incapacity, one look into Karissa's eyes indicated the unfortunate incident had made her even more determined to provide for her family.

"And what's worse," Amanda continued as she took Karissa's place beside Clint, "is that someone accused Kari of brutalizing and stealing from her own *brother!* Can you imagine anything so preposterous?" She stared up at Rafe with wide hazel eyes. "Rest assured that I told the group of vigilantes who descended on Karissa that it was her brother who had been accosted and that she would never betray her family. Of course, they disbanded straight away, feeling like fools. As well they should," she added huffily.

Rafe sorely wished he hadn't turned half of his pay over to Vanessa this week, for he would have gladly offered all of it to this struggling family. He reached into his pocket, grabbed Karissa's hand and gave her the coins he had left.

"I can't take—" she protested.

"Yes, you can," he cut in authoritatively. "I insist."

Karissa stared down at the coins. "I will repay you as soon as we show profit on our homestead."

"A simple thank-you will suffice," he told her. Before she could argue—and he didn't doubt for a moment that she intended to—he clutched her arm and towed her outside. "We need to discuss Sergeant's customary behavior so you won't be startled while you're riding him. You and he are the perfect match: feisty as hell. Now pay attention and don't go getting all stubborn on me, woman."

"Me? Stubborn?" Karissa said in feigned indignation. "How can you say such a thing?"

He slanted her a withering glance as he drew her away from the milling crowd. He halted in front of his prize horse and patted his sleek, muscular neck. "Sergeant is conditioned to react swiftly," Rafe informed her. "The sound of a bugle announcing a charge and the spitting of gunfire sets him off in his fastest clip.''

Karissa nodded. ''I'll be ready and waiting when he leaps into action.''

''A cannon will be fired at the fort, trumpets will blow and my soldiers will signal the start of the race by discharging their rifles. If you don't clamp your knees around Sergeant's flanks and anchor a fist on the pommel of the saddle this horse will run right out from under you,'' he cautioned her. ''Sergeant is exceptionally quick off the mark, and when you give him his head it takes a firm and continuous tug on the reins to force him to put on the brakes.''

Karissa reached up to scratch Sergeant's ear. The horse leaned his head against her and nuzzled her hip. ''He doesn't seem all that high-spirited to me,'' she commented as the horse soaked up her attention.

Karissa spared Rafe a glance, wishing she could hug the stuffing out of him again for allowing her to ride Sergeant and for partially replacing the money she had given to Clint for safekeeping. But she had discovered that grateful hugs and kisses caused an explosion of her senses so she had to maintain a respectable distance.

''I know you're on a very determined mission to acquire land,'' Rafe murmured beside her. ''But have a care tomorrow during this confounded race. People are bound to get hurt when they dash off hell-for-leather to stake their claims. Horses can collide and catapult their riders into the path of the stampede. Carriages and wagons can overturn, crushing bodies beneath them.'' He gazed meaningfully at her. ''Sassy and aggravating though you can be, I still prefer you in one piece.''

He glanced up sharply and stared over her head. ''Well, hell…''

Karissa watched Rafe stride off when a shouting match erupted between two prospective settlers. She knew Rafe took his duties as peacekeeper and law official seriously. Here was yet another example of his dominant personality. He grabbed the doubled fist that was aimed toward a bearded jaw and jerked it downward as he stepped between the men. In less than a minute he had squelched the dispute and sent the men to their respective tents, threatening to exclude them from the Run if they started more trouble.

She was pleased to note that the two men Rafe had dressed down were the ringleaders of the vigilantes. They had dragged her in front of their kangaroo court and accused her of accosting her own brother.

Karissa smiled to herself, remembering how Amanda had come flying to her defense. Amanda might have been dainty and with child, but she had stood up valiantly for Karissa.

When Rafe ambled back to her, Karissa helplessly appraised his powerful physique. It was no wonder he had risen through military ranks with incredible speed. With his height and commanding presence he was simply born to lead. And despite his avid dedication to following rules and regulations he was a fair, just and generous man.

''That's only a sampling of what we can expect when claim disputes erupt tomorrow,'' Rafe grumbled as he swiftly unsaddled Sergeant. ''I hope to hell that you own a firearm, Karissa. If not, you might find yourself on the losing end of an argument over who staked your claim first. If I could forbid you and the other daredevil women who insist on making this Run, I would do it in a heartbeat. Your gender is at a definite disadvantage. Please tell me you have a weapon so you can defend yourself.''

She tossed him a wry smile and said, "No, I sold mine last month, but I will be well armed, General. As you have often reminded me, I have a very sharp tongue. Although Amanda's father gave her a pistol before we left Kansas, she will need it for her own protection and Clint's rifle is exactly that. *His* rifle."

He shook his head in dismay, huffed out a breath, pulled his pistol from its holster and handed it to her. "Take this and don't hesitate to fire if the need arises. You do know how to use one of these things, don't you?"

Karissa nodded as she clamped hold of the pistol. "I taught myself to be reasonably proficient with weapons early on in life. Unfortunately, I had to sell the one I used for protection to finance our trip from Kansas."

She didn't add that she had often employed her former weapon as an imposing threat and as an improvised club when men had tried to accost her. Rafe already believed her to be a scrappy, unconventional female. No need to mention those near brushes with disaster.

Leading Sergeant behind him, Rafe carried the saddle back to the tent then staked his horse nearby. "Keep a close watch on my horse," he instructed. "The last thing you need is to have him stolen the night before the Run."

"I'll sleep beside him," she insisted. And she would, too. No one was going to steal her opportunity to run this race on such a powerful horse.

Rafe expelled an exasperated sigh. "I'm worried about your safety, damn it. Not just during and after the Run, but here in this camp."

"I've found myself in dire straits and waged lopsided battles dozens of times in my life," she informed him.

"Now, as then, there was no one to depend on except myself. I'm not your responsibility or your concern."

No, she wasn't, but that didn't stop Rafe from worrying about her. He could imagine all sorts of frightful scenarios befalling this pint-sized woman who spit in the eye of trouble and refused to back down.

True, she was resourceful and self-reliant, but she was also a woman. It was second nature for him to serve and protect. And as hard as he tried, he couldn't overcome his feelings of protectiveness toward Karissa. She had gotten under his skin and preyed on his carefully guarded emotions. When she was out of sight he still couldn't get her off his mind, not even when Vanessa tried to distract him every spare minute that he wasn't involved with his military duties.

"I should go," he said abruptly. "I have rounds to make at the Indian agency at Darlington before I return to the post."

When she nodded, the campfire light reflected off her shiny red head and he was nearly overwhelmed by the urge to sink his hands into those curly tendrils and devour her with his kiss. Damn, when had she become so irresistibly beautiful to him? Even in her faded gown and with the suntan that testified to spending time outdoors while leading her hand-to-mouth existence, he found her irresistibly attractive. He even liked that adorable crop of freckles on the bridge of her nose.

Just when, he wondered, had she become the icon of feminine spirit and perfection?

In comparison, Vanessa looked anemic, overdressed and out of place on the frontier. Not that he spent much time worrying what his family would think or how they would react, but he was curious how the dignified Hunters would perceive Karissa. His own mother was as much a socialite as Vanessa Payton, which was probably why his father thought she would make the perfect wife.

"I am truly grateful for your help," Karissa murmured, refusing to meet his gaze directly. She stared, unblinkingly at Sergeant, as if the roan gelding was the answer to all her prayers. "And I'm um…sorry that I was a nuisance and embarrassment to you while I was at the fort. I um…hope you and Vanessa will be very happy."

He studied her closely, wondering if this impossible attraction he felt for her was mutual. But, given the situation with Vanessa, Rafe couldn't ask; indeed, he shouldn't be feeling anything at all for Karissa.

But he did.

"You do?" he asked softly, watching for some sign that she longed for more than friendship between them.

"Of course. Why wouldn't I?" Karissa said with all the casual nonchalance she could muster. "You and your fiancée are a great deal alike."

Rafe winced. "Vanessa is insisting on having the ceremony at the post rather than in Virginia," he declared.

"I'm sure with her background and good breeding it will be a splendid affair, no matter where the wedding takes place," Karissa muttered.

She should be grateful that Rafe would soon be wed so she could put aside this secret whimsy. Her life was no fairy tale and there was no handsome prince in her future. The sooner she accepted that reality the better off she would be.

"Again, thank you," Karissa whispered.

She pivoted on her boot heels and headed for the tent. She had supplies to pack in preparation for making the Run and setting up camp on her claim. She had to focus on her objective and put Rafe out of her mind. She refused to get mushy and sentimental over a man who undoubtedly was relieved to have her out of his hair once and for all.

She didn't glance back when he wished her good luck in the race; she just kept walking right out of his life. It was for the best, after all, and if she had a brain in her head she wouldn't let herself forget it.

"How is Karissa holding up under the anxiety of tomorrow's race?"

Rafe flinched then scowled when Micah materialized from the shadows of the stable like a wraith. "Damn it, I swear you enjoy sneaking up on people and giving them a start."

Micah's teeth flashed in the moonlight. "Part of my training as a Choctaw warrior. I excelled at sneaking up on folks unaware. Head of my class, in fact."

Rafe was in no mood for Micah's teasing. During the ride back to the garrison he kept mentally listing all the worst-case scenarios that might befall Karissa and the other independent-minded women who were intent on making the Run.

Hell, if he weren't in charge of monitoring this crazed race he would volunteer to stake a claim for Karissa—anything to insure her safety when the wild stampede began.

"You're in a sour mood," Micah observed as he watched Rafe stable his mount. "Did you and Karissa have another argument?"

"No, we did not. We were exceptionally civil to each other."

"What a shame," Micah taunted mischievously. "I enjoy watching you get all worked up after she sets a fire under you." Before Rafe could jump down his throat, Micah hurried on. "Your fiancée has been looking for you and she is dressed fit to kill. My guess is that she plans to seduce you this evening, just in case you're having misgivings about the upcoming wedding." He grinned outrageously. "Someone around here is definitely going to get lucky tonight."

Rafe locked the horse in the stall and turned to see Micah's vivid blue eyes twinkling with deviltry. "I do not *choose* to get lucky, as you so crudely put it. I have a long, harrowing day ahead of me and so do you. Why don't we both call it a night?"

"Fine by me, my friend." Micah ambled alongside Rafe as they crossed the parade grounds. "I *am* going to get to be your best man, aren't I? Wouldn't want to miss the upcoming nuptials, ya know."

"Knock it off, Micah. You're spoiling what's left of my disposition," Rafe muttered.

"Well, here goes the rest of it," Micah murmured as Vanessa appeared from the shadows near the officers' quarters, her bejeweled neck and wrists sparkling in the lamplight. "If her plunging neckline isn't an invitation to look and touch I don't know what is."

"Rafe, there you are!" Vanessa called out as she wiggled and jiggled her way toward him. "Did you just now return from patrol, you poor dear? You really should delegate some of your duties to your subordinates." She stared surreptitiously at Micah. "I'm sure Captain Whitfield wouldn't mind covering your evening duties so that we can spend some time together."

"Glad she's marrying you and not me," Micah muttered aside, before he veered around Vanessa and hurried off to his quarters to bed down for the night.

"I'll escort you to your room," Rafe volunteered as he grasped her arm to reverse direction. "I won't be around at all tomorrow so you'll have to entertain your-self, I'm afraid. Overseeing the Run and quelling dis-putes will demand all of my time and attention.''

"Then it's important we make the most of this eve-ning," Vanessa cooed, then flashed an inviting smile.

Rafe halted at the door, opened it then gestured for Vanessa to enter. "I'm sorry to disappoint you, Vanessa. I know I have left you to your own devices for hours on end, but you've come at a bad time. Good night.''

When she looped her arms around his neck and pushed up on tiptoe to kiss him, Rafe didn't respond to the obvious invitation. He set her away from him, bowed politely and beat a fast retreat. It tormented him no end that enduring Vanessa's kiss felt like a betrayal to Kar-issa.

Now that was irony for you, Rafe thought. He wanted nothing to do with his fiancée, because he felt stronger sentiments toward the woman everyone at the post pre-sumed to be his mistress.

When Rafe turned and walked away, Vanessa glared daggers at him. Never in her life had a man rejected her. She had been a much-sought-after debutante and it was infuriating to realize her practiced charm had no effect on Rafe.

Damn him to hell and back! Surely he hadn't been tumbling in the hay with his whore again. How could he? By now he must have heard that she'd been accused of assault and theft.

Either that or Harlan had lied to her when he claimed he'd framed Karissa for robbery, Vanessa thought sus-piciously. Men! You couldn't trust them to do what you told them to do. If Vanessa knew where to find that harlot she would ride off to wring the woman's neck, once and for all.

This situation was getting desperate, she mused as she dressed for bed. There was nothing to do but put her wedding plans in motion while Rafe was busy tending this ridiculous race for land. She would spend her time hand-printing invitations and making arrangements with the cooks to prepare the semblance of a wedding feast at the mess hall.

Vanessa snorted distastefully. This was likely to be the wedding reception from hell. Well, offensive as the thought was it didn't matter. All that mattered was that Rafe signed the marriage license. It was all she needed when she returned to Virginia. She certainly didn't need him as a companion when the men of her acquaintance fell all over themselves to escort her from one grand ball to the next and begged for a dance in her arms and a tryst in her bed.

She would be back where she belonged and that pesky Harlan Billings could send all the blackmail notes he wanted. It wouldn't matter to her. She would have what she wanted.

The comforting thought wiped the snarl off Vanessa's face as she stretched out on her cot. She was playing for high stakes and she had no intention of losing the meal ticket that went by the name of Commander Rafe Hunter.

Chapter Nine

Karissa hadn't managed to get much sleep the previous night. Eager apprehension had her nerves strung tighter than fence wire. She was anxious to approach the starting line and begin the Run, but she couldn't saddle up and ride away until she helped Clint and Amanda disassemble the tent and pack their few worldly possessions in the wagon.

As Karissa requested, Clint and Amanda would wait at least an hour after the wild stampede for land. They would follow at a slower pace that wouldn't endanger their unborn child and cause undo stress on Clint's mending leg and aching head. Once Karissa staked their claim—and she refused to consider that she wouldn't reach their prospective homestead ahead of the thundering hordes—her brother and sister-in-law would arrive to help her set up the tent on their new property.

Two hours before the race, Karissa saddled Sergeant, grabbed the peeled willow stick that Amanda had decorated with colorful ribbons from her own gowns and printed the name Baxter in bold letters. The eye-catching stake was to be placed at the corner of the property to prevent other would-be settlers from attempting to secure the same homestead.

Sergeant tossed his head and pranced sideways as he jockeyed for position among the other horses and riders who were headed toward the boundary that had been marked by stones and protected by a picket line of soldiers who formed a human wall along the western border to Oklahoma Territory. It didn't take Karissa long to realize that Sergeant was as much a born leader as his master, for the horse quickened his pace reflexively when one of the other mounts tried to surge past him.

Sergeant, it seemed, preferred to lead the pack, not follow dutifully behind the herd. That, Karissa was sure, would work to her advantage when the wild race began. All she had to do was clamp herself to the powerful gelding and he would do the rest.

Karissa inwardly groaned when she noticed the multitude of settlers migrating toward the boundary line. Sweet mercy, there were thousands of would-be settlers descending like a swarm of locusts. There couldn't possibly be enough homesteads in the area to accommodate all these settlers who carried their colorful stakes like banners to mark their claims.

Some of these people were doomed to disappointment, she realized. Karissa sent a quick prayer heavenward that she wouldn't be one of them.

Her anxious thoughts scattered when she saw Rafe mounted on the black gelding he had been riding the previous night when he arrived in camp. He was directing traffic as he trotted back and forth across the prairie, behind the picket wall of uniformed soldiers. When their eyes met across the distance he sent her an encouraging smile. Karissa sucked in a calming breath and tried to control her nervous jitters.

Resolutely she focused absolute concentration on Rafe, watching him move like a centaur on his mount. She tried to stop fretting about all the prospective settlers that were crowding in around her, causing her to slam against the riders on either side of her.

"I'm apologizin' in advance, ma'am," said the be-whiskered man to her right. "My mamma taught me to be gracious to ladies, but I can tell ya right now that if you git in my way durin' the race I won't be worryin' about my manners."

"Me neither, ma'am," the man on her left spoke up. "All's fair in races such as this, and I got a family depending on me to find a homestead."

"I understand perfectly," Karissa told them as she settled more comfortably in the saddle. "And you'll understand that I won't be apologizing when I leave the both of you choking in my dust."

The men snickered good-naturedly.

"Best of luck to ya, then, ma'am," said the man on the right. "It's every man—or woman—for hisself in this free-for-all. Just don't git in my way."

Sergeant half reared when the horse behind him gouged him in the rump. Like falling dominoes, the entire line of hopeful settlers shifted and resettled into their positions.

Karissa swore her heart was about to beat her to death when the man on her left checked his timepiece and announced that it was five minutes until noon. Five minutes before all hell broke loose on this virgin prairie, Karissa thought. Five minutes until dreams were fulfilled—or shattered beneath thundering hooves.

She swallowed apprehensively then returned her attention to Rafe. Her pulse leaped into double time when he lifted his pistol in the air and ordered his soldiers to do the same. Micah, who had shifted position so that he was almost directly in front of her, tossed her a wink and an encouraging smile.

Karissa was so tense that she wasn't sure she could have smiled if her life depended on it. Clint and Amanda were counting on her and she couldn't bear the thought of disappointing them. She silently hoped that half the settlers crowding the line were headed for the fifty-foot town sites that had been plotted in advance and that they weren't interested in a homestead. The less competition the better.

"Ready, aim, fire!" Rafe yelled at the top of his lungs.

The explosion of the cannon from the fort split the air and smoke from the soldiers' pistols drifted in the breeze. Karissa yelped in surprise when Sergeant, without her command, plunged into a gallop.

Rafe had been right on the mark when he cautioned her to hold on for dear life when Sergeant took off from the starting line. She had never been on the back of such a swift, powerful horse. Sergeant's long-legged strides ate up the ground and the wind roared in her ears as she thundered across the prairie with thousands of settlers breathing down her neck.

Behind the wall of laboring horses, the wagons and carriages bounced precariously over the uneven terrain. Karissa heard the pained cries of settlers who had been catapulted from their wagons and had to scramble for their lives to prevent being trampled. Beside her, one rider screamed in terror when his horse stumbled.

Karissa was assailed by the instinctive need to stop and help those who had fallen, but trying to rein in Sergeant was next to impossible. The gelding had lowered his head, laid back his ears and increased his speed. The horses that had been racing neck to neck with him were left to stare at his departing rump.

When Karissa veered southeast to reach her claim, she noted the human wall of riders had begun to fan out in all directions. Stakes clutched in their fists, eyes gleaming with expectation, the settlers thundered across the prairie, searching for the property that appealed to them most.

Some riders hurled their colorful stakes like lances when they spied a cornerstone that marked a homestead. Foul curses and angry shouts erupted when rival settlers attempted to claim the same plot of land. But Karissa rode on, vowing that wouldn't happen to her. With Sergeant's help she would outrun the greedy masses and stake her claim minutes before the other riders caught up with her.

She galloped over rolling hills that stood knee-deep in grass. She clamped herself around Sergeant as he took the narrow creeks in a single bound and scrabbled up the steep slopes to stretch out in a canter.

There in the distance, a quarter of a mile ahead of her, Karissa spotted the cornerstone of the property she had selected. To her dismay, she saw a man on foot, emerging from the tree-choked creek with his long coat-tails flapping. He sprinted toward the cornerstone to claim the land before she could reach it.

"Damn Sooner!" she shouted furiously.

She knew perfectly well that the settler had sneaked inside the line during the night to stake the claim. It was impossible for a man on foot to outrun Sergeant, who was leading the pack by five lengths.

"The place is mine!" the man yelled as he scuttled toward the cornerstone. "Go find another homestead, missy!"

Teeth gritted, stake raised like a lance, Karissa gouged Sergeant in the flanks, urging him to run like he had never run before. When the Sooner cocked his arm to hurl his stake toward the cornerstone, Karissa did likewise. Her stake sailed through the air, its sharp point sticking into the ground, its colorful ribbons rippling in the breeze.

Her triumphant shout transformed into a shriek when her rival's stake grazed her thigh then cartwheeled over Sergeant's head. The horse reared up and Karissa, unprepared, somersaulted over his rump and landed with a thud and a groan. Gasping to draw a pained breath, she watched her rival charge toward his fallen stake. She knew his intent, the sneaky claim-jumper! He planned to yank her stake from the ground and replace it with his own.

Karissa surged off the ground, favoring her injured leg, and gave chase. "That's cheating!" she railed furiously.

When the man in the floppy-brimmed hat screeched to a halt and reached for her stake, Karissa launched herself at him, knocking him facedown in the grass. Before she could whack him over the head with the butt end of her borrowed pistol, he grabbed a handful of her hair and jerked her sideways. Karissa struggled to upright herself, but the scoundrel backhanded her, sending her rolling downhill.

By the time she gathered her feet beneath her, the jeering claim-jumper had drawn his pistol and pointed it at her head. "Don't think I'm gonna grant you any favors, just because you're a woman," he snapped at her. "I was paid damn good money to sneak in here and stake this claim."

"That's cheating, too," she muttered at him.

"Well, that's life, honey. Now git on yer horse and git outta here before I turn you into a casualty of this Run."

"Put the gun down. Now," came a booming voice from the distance.

Karissa glanced sideways to see Rafe thundering toward him, his Winchester in firing position and his handsome face scrunched up in a menacing snarl.

"She's tryin' to steal my claim," the man shouted. "Woman or not, I won't let her get away with it."

Rafe skidded his laboring steed to a halt and took the man's measure. "I witnessed your scuffle," he growled. "The lady put her stake at the cornerstone first."

The fence-rail-thin claim-jumper smirked as he lowered his gun. "I'm sure you'll expect her to be immensely grateful for coming to her rescue. A word of caution, soldier, she fights dirty, so you might want to rethink samplin' her charms after ridin' in here like her white knight."

When the scrawny man snatched up his stake and darted off, Rafe slammed the rifle into its sling on the saddle and dismounted. Karissa had scared another ten years off his life while he watched her battle the claim-jumper.

"Damn it to blazing hell, woman, this claim is not worth your life!"

Karissa clambered to her feet, dusted off her ill-fitting breeches and said, "Thank you for settling the dispute."

The beaming smile that lit up her face stole the breath from his lungs and melted his anger like butter in a hot skillet. He could tell that she was so pleased with her success she was damn near bursting with it.

Seeing her this happy, her eyes twinkling like emeralds in the sunlight, Rafe couldn't bring himself to scold her further for her daring and determination. He simply had to accept the fact that Karissa Baxter was who she was—a woman on a self-sacrificing mission to help her family. A resourceful, independent woman who had been forced to learn to survive at an early age and had developed the courage to face whatever battles she encountered.

In his mind, Karissa epitomized the pioneer spirit. She had weathered the hardships of her exodus from Kansas, faced difficult odds and looked to the future with unfaltering hope.

Rafe was so damn proud of her that he wanted to hug her. Of course, at the same time, he wanted to shake the stuffing out of her for squaring off against that scrawny ruffian who had looked as if he had every intention of shooting her, dragging her lifeless body down to the creek and dropping her into a shallow grave.

"I did it!" Karissa declared, excitement bubbling up in her voice. "It was worth the struggle. And I have you to thank for lending me your horse. I swear Sergeant had wings when he took off from the starting line. He was magnificent! Oh, Rafe, thank you so much!"

When she came flying toward him, her wild hair billowing behind her, her manly breeches covered with dirt and grass, he felt his heart dissolve in his chest and dribble down his rib cage. He scooped her up in his arms and swung her in a dizzying circle while she nuzzled her cheek against his neck.

"On top of the world, are you?" he chuckled as he held her close.

He felt her smile against the side of his neck before she nodded her head. "Can you possibly imagine what it's like to own little more than your own name and suddenly lay claim to a hundred sixty acres of fertile farmland?''

No, he couldn't. He'd been born into a wealthy family, the only son of an only son. He had never had to scratch and claw for anything in his life. He'd had to fight like the very devil a few times to survive in battle, but he had never doubted where his next meal would come from or how he would pay for it.

Oh certainly, he had worked hard to earn promotions on merit, although there were always those—like Harlan Billings—who insisted his family name and wealth were the reasons he had made the rank of major by the age of thirty-three. He had a few battle scars to prove that he didn't believe in waging war from the sidelines. He led his men into battle; he didn't watch them fight while staring through a spyglass and standing well out of cannon and rifle range.

He knew the self-satisfaction of seeing a job well-done. So yes, he could imagine how elated Karissa felt at the moment. The fact that he was here to share her joy and excitement was a memory he would savor for a long time.

He wondered if she was glad that she had earned the right to file a deed for this property legally—instead of sneaking in like a thief in the night to take advantage of the other settlers who made the race.

As if she could read his mind, she said, ''I cursed you mightily in the beginning, but I'm ever so glad you made me follow your rules.'' When he lowered her to the ground, she stepped back to peer up him at from beneath long curly lashes. ''I doubt my conscience would let me sleep at night if I had managed to avoid your patrols and cheated the other homesteaders.''

Rafe brushed his fingertips over the welt on her

cheek—compliments of the vicious claim-jumper. "Glad to hear you say that, Karissa. If not for rules and regulations, undesirables would own most of these homesteads and town sites. The honest citizens wouldn't stand a chance against them."

Although he was hesitant to leave Karissa alone, for fear other claim-jumpers would descend upon her, he needed to keep surveillance so that other settlers weren't victimized. "My men and I will have a long afternoon, riding herd over the area," he said as he swung into the saddle. "Keep that pistol handy, in case someone else decides you look like an easy mark."

"Clint and Amanda should be here soon," she assured him as she glanced west. "I'll bring Sergeant back to you this evening." She glanced fondly at the horse. "I'm going to let him graze our property to his heart's content and give him the chance to rest before I return him. And Rafe?"

He stared down into her animated face and felt another corner of his heart crumble. "Yes?"

"I wish I could repay you."

"You already have," he murmured as he memorized the radiant expression on her face. Damn, he was going to miss this lively female like crazy.

Rafe nudged his mount and trotted away. Seeing Karissa's smile of pure delight was worth more than he dared to admit aloud. So he kept it to himself and rode off to protect and defend other settlers who encountered disputes over their claims.

When Clint and Amanda arrived an hour later, Karissa watched her brother stare across the rolling hills that tumbled into the heavily timbered, spring-fed creek. These would provide lumber for their new home and a fresh water supply. It was the first time she had seen Clint smile since the day before he had been thrown from the gray mare and landed in a broken heap. She swore she would tangle with that pesky claim-jumper all over again if she could bear witness to this expression of pride and elation that settled on her brother's face.

"My God, you did it, Kari!" Clint whooped as he awkwardly climbed down from the wagon then hobbled around to help Amanda to the ground. "This place looks like paradise."

Beaming in satisfaction, Karissa nodded. "That's exactly what I thought the first time I saw it." She gestured to the rise of ground to the east. "I can envision a house tucked up against the hill to block the cold north winds of winter and provide a spectacular view of the creek."

Amanda clapped her hands together in delight. "That would be perfect! Oh, Kari, this is incredible! How can we possibly thank you enough for braving that wild stampede and staking this marvelous homestead?"

When tears sprang from Amanda's eyes and trickled down her flushed cheeks, Karissa strode over to give her an affectionate hug. "I've been properly thanked already. Together we can make this land our new home." She looked over Amanda's shoulder to stare meaningfully at her brother. "No more wandering from town to town like vagabonds and gypsies. We can put down roots, raise cattle and sheep and plant crops."

Clint smiled, nodded then drew in a deep breath and admired the land. "Home," he murmured appreciatively. "A place to call our own."

Amanda wiped away her tears then blinked in shock. "Kari, what in the world happened to your cheek!" She brushed her fingers over the welt then jerked back her hand when Karissa winced. "It looks as if someone struck you."

Karissa shrugged nonchalantly. "I had a run-in with a claim-jumper, but Rafe...um...Commander Hunter came by to send him on his way. We will have to take turns standing guard tonight so no one tries to sneak in to steal our claim again. I predict there will be a great number of disgruntled settlers who weren't able to stake a claim and have become desperate enough to resort to drastic measures."

"At least that's one duty I can handle around here," Clint said as he hobbled to the back of the wagon to drag out the tent. "Kari deserves a good night's rest and so do you, Amanda. I'll keep the night vigil."

Together the threesome pitched the tent near the location on which they hoped to construct their home. Together they built the campfire to enjoy their first meal at their new homestead. Karissa couldn't remember the last time she had felt so content and happy. Well, except those few times when she had become the recipient of Rafe's mind-boggling kisses.

She quickly stifled the thought. She had no future with Rafe. But at least she would have the pleasure of helping Clint and Amanda build their house and stock their pastures. For a time, this would be her home, too.

Karissa refused to spoil her grand mood by wondering where she would settle after Clint and Amanda had a roof over their head, crops in the field and cattle grazing the lush pastures. For now, she was simply going to live for the moment and savor her dream of making a fresh new start with her family.

Under the pretense of patrolling the area to settle disputes over claims, Harlan made his rounds to collect his fees for pointing settlers in the right directions. In addition to helping Vanessa with her plot to secure her marriage—and blackmailing the snippy chit—Harlan had discreetly accepted money to aid a handful of men in locating plots that would provide fertile soil and an abundance of water.

He had insisted on half of his payment before the Run and now he intended to acquire the balance due. Most of his secretive business associates were so elated to have staked prime land they handed over the money without batting an eye. However, there was one persnickety old goat who balked at paying Harlan his fee.

When Harlan made the mistake of threatening to use the power of his position with the army to block the legal registration of the deed for the land Arliss Frazier acquired, the rascal sniffed arrogantly. When Arliss lifted his pudgy hand, three armed men appeared from the underbrush to take aim at Harlan's chest.

"Now then, Corporal," Arliss said in gloating satisfaction, "you can ride off the land my friends claimed for me or we can bury you down in the ravine. As it turned out, I wasn't able to claim the adjoining piece of property, as I'd hoped. A feisty red-haired female and an intimidating soldier forced Chester Gentry to run for his life."

Arliss gestured toward the thin, wiry man who stared at Harlan from the barrel of a shotgun. "You've been paid more than enough for land I claimed. Since I wasn't able to claim the property I wanted most, *you* actually owe *me* money."

Harlan silently seethed when he realized it was that pesky Karissa Baxter—with the help of Commander Hunter, no doubt—who had staked the claim that Arliss wanted most.

Wouldn't you know that witch would be involved? For the life of him, Harlan couldn't figure out why Karissa hadn't been charged for robbing the crippled man he had knocked over the head. Probably slept with every man who accused her of thievery, Harlan decided bitterly. She had resisted *his* sexual advances, but she had undoubtedly used her charms to get off scot-free.

"Take yourself off, Corporal," Arliss said with an impatient flick of his wrist. "I have arrangements to make with my unwanted neighbor. That piece of property she claimed has the best source of water. I need that land to develop a stage station and trading post that will sit halfway between the town plotted to the north and the one plotted to the south."

"A word of caution," Harlan said with a smirk. "I know the woman in question and she is difficult to deal with." He glanced at Arliss's scraggly henchmen. "And one more thing—I'll be back to collect my due when you don't have your thugs to protect you. In fact, I might just tell the commander at the fort that I witnessed underhanded dealings. You might find yourself stripped of the property you did manage to claim—with *my* help."

Arliss snorted at the threat. "Blackmailing me into paying you will force me to explain your involvement, Corporal. You could find yourself demoted or court-martialed before you know what hit you." His face contorted into a sneer. "Just try to cross me, Harlan, and I'll make you regret it—in spades!"

Muttering curses, Harlan retreated, refusing to turn his back on Arliss and his henchmen for fear of being pelted with buckshot. That sneaky bastard had backed Harlan into a corner. Well, Arliss might have won this round, but Harlan never had been able to tolerate being out-

smarted. He would have his revenge—and the rest of
his money. Arliss Frazier could damn well depend on
it.

Just before dusk, Karissa saddled the plodding gray
mare, grabbed Sergeant's reins and headed for the fort.
She sincerely hoped she could return Rafe's horse without having to see him with his fiancée.

Although Karissa kept telling herself that her infatu-
ation with Rafe was a waste of emotion, his memory
would forever be attached to the thrilling moment when
she had claimed the homestead. He had been there to
share her elation. He had prevented that sneaky claim-
jumper from stealing her property. He had also been
there to offer his swift horse and his pistol for her protection.

"Since when did you become a hopeless romantic?"
Karissa muttered at herself as she rode northwest. She
was the farthest thing from a fairy-tale princess, even if
she had begun to perceive Rafe as her Prince Charming.
"He doesn't belong to you, nor you to him. Accept that
and get on with your life."

After bolstering herself, Karissa reached the garrison.
There was only a skeleton crew of soldiers on hand to
greet her. Most of the cavalry was still patrolling the
new territory. She had nearly made it around the perimeter of the parade grounds to reach the stables when
Vanessa Payton, dressed in one of her eye-catching
gowns, walked from the officers' quarters. Damnation,
talk about lousy timing, Karissa thought glumly. This
was one individual she preferred not to encounter.

Vanessa broke stride when she noticed Karissa. She
looked down her nose at Karissa's faded cotton gown
and sniffed disapprovingly at the very idea of a woman

straddling a horse. Her gaze narrowed when she realized Karissa was leading Rafe's prize gelding.

"You have nerve," Vanessa sneered as she closed the distance between them. "I don't even have to ask how you repaid my fiancé for the use of his horse. I distinctly remember telling you that I never wanted to lay eyes on you again."

"Believe me, Vanessa," she countered, "nothing would make me happier, either. I have enemies for whom I have developed fonder affection."

Vanessa thrust back her shoulders and emitted a hissing oath that condemned Karissa to a place where the hottest of climates prevailed.

Karissa thought it was a crying shame that a woman who looked like a grounded angel, with her vivid blue eyes and shiny blond hair, had been cursed with a vile personality. Of course, Rafe wouldn't be privy to Vanessa's waspish tongue and condescending glares. He probably had no idea that Vanessa was a full-fledged witch in hiding.

In her opinion, the one true lady in the area was Amanda Baxter, who was an eternal optimist and rarely had an unkind word to say to—or about—anyone. Amanda should be the one who was dressed in elegant finery, sporting expensive jewels and receiving preferential treatment.

Karissa smiled wryly, picturing Vanessa in *her* rightful place as a harried, gray-haired old hag who spent the better part of her days croaking incantations over her boiling caldron, burning her tongue on her hot brew and flying around on her broom.

"And what can you possibly find so amusing?" Vanessa snapped as she jerked Sergeant's reins from Karissa's hand. "You have no pride and no shame. Just look at you, a working-class harlot who isn't good enough to polish Rafe's boots, much less share his company.''

Karissa had been insulted and called frightful names a few times in the past. She had been mocked and ridiculed because of her father's lowly reputation as a vagabond and gambler. But she had shrugged it off, assuring herself that she was nothing like her father, who had proved to be a weak, selfish individual. But it hurt to hear that she wasn't worthy of Rafe's affection, much less his friendship.

If she didn't harbor affection for Rafe, she knew Vanessa's cutting words couldn't have touched her. Hadn't she told herself a thousand times in the past that the only way to prevent being hurt was not to let someone close enough to touch her carefully protected emotions?

"Leave this garrison before Rafe returns," Vanessa demanded hatefully. "If you ever come here again, I will make your life more miserable than it is already. Rafe and I will be married in less than a week. The arrangements are under way and I don't want you to go near him ever again!''

The news threw Karissa off balance. She knew Rafe would soon be wed, but not *that* soon! The impending reality was worse than a hard slap in the face—and Karissa had suffered from stinging blows twice recently. But neither of them hurt as deeply as knowing Rafe would be forever beyond her reach when he married this pretentious chit.

"He deserves better than you," Karissa said.

"For certain, he deserves far better than the lowly, ill-bred likes of you," Vanessa retaliated scornfully.

When Vanessa called to one of the soldiers to take Sergeant to the stables and have him washed down to remove the offensive stench, Karissa winced at the snide insult. Turning away from Vanessa's loathing glare, she trotted through the gate. Only then did the tears of frustrated humiliation flow freely.

God! She'd gone from the pinnacle of excitement after the Land Run to the blackened pits of rejection in the course of one day. And why hadn't she lowered herself to exchange a few more stinging insults with Vanessa? Why had she sat there and taken that demeaning tirade and allowed her to have the last word?

Karissa's shoulders slumped as she rode through the darkness. Perhaps she really was nothing more than a gambler's daughter—and a lousy gambler at that. Karissa decided that even in a newly formed territory you couldn't outrun your heritage or your past. You simply were what you were. She was going to have to make peace with that, she decided as she swiped at the infuriating tears of self-pity.

Karissa inhaled a cathartic breath and squared her shoulders as she trotted through the darkness. She had to put all whimsical thoughts of Rafe behind her and get on with her life. Clint and Amanda cared about her, needed her, and she cared about them. She was going to devote her time to building a home and acquiring money to purchase seed for crops. And she was *not* going to harbor delusions of Rafe Hunter being anything except one of the many fleeting acquaintances who passed through her life.

Even if his kindness, generosity and inborn need to protect and defend had touched the deepest reaches of her soul she *had* to forget him. If she couldn't remember that she didn't deserve to love and be loved, she could always depend on Vanessa Payton to remind her of her place.

Chapter Ten

Rafe was three miles from the fort when he encountered Karissa. Instantly, he knew something was amiss. He could tell by the way she sat her horse, the way she withdrew into herself when he hailed her.

It was difficult to believe this was the same woman who had been so overjoyed at staking her property that she had thrown herself into his arms and laughed with pure delight.

"What's wrong? More trouble with claim-jumpers?" he asked in concern.

"No, everything's fine," she mumbled, staring at the air over his left shoulder. "I have all I dreamed of, don't I? What else could I rightfully hope to want?"

"Rightfully?" Rafe frowned, disturbed by the way she phrased the question. This didn't sound like the free-spirited woman he had come to know. Even her voice sounded subdued. Where was the lively animation he had come to expect from her?

She evaded his question by saying, "I should go. I'm keeping you from your duties and your fiancée."

Ah, now he was getting somewhere. He would bet the entire Hunter family fortune that Karissa had encoun-

tered Vanessa. No doubt, Vanessa had taken grand pleasure in rubbing the wedding plans in Karissa's face.

A wry smile pursed his lips as he eased his mount
forward until he and Karissa were sitting knee to knee.
Could it be that Karissa had become so fond of him that
the prospect of his marriage tormented her? That was
encouraging, because he was more than a little fond of
her, too.

The fact was that he had reached the point where he
was willing to do just about anything—aside from
breaking the laws he was obliged to uphold—to become
the recipient of her blinding smiles. They provided a
warmth and pleasure that surpassed anything he had ever
experienced. That was saying a lot, because his life had
been rife with vast and varied experiences.

Impulsively Rafe brushed his fingertip over Karissa's
dewy lips. And suddenly she was tumbling toward him
and he was lifting her off the mare to plant her in his
lap. His horse shifted sideways as Rafe guided her legs
around his hips and cuddled her in his arms.

He didn't know what prompted the urgency he sensed
when she kissed him, as if she needed to share his breath
in order to survive, but the impact of having her in his
arms, her lips hungrily merging with his, left him hard
and needy in one second flat.

There was no tenderness in the way they kissed. They
devoured each other. She tried to consume him as completely as he tried to consume her. His hands, as if they
possessed an ungentlemanly mind of their own, roamed
over her lush curves and generous swells. Rafe pulled
her hips to his, settling the apex of her thighs atop his
rigid manhood. Damn but he resented the fabric that
separated him, resented the fact that he couldn't see the
feminine flesh that he touched so familiarly.

"This is goodbye," she whispered when he allowed her to come up for air. "I'll never forget you, never forget all you've done for me and my family."

Rafe didn't like the sound of that, didn't like it one whit, but his senses were exploding like a Gatling gun. The taste of her, the feel of her body pressed intimately to his, made it impossible to think, only respond in hungry desperation.

He couldn't recall how or when he had loosened the buttons on the back of her gown, but the garment gaped, granting him a view of her tattered chemise and the supple curve of her breasts. Angling her sideways, he skimmed his mouth over the column of her throat and nuzzled his cheek against her breast until he had moved the fabric aside so he could claim her nipple.

Her breath broke as she arched upward, as desperate for his brazen touch as he was to suckle her greedily. "Sweet mercy, I—"

He didn't let her complete her sentence. He wanted her mouth again—and he needed it now. Rafe forgot the meaning of noble restraint as his hand dipped beneath the hem of her gown to caress the silky flesh of her thigh. When she gasped at his bold touch, he plundered her open mouth. Kissing and touching Karissa was like devouring a succulent feast after weeks of fasting.

She was driving him crazy. Or maybe he was driving himself crazy for wanting her beyond reason. Rafe found himself comparing the impersonal couplings of his past, for the sake of sexual gratification, to the incredible sensations he was experiencing with Karissa. There was no comparison. He had never desired a woman the way he desired Karissa.

He wanted to tap into the passionate spirit that made her the remarkable woman she was and greedily hoard it for himself. He wanted to know that she, like him, was so caught up in the compelling sensations that nothing on earth was quite as important as satisfying a need that raged through him like wildfire.

Breathing heavily, he lifted his head and surged helplessly toward her. He watched her eyes fly open as he moved rhythmically against her, despite the infuriating barrier between them. He swore he would never forget the astonished look on her face as she curled her arms around his neck and sought his mouth as hungrily as he sought entrance into her body. He didn't care if they came together on the back of his horse. It didn't matter where they were, because he had become a senseless slave to passion.

As his free hand lifted to capture the full mound of her exposed breast he became vaguely aware of the thunder of hoofbeats in the distance. Karissa reacted more quickly than Rafe did. He was still lost in a desperate haze of unfulfilled desire.

And suddenly his hands were empty of her satiny flesh. Only a drifting breeze greeted his lips and he realized his pulsating body was perched—alone—on his horse. Like a man emerging from a hypnotic trance, Rafe blinked and glanced sideways to see Karissa fumbling to fasten her dress as she resituated herself on her mare.

"Here's your pistol," she said on a seesaw breath. She clutched his hand and dropped the weapon into it. "Thanks for the use of it." Her passion-drugged gaze swung to him then flitted away. "I have to go home."

"Karissa, I'm—" He wasn't allowed to apologize for losing his head because she gouged the mare and galloped off without a backward glance.

Rafe twisted in the saddle, watching her pass six soldiers who were returning from patrol. God! He needed to pull himself together!

Scowling at his bewildering loss of control, Rafe dragged in a few shaky breaths and prepared himself to encounter his men. He couldn't remember what he said to them as they rode toward the garrison. His mind was still numb with forbidden pleasure and his body was still thrumming with sensations that defied description.

Damn, he thought as he gingerly dismounted, he needed a dousing in a cold bath and he needed it quickly. He was so determined to closet himself in his quarters that he broke his established routine and asked one of the soldiers to tend his horse.

Rafe sighed in frustration when he realized Vanessa was dogging his steps into the officers' quarters. Well, so much for the time and space needed to regather his composure.

"Hello, Rafe," Vanessa called out before he could open the door and seek the solitude of his room. "I'm so relieved that you're back safely. Some of the soldiers described that wild stampede for land and I was deathly afraid those land-hungry heathens would trample over you to stake their claims." Her nose wrinkled distastefully. "It sounded like desperate folly to me."

Rafe couldn't picture Vanessa breaking a sweat or dirtying her hands in any manner whatsoever. She would never lower herself to racing cross-country to stake free land. She had been raised like a princess. Struggling to make ends meet was beyond Vanessa's comprehension.

With a trill laugh, Vanessa swept, uninvited, into his room and he politely refrained from voicing his objection to being alone with her. He made a point to leave the door wide-open. He had no reason to believe Vanessa would stoop to devious means by claiming they had been intimate, thereby creating the need for a wedding. No, he left the door open because, having come straight from Karissa's arms, with the intoxicating taste of her on his lips and the feel of her lush body branded on his skin, it was inconceivable to imply intimacy between him and Vanessa.

Primly, Vanessa spun about, graced him with an enchanting smile and said, "Now that the hurdle of the Land Run is behind you we can finalize the wedding date. I think this weekend will be perfect. I have had a grand time making preparations and writing invitations to distribute around the garrison. I think a military wedding will be most impressive."

Feet askance, arms crossed over his chest, Rafe stared at his fiancée. "I'm sorry, Vanessa, but this just isn't going to work."

She smiled a little too brightly. "If there are duties that demand your attention, then I'll select another date. But I see no need to wait." She batted her lashes and peeked up at him with practiced charm. "But surely you realize that I have no objection to being a wife to you in every sense of the word. I think I have fallen in love with you already, Rafe."

Rafe nearly strangled in an effort to prevent bursting out in incredulous laughter. Did she really think him so egotistical to believe that nonsense? He appraised his crude living quarters then focused his attention on the attractive woman who appeared hopelessly out of place in his room, in his life.

"There isn't going to be a wedding, Vanessa. I'm a different man than I was when I left Virginia and the hallowed halls of West Point behind," he told her as gently but firmly as possible. "I'm as much a part of this last frontier as these settlers. I have no intention of requesting a transfer, and I doubt you could ever be happy here.''

Melodramatically, her hand swept up to her brow and she braced herself against the back of the chair. "You are breaking our engagement? But you can't! I told you that I have grown immensely fond of you, even if I've only been here a short time. I can be happy here, as long as I'm with you.''

Rafe suspected she nearly choked on that declaration, but he gave her high marks for her theatrics.

He had been pursued several times in the past because of his wealth and his family name. And just because he had spent the better part of the week dodging Vanessa and ignoring her insistence to set a wedding date didn't mean he had turned into a complete idiot. He knew what she ultimately wanted from him—financial security.

Maybe it wasn't even Vanessa's fault that wealth and prestige were so vitally important to her, when it came to prospective husbands. But Rafe's indifference toward marriage had changed radically the past few weeks. So had his perspectives.

He gestured toward the open door and smiled kindly. "I think it would be best for both of us if you returned to Virginia. Your life is in the East, Vanessa, and mine is here. We simply will not suit, I'm afraid.''

For a moment he swore she was going to lash out at him. He noted something less than attractive in her snapping blue eyes and the sour curve of her lips. But dignified lady that she was, she drew herself up to a proud stature, grabbed the front of her silk skirt and swept regally toward the door. "I think I picked a bad time to discuss the arrangements with you, Rafe. Perhaps tomorrow, when you aren't thoroughly exhausted, we can continue this conversation in a more reasonable manner.''

''Nothing is going to change, Vanessa. I'm sorry,'' Rafe said to her departing back.

Vanessa employed every oath in her repertoire as she stalked from the building. When she saw Micah coming toward her, she was tempted to club him over the head with her fists. This half-breed was partially to blame for Rafe's infuriating decision, she mused angrily. The man was a bad influence on her fiancé. Rafe had become so conditioned to consorting with a lower class of individuals during his assignments on the frontier that he had befriended the likes of this ill-mannered subordinate.

Refusing to acknowledge Micah's presence with even a passing glance, Vanessa stormed away, and then glanced around frantically. She needed to summon Harlan immediately. Blackmailed or not, she was forced to resort to relying on that weasel's services once again.

No marriage? Indeed! No one, including the illustrious Rafe Hunter, was going to break the engagement. If Vanessa decided she would marry the man then she would, no matter what lengths she had to go to secure the match.

If she could get her hands on that redheaded tramp this minute she would strangle the life right out of her! Karissa had sunk her claws into Rafe, had bound him to her with her risqué antics in bed, no doubt. And if Rafe hadn't left the door to his room standing wide-open, Vanessa would have made a play for him. Or at the very least, let it be known around the fort that she and Rafe had become intimate so that marriage became necessary to protect her reputation.

Vanessa was so blinded with fury that she plowed into a soldier who passed her in the shadows. She bit the man's head off for not watching where he was going—and then realized it was Harlan who had rammed her broadside.

Vanessa clutched his skinny arm and towed him toward her quarters. "We have arrangements to make," she muttered.

"Fine, but remember that it's going to cost you," Harlan said as he quickened his pace to keep up with her pelting stride.

No matter the cost, it would be worth it, Vanessa assured herself. When Karissa Baxter was out of the picture, Rafe would give up his ridiculous fascination with her and come to his senses. And when he did, Vanessa would still be here to make the last-minute arrangements for the ceremony. She was not leaving this god-awful frontier post without a marriage license in hand and a ring on her finger!

Karissa spent the day after the Run helping Clint and Amanda dig postholes and build a corral to hold their livestock—an aging mule, the gray mare and milk cow. They formed a pitiful-looking crew, what with Amanda's delicate condition and Clint's injuries. But they managed to make the necessary improvements on their property that would allow them a legitimate deed to their homestead.

The hard labor and long hours served a second purpose—keeping her thoughts occupied. She was thoroughly ashamed of herself for the way she had behaved the night she encountered Rafe outside the garrison.

Since she had realized that it was best if she never saw him again, she had been overwhelmed by the impulse to hold him close to her heart for a few minutes before she rode away and left him to his spiteful fiancée.

Karissa still couldn't believe how wildly she had responded to Rafe, right there on the back of his horse. She had behaved like the shameless trollop Vanessa accused her of being.

After they had shared that first mind-boggling kiss, Karissa had forgotten the meaning of self-restraint. No doubt, her flighty emotions—the result of her confrontation with Vanessa—were responsible for sending her cartwheeling into the dizzying vortex of newly awakened desire. When Rafe had touched her intimately, her inhibitions had launched into outer space. She had craved his touch, savored the unprecedented sensations that assailed her.

She had never known there could be such phenomenal degrees of pleasure when in the grip of desire. She, who customarily balked at the slightest domination of a man, had been ready to scream, "Take me. I'm yours!"

Lost to the erotic memories she had shared with Rafe, a crimson blush worked its way up her neck and didn't stop until it reached her hairline. No doubt, her lack of self-control and uninhibited responses had convinced him she was accustomed to sharing her body with men.

Of course, she had unintentionally left him with that assumption the first night they had met. What else was the man supposed to think?

Well, it was too late to correct his erroneous assumption, Karissa told herself as she led the mare to the corral. There would be no future contact—especially of a physical nature—with Rafe. She had said her last goodbye and had gotten carried away. To the extreme.

"Kari, I think you should sit down and take a rest," Amanda advised, studying her sister-in-law closely. "Your face is beet-red and you've set such a furious working pace all day that you've obviously worn yourself out.''

"I'm fine," Karissa insisted as she latched the gate. She wasn't about to confide in Amanda that thoughts of her steamy encounter with Rafe had heightened the color in her cheeks and left her body pulsing with unappeased need.

"Who do you suppose that is?" Clint questioned as he stared at the four riders in the distance. As a precaution, he hobbled over to grab his rifle.

Karissa frowned warily when she recognized the scarecrow-thin scoundrel—dressed in brown breeches, long coat and floppy-brimmed hat—who had tried to steal her claim and had left a welt on her cheek as a souvenir of their disagreement. She critically assessed the overweight dandy who was decked out in an expensive suit and wore an undersize bowler hat that emphasized his round face.

"Miss Baxter. I'm Arliss Frazier," he greeted as he drew his steed to a halt in front of her. "These are my business associates, Sam Pickens, Delmer Cravens and Chester Gentry. I've come to make you an offer for your property."

"Don't waste your breath," she said. "I dealt with one of your associates yesterday." She flashed Chester a grievous frown. "He mentioned you briefly during our fracas."

Arliss shrugged and smiled blandly from atop his horse. "Emotions were running high yesterday, my dear. Chester Gentry was simply trying to carry out my wishes. He didn't want to disappoint me."

Karissa scoffed irritably. She wasn't going to stand here waxing polite with this Sooner, who had obviously hidden out in the underbrush, lying in wait to stake his claims. "I suspect you illegally acquired your home-steads, so your fancy apology is wasted on me. We have no intention of pulling up stakes and leaving our claim." She hitched her thumb toward Clint. "My brother is a crack shot, by the way. I'm sure that if push comes to shove you'll be the first to fall. Start at the top, we Baxters say, and work your way down to the hired help."

All pretense vanished from Arliss's pudgy face. "I intend to develop a thriving community on this site," he said. "I'm offering to transfer the deed of one of my other properties to you, in exchange for this land."

Karissa was no one's fool. She knew this homestead was prime real estate because of its abundant water supply. She also suspected Arliss intended to make a killing by selling off small plots to businessmen.

"I suggest you focus your efforts on building your town site a mile east, because I don't have the slightest interest in selling to you or to anyone else."

His eyes narrowed and his full jowls wrinkled like an accordion. "There are ways, young lady, to encourage your cooperation. Do not force me to resort to drastic measures."

"Are you threatening me and my family? If you are, I will register a complaint with the commander at Fort Reno, just in case. He will know exactly whom to question about whatever unfortunate mishap befalls me." Karissa took a daring step forward and glowered at Arliss. "If you dare lay a hand on my family, the only place you'll see your name recorded is on your head-stone."

When Arliss raised his hand, as if to signal his hench-men to shut Karissa up—permanently—Clint cocked the trigger of his rifle. "Not a good idea, Arliss," Clint called out. "I'm not feeling very neighborly myself."

When Amanda retrieved the concealed pistol from behind her back and pointed it at Chester, Clint nodded in his wife's direction. "By the way, I've taught Amanda everything I know about marksmanship. I wouldn't want to wager how many of you will be dead before you can draw and fire."

Arliss swore sourly as he backed his horse away. "You haven't seen the last of me, Miss Baxter," he growled menacingly at her.

Karissa didn't move from the spot until the foursome disappeared over the hill.

"Oh dear," Amanda chirped as she half collapsed on the ground.

Clint cast aside his rifle and crutch to kneel beside his wife. "Are you all right, sweetheart?"

Amanda gulped and nodded. "I will be in a minute."

"Perhaps you should go inside and lie down," Karissa suggested as she hurried to Amanda's side. If Arliss caused complications in Amanda's pregnancy, he would discover that hell had no fury like an enraged aunt-to-be.

"I think you're right. I do need to lie down," Amanda wheezed as she grasped Karissa's outstretched hand and came clumsily to her feet.

When she swayed unsteadily, Clint wrapped a supporting arm around her waist to hold her upright. He glanced at Karissa in wry amusement. "A crack shot, am I? You lie very convincingly under pressure, sis."

"Thank you," Karissa said unrepentantly as she assisted Amanda to the tent. "First thing in the morning I'm riding north to the new town that was established near the North Canadian River. I want our deed registered—and in hand—as soon as possible. Once the deed is registered it will be more difficult for Arliss and his henchmen to cause trouble.''

"Riding off alone?" Clint snorted. "I think not."

"Don't argue with me," Karissa muttered. "I'll wear my disguise so I won't be recognized. But I am definitely going to register our claim." When he opened his mouth to object, Karissa shot him a silencing glance—like the ones she'd employed when he was just a child and she had to be both mother and sister to him. The look was enough to give him pause, and she hastily added, "Do not argue with logic, Clint. Someone has to stay here to defend our claim and I'm the only one with two steady feet beneath me. So that's that."

"That might be that," Clint grumbled as he gently settled his wife on the cot. "But I don't have to like it."

"Which we don't," Amanda chimed in. "You be careful, Kari. We would never forgive ourselves if you came to harm."

Better her than them, Karissa mused as she walked back outside to gather wood for the campfire. She had come too far and sacrificed too much to stake this homestead. This was her promised land, and it was going to be registered in the Baxter name.

Arliss Frazier could establish his community on a piece of land he obtained illegally. But if he wanted to purchase spring-fed water for his town then he could pay for it. That was the one commodity Karissa had to sell until the first crop was harvested in the fall. And if she didn't have so much to do around the campsite, plus a long ride to the new town to the north, she would indeed register a complaint with Rafe at the fort. Unfortunately, she had said her last goodbye to him. And anyway, Vanessa was guarding her fiancé like a fire-breathing dragon.

Poor Rafe, she thought—and not for the first time. He was so wrapped up in his military duties that he probably hadn't taken the time to look past Vanessa's imperial demeanor to see her for what she was. Maybe Karissa should relay her warning to Micah and let him break the news to Rafe. It would still make her come off sounding like a jealous rival, but at least Rafe wouldn't be stuck with that witch for the rest of his life.

That's what she'd do, she decided as she built the campfire. Micah seemed to have Rafe's best interests at heart. The news would be easier to take from a loyal friend.

Now, if Karissa could only deliver the message and make it to town to register the deed without getting her head blown off by Arliss and company, she was certain tomorrow would be a very productive day.

Chapter Eleven

Rafe was astounded when he rode into the boomtown that had been established overnight—literally. The community that had been named Reno City, in honor of the nearby fort, sat on the riverbank and bustled with activity. Hastily constructed clapboard false fronts were staked as entrances to the canvas-walled stores that provided necessary supplies and lumber. Most of the new businesses were restaurants or saloons. And some were a combination of both.

The buffalo grass of the prairie had been stamped down and ruts from wagons and imprints from hooves marked the newly formed streets. Horses were lined up at hitching posts, and wagons, stacked with supplies, turned the avenues into a busy maze.

Rafe had been obliged to make the jaunt to town to question witnesses about the two shootings Micah had reported the previous evening. A female settler had been shot in the arm during a dispute over a homestead. A male settler hadn't been so fortunate in his argument with claim-jumpers.

Although Jake Horton, the deputy marshal, had arrived to keep the peace, he had sent a request to the fort, asking for Rafe's assistance. Stacks of complaints about claim-jumpers and thieves were piling up in the tent the marshal had erected as his makeshift office.

Rafe could well imagine how much time would be required to investigate and settle the inevitable disputes. Here, he mused as he listened to various arguments to the right and left of him, were the headaches he had predicted he would encounter after the Run.

And speaking of headaches, Vanessa still hadn't purchased a ticket on the stage line that stopped twice a week at the fort. She claimed she hadn't had time to gather her belongings the previous morning before the coach rumbled off to the East. He hadn't been at the fort long enough to insist that Vanessa cease harboring false hopes of a wedding and return to Virginia.

His thoughts trailed off when push came to shove in an argument that erupted outside a dance hall. Rafe dismounted in time to deflect a flying fist before it landed squarely on a furious face.

"If you can't resolve your differences peaceably then you can join me in the marshal's office," he said brusquely.

The men cast a begrudging glance at Rafe's blue uniform then backed off, but not before he caught a whiff of whiskey and made note of two pairs of bloodshot eyes.

Celebrating the claims of a town site or homestead was one thing, but these men had been drinking excessively and their manner of dress indicated they were professional gamblers, not farmers or ranchers. There were definitely more scalawags swaggering down the streets than law-abiding citizens. The gamblers and shysters had turned out in full force to prey on unsuspecting settlers. The undesirables were crowding one another's space and stealing one another's marks.

For a brief moment Rafe couldn't recall why he had forsaken polite society back East to ride herd over this last frontier. Ah yes, he remembered now. He thrived on challenge. Well, he had gotten a tad more challenge than he had bargained for when the government reduced the size of the Indians' tribal holdings and then opened the Unassigned Lands in the heart of this territory.

Rafe strode toward the marshal's office—such as it was—and then stopped in his tracks when he recognized the female voice that rose to a shout. He wheeled around, searching the crowded street until he spied a red head glinting in the sunlight. Karissa, dressed in men's clothes, stood toe-to-toe with a plump gent who had clamped his beefy hand on her forearm.

"I told you to stay away from me or you'd be sorry," Karissa spouted off.

"I offered you a fair amount, you little hellion," Arliss Frazier growled into her stubborn face.

"Fair?" she scoffed at him as she squirmed for release. "Your offer is laughable and I've told you I have no intention of selling out to you. Now let me go! If you try to detain me from entering the claim office one more time, I—"

"Is there a problem, Miss Baxter?" Rafe cut in before she threatened to take her adversary apart with her bare hands. Worse, the argument had drawn a crowd of curious bystanders.

When Arliss released her instantly, Karissa made a big production of straightening her shirtsleeve. "Mr. Frazier is trying to strong-arm me into selling my homestead before I can file a deed," she huffed. "He showed up with his three henchmen at our farm to insist I sell out to him. In addition, he and his ruffians tried to over-take me before I could reach town this morning. It was pure luck that I arrived in one piece!''

"She is exaggerating. We did not try to overtake her. We only wanted to discuss the matter with her. It was Miss Baxter who threatened bodily harm, just for making her a reasonable offer," Arliss snapped back. "The woman is half-crazed, if you ask me."

Rafe, trying to remain the unbiased mediator, stepped between them. "Miss Baxter, allow me to escort you to the claim office."

"Thank you," she said to Rafe.

When she flashed Arliss a venomous glare, he smiled craftily at her. Her fists curled in frustration. She didn't trust that overweight scoundrel as far as she could throw him. His sly expression indicated that she hadn't seen or heard the last of him and that he intended to hound her unmercifully until she gave up and sold out to him. Over her dead body!

"I swear, woman," Rafe said as he hustled her across the street. "I'm beginning to think that if trouble doesn't gravitate toward you then you feel obliged to flag it down."

"I've had to stand up for myself since I can't remember when," she informed him crisply. "And for the record, Arliss and his ruffians were hot on my heels during the jaunt to town and they didn't look the least bit friendly. And if you think I'm going to let that rascal walk all over me and attempt to intimidate me then you had better think again."

"Ah, here we are." Rafe physically placed Karissa at the back of the waiting line. He leaned down to wag his finger in her fuming face. "Do not try to cut in line or pick a fight with these good people. And if that gent in the ridiculous bowler hat tries to harass you again, start screaming your head off and I'll be back here in a flash." He leaned in even closer, his lips twitching with barely concealed amusement. "But absolutely no biting or clawing, wildcat."

A reluctant smile pursed her lips as she stared into his handsome face. "You are absolutely no fun at all, General. You're bossy and overly authoritative to boot. But I promise that I won't start any trouble. All I'm going to do is use two of the silver dollars you gave me to pay the fee to register our deed."

"Just don't let yourself be drawn into a shouting match that I have to break up," he warned. "I'm not kidding about that, Karissa. Mind your manners, if at all possible."

"What manners?" she teased mischievously.

Rafe chuckled as he tapped his forefinger on her freckled nose. "You have them, all right. You just delight in letting everyone think you don't."

Karissa watched him walk away and felt her heart do a somersault in her chest. She had fallen in love with this man and she hadn't been able to talk herself out of it.

Way to go, Karissa. You and your impossible dreams.

She heaved a sigh as she impatiently waited in line. It was going to be difficult to live in the same area as Rafe without seeing him occasionally. How was she ever going to recover from this ill-fated love that had mushroomed inside her when she kept bumping into him?

It wasn't going to be easy, she realized. But then nothing in life had come easily. Why should getting over Rafe be any different?

* * *

Bubbling with feelings of elation and accomplishment, Karissa exited the tent that served as the land office. She had registered her deed in Clint and Amanda's name. She was disappointed that she hadn't been able to make the Run to claim her own land and see *her* name on the deed, but Clint having a place of his own was the next best thing.

Using the last of the money Rafe had given to her, Karissa purchased food supplies and then found herself standing in front of a boutique. Inside the large tent was an impressive collection of dresses.

What in heaven's name was she doing in here? She couldn't spare money for clothes, especially the sunflower-yellow gown that caught her eye. Of course, it wasn't as fine as the dresses Vanessa Payton paraded around in at the fort, but it suited Karissa's taste. Impulsively she ran her hand over the soft fabric, remembering that Rafe had never seen her in anything except baggy breeches, borrowed gowns and cast-off dresses that she had picked up at bargain prices in cow towns.

Now why was she standing here, wishing Rafe could see her in that frilly dress, as if she wanted to bedazzle and impress him? He belonged to someone else. Her only consolation was knowing that, while Vanessa might become his wife, she would always be a distant second to Rafe's military career. Why else would he give up the luxuries of his family's elite social circle if he didn't live for the unexpected challenges on the frontier?

"Would you like to try on the gown?" the gray-haired dressmaker asked from behind her. "My husband constructed a makeshift dressing area at the back of the tent."

Karissa pivoted to meet the older woman's smile.

"It's a lovely gown, but since I can't afford it I don't want to tempt myself."

"It would look wonderful on you. Try it on, just for the fun of it," the woman encouraged her.

She was truly tempted, but in the end she shook her head and smiled. Bidding the kindly woman a good day, Karissa stepped outside and caught sight of Rafe standing across the street, conversing with a man who had a badge pinned on his chest. To her surprise, Rafe glanced at her then looked up at the clapboard false front of the store to read the sign that read Gertie's Boutique. He cocked a thick black brow and then stared at the sack of cornmeal, lard and flour she had clamped under one arm.

Feeling utterly foolish for being caught browsing through dresses she didn't need and couldn't afford, Karissa spun on her heel and strode toward the gray mare she'd left tethered in front of the dry goods store.

She cursed herself soundly for not scraping her long hair up on her head and cramming on the cap that made it difficult to tell if she was male or female. For, sure enough, Arliss Frazier caught sight of her red hair and waddled in her direction. Damn, the man was making a nuisance of himself.

"Deed or not," Arliss huffed and puffed as he scurried toward her, "I need that property and I want to close our business deal immediately."

"You are never going to close this deal," she said in no uncertain terms. "You need to get it through your thick skull that my family and I are here to stay."

His expression changed from semi-pleasant to downright mean and nasty. "Don't think that just because you're a woman, your brother is crippled and your sister-in-law is with child that I intend to be lenient with any of you. I will find the path of least resistance to gain your cooperation.''

Karissa wheeled around and started forward, but Arliss slammed his oversize body into her, causing her to stumble forward and fall facedown on the ground. She knew he had done that on purpose to drive home his point.

While he stood over her, grinning nastily, her temper hit its flashpoint. She bounded to her feet, bowed her neck and plowed into him. With a squawk he teetered sideways then rolled like a barrel.

''Did you see that?'' he railed as he fumbled like an overturned beetle to gather his tree-stump legs beneath him. ''The woman knocked me down after I accidentally bumped into her!''

Hands on hips, Karissa glowered at him. ''I did no such thing, you conniving scoundrel. You don't have the decency God gave a mosquito. If you come near my family or me again you won't be sprawled on the ground. You'll be buried beneath it.''

Ignoring the crowd that had gathered around her, Karissa plucked up her scattered supplies and stalked off. The very thought of Arliss's men holding Clint or Amanda for ransom to induce her to sell out had her seeing red. Just because she was a woman, trying to make her way and hold her own in this man's world, did not mean that she would tolerate threats without voicing a few of her own.

Karissa had learned early on in life that the only way to stand up against men who had evil designs on her was to act as tough as they did. Furthermore, she had been pushed around and knocked down too many times in the past twenty-six years and she was sick to death of it.

By the time Karissa reached the gray mare, Rafe was waiting for her and he didn't look happy. Well tough, neither was she.

"I do declare, woman," he drawled sarcastically. "You missed your calling in the theater. You have been in town for only a day and already you have given two attention-grabbing performances." Rafe sighed audibly and shook his head. "Half the folks in this community, the deputy marshal included, know who you are. By sight, at least, if not by name."

Karissa stuffed her food supplies in her saddlebag and muttered, "Arliss threatened to harm Clint and Amanda if I didn't sell out. Then he knocked me flat and claimed it was an accident. I have no intention of allowing him to think I'm a pushover." She tossed Rafe a frustrated glance. "In the event that I wind up dead I suggest that you question him and his thugs about my untimely demise."

"And vice versa?" Rafe asked, a smile twitching his sensuous lips.

She shot him a withering glance as she pulled herself into the saddle. When his hand curled around her ankle, she glanced down into that strikingly attractive face that she had seen too often in her dreams.

"If you can find the patience to wait about an hour I'll escort you back to camp," he offered.

"No, thank you. I can find my own way."

Rafe glanced over his shoulder, trying to locate Arliss Frazier then frowned. "You've made one enemy already, Karissa. I don't want you to become the victim of ambush."

"I'll be careful," she assured him as she reined the mare away. "Besides, I spent the last of the money you gave me on supplies and to register the deed in our name. There is very little left for someone to steal from me.''

Rafe swore under his breath as he watched Karissa weave around the wagons and carriages that filled the street. Damn it, that woman was too proud and independent to accept assistance. He didn't fault her for that, knowing she had grown up the hard way, but it still frustrated him no end to see her gallivanting about without a chaperone.

Grumbling, Rafe headed toward the deputy marshal's tent to sort through the complaints then halted abruptly. Struck by sudden impulse, he reversed direction and jogged across the street to tend to his errand.

Karissa was exceptionally cautious during her jaunt back to the homestead. She kept expecting Arliss or one of his ruffians to leap from the shadows of the trees and pounce on her for pure spite. Thankfully, however, she arrived home in one piece. To her dismay, Clint was trying to hitch up the mule to the plow, preparing to break ground.

''I'll take care of that,'' Karissa insisted as she slid off her horse. ''You go sit down and stay off your leg.''

''No,'' Clint muttered. ''You've been carrying the lion's share of responsibility and I want to do my part.''

When Amanda exited the tent, Karissa hitched her thumb toward Clint. ''Will you please talk some sense into your husband?''

''I tried,'' Amanda grumbled. ''You can see how successful I was.'' She dug into the pocket of her dress then opened her palm. ''I did, however, sell a keg of water to travelers. They were very grateful for the spring water.''

Income. Good. They could use every penny they

could get. Karissa smiled approvingly at Amanda before turning her disgruntled frown on Clint. "Working the ground will get done twice as fast if I do it," she insisted. "You can put your strength to use by going down to the creek to fell trees. We can use the lumber to construct the cabin."

"Fine," Clint scowled. "I'll take the ax and you take the mule and plow. But I swear, Kari, this is damn hard on my male pride. I was hoping to take care of *you* for a change.".

Karissa smiled fondly at her sulking brother as he hobbled over to retrieve the ax. Together Amanda and Clint walked toward the creek, leaving Karissa to follow the mule around in circles, stumbling over the upturned earth.

Despite the long hours and exhausting labor, Karissa savored the smell of freshly turned earth beneath her feet. To her, it was the scent and symbol of success. This was Baxter land and she had the deed to prove it. They owned something of value for the first time in their lives. They had a place to put down roots and to call home.

Although she wouldn't intrude in Clint and Amanda's lives indefinitely, she would have a place to return to, a place that would always feel like home to her. That was something, she consoled herself as she wiped the beads of perspiration from her brow and urged the mule to quicken its pace.

Rafe managed to dodge Vanessa after he returned to the fort to catch up on his duties. She still hadn't caught the stagecoach and she kept insisting that he would come to his senses when the activity in the new territory died down. Rafe held the hope that Vanessa would give up and go home, once she accepted the fact that he wasn't interested in marriage.

It had been three days since he had watched Karissa square off against Arliss in Reno City, and, as a precaution, Rafe had sent Micah to the homestead to check up on the struggling family. Rafe had snorted in disbelief when Micah informed him that Karissa was plowing the field like a farmhand while Clint and Amanda were hitching logs behind the mare and dragging them to the construction site for their cabin.

Was there nothing that woman refused to do? Rafe wondered as he finished double-checking the duty roster for the following day. After impulsively asking Micah to cover for him, he swung by his room for a moment then hurried to the stables to saddle Sergeant. He cantered through the gate and headed southeast at a fast clip. He needed to see for himself that Karissa hadn't worked herself into an early grave by assuming farm duties and only God knows what else.

When he arrived at the Baxter homestead, he noticed two silhouettes moving about in the lighted tent. He dismounted and tied his horse to the corral then went in search of Karissa. When he noticed the glow of a campfire near the creek, he headed in that direction. He found an unoccupied camp and a pallet stretched out on the ground, and he swore foully.

Damn that woman! She was forsaking her own protection and comfort by giving Clint and Amanda privacy. If it had occurred to him that she might set up her own camp, out of earshot of the homestead, he would have dragged a canvas tent from the supply hut at the fort and insisted she use it.

Rafe pricked his ears when he heard singing in the distance. Primed to scold Karissa for braving the wilds by herself, he went in search of the source of that voice. He stopped in his tracks when he realized Karissa was bathing in midstream.

A smile pursed his lips as he tiptoed toward the clothes that were draped over the underbrush. He snatched up the clothes, unwrapped the package he had brought with him and left the new garment in plain sight.

When he caught a glimpse of feminine flesh glistening with water droplets, his knees threatened to fold up beneath him. This woman, who'd had the starring role in his fantasies for weeks, was bare naked in the stream. Rafe couldn't help himself. He looked his fill while she paddled around, singing some ditty that she had obviously heard while sweeping floors in some nameless saloon in some nameless cow town.

Rafe sighed in appreciation when the full moon glinted over her skin and he caught a peek of her rounded bottom before she dived beneath the water. When she resurfaced his absolute attention focused on her full breasts. Rafe swallowed with a strangled gulp.

Ah, what he wouldn't give to join her in the stream and map the lush curves and silky textures of her body until he knew her by touch, by memory.

Before he succumbed to the secret fantasy, he turned away and forced himself to walk back to her camp, but the enchanting sight of Karissa frolicking like a siren in the stream still danced in his head. It was impossible to divert his attention to something else.

Rafe sank down cross-legged beside the campfire and waited for Karissa to appear. But she didn't. Instead he heard a shriek in the distance. Rafe was on his feet in a flash, imagining all sorts of disaster that might have befallen her while she was undressed and unarmed.

Pistol drawn, Rafe plowed through the underbrush to see Karissa clutching the sunflower-yellow gown he had purchased for her against her bare body.

Wide-eyed, Karissa gaped at him as she held the dress modestly to her chest. "How?" she croaked out.

Rafe reholstered his weapon and smiled. "I noticed that you exited the boutique so I inquired inside and Gertie pointed out the gown you favored."

"And you bought it for me? Why?" she asked, incredulous. "No one has ever given me a gift before, and certainly not one so expensive. Why did you do that?"

It damned near broke his heart to learn that no one had given this remarkable woman much of anything. Furthermore, the gown wasn't all that expensive, but Karissa was staring down at it as if were spun gold.

"Put it on," he insisted.

Karissa shook her damp head. "Give me my own clothes. I'm taking this back to Gertie's Boutique, first chance I get."

"It's a gift, Rissa, I want you to keep it," he insisted.

"I cannot accept a gift from you," she grumbled.

"Why not?"

"You know perfectly well why not."

"I do?" he said stupidly.

"Of course, you do. You're getting married, if you aren't already."

"No, I'm not," he informed her. "Didn't Micah tell you?"

"No, and I didn't ask. Why aren't you?" she questioned.

"Well," he said, "I can't very well marry one woman when I can't keep my hands off another, now can I?"

Karissa was so astonished that her arms sagged before she remembered she was naked. Quickly she pulled the gown under her chin to cover herself. Was he saying that he had canceled his wedding because of *her?* Surely not. That was wishful thinking on her part.

When Rafe moved deliberately toward her, Karissa all but stopped breathing. His silver-gray eyes burned like brands on her exposed flesh. For the life of her, she couldn't think of one thing to say when he reached out to trail a lean finger over her bare shoulder.

"I've changed my mind," he said with a devilish grin. "I want the dress back. Now. Give it to me, Rissa."

Flustered, she clutched the gown closer. "You know perfectly well that I can't give it back *now.* I don't have any clothes on."

His index finger skimmed her neck then traced the curve of her lips. "I know," he whispered huskily. "That's why I want the dress back. I want to know if the reality of seeing you naked is as erotic as my dreams."

When his dark head angled toward hers and his lips claimed her mouth, she felt living fire coil deep inside her. And when his arm slid around her waist, drifting over her bare flesh her pulse thundered like a racehorse.

There was no fighting the obsessive desire that one kiss and one touch aroused inside her. She had never wanted a man the way she wanted Rafe. She had never allowed any man to wield power or control over her, but the way he made her feel when she was in his arms demanded willing surrender.

Karissa glided her arms around his neck and gave herself up to the scalding heat of his kiss, the tantalizing feel of his prowling hands moving, unhindered, over her flesh. When he pulled her full length against him she became aware of his rigid arousal.

"I want you, Rissa," he murmured against her lips. "This time I want all you have to give. If that's not what you want, then say so now, because in another minute I won't be able to find the noble restraint to turn and walk away."

He pressed another searing kiss to her lips then said, "And knowing how wary and suspicious you are, don't you dare think I gave you that dress in exchange for favors. That has nothing to do with this."

He looked so determined to be believed that she smiled up at him. "And so, if I said I want you to let me go and return to my camp, you would go? Just like that?"

Rafe gritted his teeth, eased his fierce grip on her and nodded. "If that's what you want."

No one had cared much about what she wanted. Until Rafe. If she hadn't fallen in love with him already, she *would have* the moment he stepped away and allowed her to cling modestly to the frilly dress. He was offering her a choice and accepting her decision. My, wasn't that something?

Without a word he turned and strode away. Hurriedly Karissa pulled the dress over her head and smoothed it into place. Although it was too dark to see how she looked in the gown, it made her feel wondrous. Not as wondrous as Rafe's kisses made her feel, but nothing, she had discovered, remotely compared to that.

Karissa stared toward the glowing light of her camp-fire and made her decision. She knew she wasn't a woman of quality and she would never be considered good enough to be Rafe's wife. Not that he had asked. But she wanted him. She wanted to experience the close-

ness that Clint and Amanda shared and she was tired of
being alone…and tired of pretending she didn't care.

Resolved, but a mite nervous, Karissa trekked through
the trees and underbrush to return to camp—and to the
man who awaited her arrival.

Chapter Twelve

Rafe glanced up from where he sat on Karissa's pallet when she halted a few feet away from him. He feasted his eyes on the vision of lively beauty before him and felt hot chills slide down his spine. Lord, sometimes when he looked at her it took his breath away.

This was definitely one of those times.

Smiling saucily, she spun in a circle. "So what do you think, General? Do I look presentable?"

Rafe smiled appreciatively as his gaze swept from the top of her curly red head to her bare feet. God, she was something. She had always reminded him of a pixie or leprechaun with that pint-sized body of hers, that magical spirit that just wouldn't quit. But the dress emphasized her beauty and accentuated her curves. She was like the personification of radiance and he would gladly give his rank, pay and commission if he could sink into her dazzling heat.

"You look more than presentable, Rissa," he wheezed. "You look positively enchanting."

When she smiled in response to his compliment, Rafe was prepared to swear that the sun had suddenly burst into the night sky, bathing him in its warmth. He had been clutching at self-restraint for the past half hour, but it evaporated when she smiled and those mesmerizing green eyes twinkled.

There was no doubt about it. Karissa had captivated him and he wanted her so desperately that he was very nearly shaking with it.

"As good as you look, Rissa," he murmured as he met her gaze directly, "you look even better wearing nothing at all."

To his surprise she came toward him then knelt on the pallet. She looped her arms over his shoulders and brought her lips a hairbreadth from his. "Now you can have the dress back," she whispered, her eyes dancing with challenge, "providing I can have your uniform. I don't want either of us to be wearing anything at all."

Desire slammed into him like a doubled fist. He wanted to rip the gown off her body and make a feast of her, but it was the finest thing she owned and he wasn't about to damage it. As he closed the scant distance between them to claim her lips, he hooked his forefinger inside the bodice of the dress and drew it down.

He felt her tremble and heard her sigh as he dipped his head to flick at her nipple with the tip of his tongue. Carefully but swiftly he divested her of the dress and chuckled in amusement when she practically ripped the shoulder seam from his jacket in an attempt to get him out of it.

"Easy, wildcat," he teased as he leaned away to shed his jacket and shirt. "I'll have a difficult time explaining why my uniform is torn to shreds when I return to the fort."

Her eyes focused on his chest as he turned back to her. The instant her hand made disturbing contact with his bare flesh, throbbing heat coiled inside him. She was tormenting him to the extreme with her tantalizing explorations, bringing him another step closer to the crumbling edge of control.

Rafe knew, right there and then, that he would never last if he allowed her to touch him freely. It had been too long since he had been with a woman, and the want of this particular woman had been driving him just short of crazy for weeks. He wanted to fulfill every erotic fantasy that had been interrupting his sleep.

He drew her down to the pallet and kissed her hungrily. All the while, his hands roamed and kneaded her silky flesh. Her muffled moan fascinated him, caused his male body to clench in answering response. He longed to draw more sounds of pleasure from her, longed to arouse her to the limits of *her* sanity because he'd already lost *his*. Being with her like this was enough drive him right out of his mind.

''Rafe? Oh, my—''

Her voice trailed off when he brushed his thumb over the rigid peak of her nipple. Splinters of fire pricked her skin. Karissa struggled to draw breath as he focused intently on her and caressed her until she was trembling with sensual anticipation. His wandering hand drifted over her belly and glided over the sensitive flesh of her inner thigh. Need quivered inside her, fanning out in all directions at once.

When her lashes fluttered down and she moaned softly, Rafe whispered, ''Look at me, Rissa, I want you to watch me touch you. I need to know that my every touch pleasures you. I want to learn all the ways you like to be touched.''

Her long, curly lashes swept up and she looked him straight in the eye as he leaned down to take her lips in an all-consuming kiss. He cupped her intimately, stroked her gently. He marveled at the way she arched toward him, and he was amazed at the starburst of pleasure he derived from bringing her luscious body to life in his hands. When he dipped his finger inside her to touch the moist heat of her desire he felt her tremble helplessly, heard her gasp when pleasure radiated through her body and echoed into his.

Rafe knew that caressing her intimately wasn't going to be enough to satisfy him. He needed to taste her completely—though he had never before felt the desire to become so intimate with a woman. Being with Rissa wasn't about scratching an itch or satisfying an urge. This was so much more, something that involved intense emotions as well as breathtaking sensations.

He nudged her thighs apart with his elbow and shifted to trace the velvety folds of her femininity with the tip of his tongue. When she gasped and moved instinctively toward him, so wildly responsive to his touch, he deepened the intimate kiss and felt her burn for him. With tongue and fingertip he brought her to the pinnacle of pleasure and felt her shimmering around him like liquid fire. When she came undone beneath his hands and lips, Rafe shifted above her.

She clawed impatiently at him, but damn it, he had been so caught up in pleasuring her that he hadn't removed his breeches. He wanted to be inside her the moment she wanted him most—wanted to be flesh to heated flesh with her, seared by the flames of mutual desire.

One hand braced on the pallet, the other hand fumbling with the placket of his breeches, Rafe lowered his head and kissed her fervently. When he had finally freed his throbbing manhood and settled himself exactly above her, he plunged urgently inside her…and encountered a barrier that he hadn't expected.

His eyes snapped open and he stared into Karissa's flushed face. He opened his mouth to say something—he didn't know what. He was so stunned by the discovery of her innocence that he was struck speechless.

"I swear, Rafe," she rasped as she hooked one leg around his hips, "if you go all gentlemanly on me now I'm going to strangle you. I didn't wait this long to discover what passion was all about, just to stop when we've only started." She peered up at him with such innocent curiosity that he almost laughed. "We *have* only started, haven't we?"

"Oh yes," he said, grinning—like an idiot, no doubt. "We're just getting to the really good part."

"It gets better?" she asked as she shifted beneath him, trying to adjust to the unfamiliar pressure of masculine invasion. "I can't imagine how that's possi—"

He moved against her then withdrew slightly, and Karissa felt the crescendo of incredible sensations build all over again. It astonished her that she could feel as if she were flying while Rafe clutched her so tightly to him, while he was buried so deeply inside her and pressing her to the pallet.

The ultimate paradox, she thought fleetingly. Passion so overwhelming and wondrously satisfying that even while she felt as if she were dying, she welcomed it, reveled in it, savored it.

As pleasure burgeoned, expanded and then exploded inside her, Karissa clung to him in spellbound amazement. The fevered ecstasy that had assailed her earlier came rushing back like a tidal wave. The blind rush of inexpressible bliss consumed her as the penetrating thrust of his passionate need sent her into complete abandon.

She thought she might have cried out his name when he shuddered above her and phenomenal sensations dragged her into their swirling depths. But she wasn't sure if that strangled sound had come from her or him. She was so oblivious to everything except the incredible sensations riveting her that nothing else registered in her dazed brain.

Gasping for breath, she held him possessively to her as aftershocks of sublime passion rippled through her body to his, and back again. Her hands glided over his broad shoulders, down the corded tendons of his back, to the muscle curve of his buttocks. She kissed the ridge of his cheek, his jaw, and his collarbone and felt contentment settle over her like a feather quilt.

Karissa smiled to herself as she melted against him and absently lifted her hands to stroke the expanse of his massive shoulders. This man might well be a decorated and competent military officer, but he had proved himself to be an amazingly gentle and attentive lover. He had given of himself to arouse and satisfy her beyond her wildest expectations.

Suffused with such feelings of lethargy, Karissa wondered if she would ever gather the energy to move again. Wondered if she would ever *want* to move again. She could lie here, happily, for the next few days in this boneless trance and never once complain.

"Come on," Rafe murmured as he rolled away. "Come with me, Rissa."

"I'm not sure I can get up," she confessed. "I—"

Her voice evaporated when Rafe pulled her to her feet. She blushed in embarrassment when she found herself standing naked before him. Her blush got progressively worse when Rafe made a blatant study of her feminine body.

"Nudity becomes you," he teased rakishly. "You wear it well."

She was so flustered that she didn't object when he grasped her hand and led her through the maze of trees to reach the trickling spring that cascaded over the stair steps of rocks to form a clear pool that glistened like silver in the moonlight.

When Rafe shed his breeches, picked her up and walked into the water, she clung to his neck. "What are we doing?" she asked.

"Bathing," he said as his hands moved gently over her chilled flesh. "I bungled your first experience with passion rather badly. I assumed…well, never mind what I assumed. The point is we have no choice but to do it again."

Karissa leaned away to stare into his shadowed face, noting his roguish grin. She adored this playful side of his personality—a side that had been ruthlessly overridden by the regimented discipline of military life.

"I think I'm being had, General," she declared. "And just so you know, I thought the first time was rather grand."

"You *are* being had," he assured her, "and thank you, but this time is definitely going to be better."

"You mean this time I get to put my hands all over you?" she asked brazenly, then grinned when he choked on his breath. "It seems only fair, you know."

"Being the independent-minded woman you are, why am I not surprised that you demand equal time?"

"Beats me. You, of all people, know what I'm like. I've never deceived you. Well, except for that time when I tried to barter my body for my freedom." She gazed at him mischievously. "But I mistakenly presumed you were planning to take what you wanted from me for free and I damn well intended to get something out of it myself. Had I known what I have been missing, I definitely would have been more insistent that first night."

Rafe laughed aloud then pressed a kiss to her forehead. "Will you stop yammering, Rissa. I have other things in mind to do with you at the moment and conversation isn't on the list—"

His voice fizzled out when she dipped her hand below his waist and folded her fingers around his shaft. Despite the cool water, despite the fact that it had only been a few moments since he had been thoroughly sated, he felt himself swell in her hand.

The look of curious astonishment on her face was so endearing that he dropped a kiss to her parted lips. "You've had that effect on me since the first night we met."

"I have?" She stroked his rigid length and grinned impishly. "I think I have just gained new appreciation for military officers who stand at attention." Her voice dropped to a seductive purr. "And it is attention you shall have, General. In fact, I insist upon it."

Rafe's knees buckled as her hand glided over him. Lightning flickered through his body as she cupped him gently, inquisitively. Tormented pleasure sizzled through his nerve endings as she explored him with her fingertips, then traced her index finger around the tip of his throbbing manhood.

Fierce need left him staggering to maintain his balance. A tortured moan rumbled in his chest as she measured him from base to tip—repeatedly, more boldly with each gliding motion of her hand.

He'd had every intention of leading Karissa back to

the campsite, worshiping her luscious body with kisses and caresses and taking her gently this time. But desire clawed at him like sharp talons as she skimmed her lips over his mouth in petal-soft kisses and drew lazy circles on his aroused flesh. His blood ran so hot and heavy that he could feel his heart thudding against his ribs and his lungs shuddered in a frantic attempt to draw in much-needed air.

Her erotically tender assault had emptied his mind of all thought and filled him with incredible delight. Feeling was the only reality Rafe understood. There was only the stroke of her hand, the sweet pressure of her dewy lips upon his. He was living only through her touch, aware of nothing but the pulsating sensations that knotted in every fiber of his being. He was burning on a scalding-hot blaze that scorched all the way to his soul.

Rafe knew he would never make it to dry land before the compelling urgency to be inside her again consumed him. He was nine-tenths of the way there already. ''I need you now. I can't wait,'' he growled as he hooked her legs around his hips and moved impatiently toward her.

''Who asked you to?'' she whispered as she felt the hard, satin length of him filling her with pulsing heat.

Feminine satisfaction flooded over Karissa when she heard his panted breaths and rumbling groans. She felt his heart hammering against her breasts like a wild bird battling captivity. Now he understood how she had felt that first time when he'd sent her spiraling in reckless abandon. If she had ignited those same intense sensations in him that he had aroused in her then she would be content. Karissa needed to know that she held the power to devastate him the same way he had devastated her.

"Sweet mercy, woman, you're killing me," Rafe said on a jagged breath. "What you do to me should be against the law."

Rafe closed his eyes and surrendered to the fiery explosion of pleasure that vibrated through him as he drove frantically into her. He had wanted to give her the sun—one shining beam at a time—the second time around. But his obsessive passion for her defied the self-discipline he had spent years perfecting and left him out of control.

Why was this feisty, defensive female the one who touched every carefully guarded emotion inside him? Maybe it was because she was so tempestuous and free that she appealed to the reckless side of his nature, which he had ignored for years.

Maybe it was her fearlessness, her passion for life, her indomitable spirit, her endearing determination to provide for her injured brother that touched him so deeply and completely. Or maybe it was her amazing smile, which affected every pixielike feature of her face, that had become his hopeless downfall.

Whatever the case, Rafe had been completely bewitched. Her name was on his lips as bulletlike sensations pelted him, driving him so deeply into her that he became a living, breathing part of her and she became an essential part of his being.

When a kaleidoscope of fiery ecstasy converged on him, Rafe's legs threatened to fold up and leave him floundering in the stream. He shuddered helplessly as he clutched Karissa to him in the aftermath of passion beyond reason, beyond all previous experience, beyond his wildest imagination.

When he recovered his senses and his strength, he carried Karissa to solid ground and let her slide sensuously down his body. There weren't words enough to convey what he was feeling so he kissed her tenderly and hoped she understood that being with her was incredibly special to him.

"I should go," he whispered then kissed her again.

"I know," she whispered back, before her warm lips skimmed over his in a tantalizingly sweet kiss.

"But I'll be back," he assured her. He dropped one last kiss to her swollen mouth. "If that's all right with you."

"It's more than all right. I'd like that very much." She glided her arms over his bare shoulders, pressed intimately against him and kissed him until he swore his eyes crossed and his body boiled into mush—again.

When Rafe finally gathered the willpower to release her, he was still fully aroused. She raised a perfectly sculpted eyebrow and stared pointedly at him. Embarrassed for the first time since he couldn't remember when, Rafe grabbed her hand and led her back to the campfire.

"You should be ashamed of yourself," he teased her. "You are making a mockery of my gentlemanly restraint."

She laughed impishly. "You don't need my help on that count, General. Besides, I like you better when you're out of control and out of uniform."

Rafe pulled on his breeches—carefully. Then he grabbed his discarded shirt and jacket. "I would prefer that you bunk with Clint and Amanda," he said as he put himself together hastily. "Then I won't worry so much about you."

"No," she said as she shimmied into her cotton nightgown. "I'm staying here and that's that."

Rafe tucked his shirt into his breeches and stared her

down—not that it did one whit of good. He was sure the word *stubborn* had been invented to describe Karissa Baxter.

She grinned at him as she snuggled beneath the quilt. "Knowing what I know now, I have no intention of depriving Amanda and Clint of pleasure. Good night, Rafe," she whispered.

Reluctantly Rafe walked uphill to retrieve his horse. Leaving Rissa alone was one of the most difficult things he had ever done. He wanted to stay with her all through the night, wanted to hold her against him and fall asleep with her nestled possessively in his arms. He also needed to know that she was safe from harm. But she wouldn't hear of bedding down in the tent with Clint and Amanda.

He was definitely going to see that she had her own tent, he vowed as he rode through the darkness. He wished he could give her a castle fit for a princess. And that was saying a lot, because he had never invested so much emotion in a woman that he had felt compelled to lay the world at her feet.

During the ride back to the garrison, Rafe asked himself at what point his single-minded focus on his military career had shifted to that feisty but adorable female who had chosen him to be her first experience with passion.

And her second. All in the same night, he thought as the intoxicating memories poured over him in waves and left him fully aroused during his ride to the post.

Cold fury blazed in Vanessa's eyes while she stood at the window of her second-story quarters, watching the lone rider return to the garrison. She had recognized Rafe the instant he rode beneath the lantern that hung outside the barracks. Damn him to hell for sneaking off to take a tumble with his tart.

Swearing, Vanessa whipped around to grab a gown. She had tried to prove her patience and devotion to Rafe by remaining at the fort, even after he had called off the wedding. She had assumed that he would tire of that shabbily dressed little nobody and realize that his marriage to Vanessa was not only expected but also sensible. He was a Hunter, after all. He had a family name to uphold.

Vanessa jerked open the door and stalked down the steps. She was so furious with the situation that she was halfway down the staircase when she remembered to glance this way and that. She did not want the patrolling guards to see her.

"Going somewhere, miss?"

Vanessa sagged with relief when she recognized the guard's voice. Harlan, thank God. The very man she wanted to see. She grabbed his arm and tugged him into the shadows beneath the gallery of the mess hall.

"I am tired of waiting for you to make your move," she muttered at him. "This liaison between Rafe and that trollop is making it impossible for me to arrange the wedding. You have to do something drastic and you need to do it now!"

"It's already been taken care of," Harlan assured her.

Vanessa snorted in contradiction. "If things have been taken care of, then why did I just see Rafe riding back to the fort? As if I don't know where he's been. And with whom! I paid you good money to get that tramp out of my way. I expect to see results!"

When her voice rose to a near shout, Harlan clamped his hand over her mouth. "Keep your voice down, damn it. Do you want to wake every man in the barracks?"

Vanessa slapped his hand away, appalled that this lowly soldier would dare touch her. He wasn't fit to be within ten feet of her and he wouldn't have been if she hadn't had to resort to conspiring with him to achieve her goal.

"Why isn't that harlot locked in jail somewhere?" she wanted to know. "You assured me that you would see her framed for crimes that even a woman would be punished for."

"I said it's been taken care of," Harlan repeated gruffly.

"Of course it has." she smirked. "Well, I've changed my mind. I want her away from here, away from Rafe. I don't care what you do with her, but I want her to disappear. Surely you can find someone who will accept payment to haul her so far away that she can't possibly return before I convince Rafe to go through with the wedding."

"You have no patience, Vanessa," Harlan snickered.

"I've had more than I should have." She scowled at him. "See to the matter immediately."

Harlan doubled over in a mocking bow then held out his hand. "You'll need to make it worth my while."

She stared at his outstretched hand, cursed under her breath then dug into her reticule for more money. "This is the last of it until after the wedding," she informed him. "Now make that trollop disappear and make it quick!"

"Oh, it should be quick, all right," he insisted as he walked away. "By tomorrow you should see results."

"I damn well better," she grumbled as she ascended the steps, a little lighter in the pockets—thanks to her association with the treacherous corporal.

Chapter Thirteen

Rafe glanced up from his desk when he heard footsteps approaching. Unease sluiced through him when he noticed Micah's somber countenance. Rafe could tell by the expression and the way his friend held himself that he had come bearing bad news.

"Now what?" Rafe demanded as he slumped back in his chair.

"I just returned from Reno City," Micah said. "Karissa Baxter has been arrested for the murder of a man named Arliss Frazier and his business associate, Sam Pickens."

"What!" Rafe was on his feet in less than a heartbeat.

Micah nodded stonily. "Two witnesses claimed they saw the confrontation. They described her clothes, her hair color and the horse she rode off on. They say she stole money and a pistol."

"Son of a bitch," Rafe hissed as he stalked toward the door.

"My sentiments exactly," Micah muttered.

"Where is she?"

"The deputy marshal arrested her yesterday afternoon." Micah fell into step behind him. "Jake is holding her in custody with a bunch of men that he keeps strung together like a team of horses in that tent that serves as his office.''

Rafe grimaced at the thought of Karissa being tied up like an animal and left to defend herself against a crowd of ruffians. Which is why he had kept her separated when he hauled her in for squatting on that homestead before the Run.

For God's sake, you didn't tie up a temperamental but very attractive female with a bunch of hooligans! Jake Horton was damn well going to hear about this.

Fuming, Rafe jogged to the stable to fetch Sergeant. Micah was still one step behind him. "You stay here and keep this place under control," Rafe commanded.

"Sorry to disobey your order," Micah said as he slung a saddle on his horse. "But I'm going back to town with you. I already told Lieutenant Johnson to hold the fort. If worst comes to worst, you can distract Marshal Horton while I bust Karissa out of that makeshift jail."

Rafe shot his friend a withering glance.

"Oh, right. I forgot," Micah said. "We can't break the laws we are supposed to enforce. Well, I've got news for you, Rafe. Someone has stirred up a bunch of self-appointed vigilantes who have decided that maybe Karissa should serve as an example in this new territory. They are ready to hang her, just to prove to the shysters and ruffians around here that no one, man or woman, is gonna get away with murder."

Rafe gouged his steed and thundered through the gate. He didn't care how much evidence was stacked against Karissa or how many witnesses claimed to have seen her blow Arliss Frazier and Sam Pickens to smithereens. He knew in his heart that she was innocent.

Yes, he believed she would defend herself if the need arose. Rafe had seen her do it twice. And yes, that sassy mouth of hers was twice the size of her curvaceous body, but she used her fiery tongue as a convincing bluff. It kept her alive and kicking when odds were against her. But she wouldn't shoot two men down in cold blood, and commit robbery and theft, he assured himself. She might have been short on funds and without a weapon for protection, but she wouldn't resort to such brutal means to acquire cash and a pistol.

When Sergeant began to labor, Rafe relented and drew the winded steed to a walk. He glanced sideways at Micah. "When did these murders take place?" he asked.

"Two nights ago," Micah reported. "Just before dusk. According to the witnesses, they could see her plain as day when she shot her victims, stole the money from their pockets and rode off on a gray mare. Marshal Horton questioned several townsfolk who claimed they had overheard at least two arguments between Arliss and Karissa. Some even went so far as to say they saw her shove him off his feet and heard her threaten to kill Arliss."

Rafe groaned aloud. Damn it to eternal hell! He had witnessed those shouting matches himself and he had chided Rissa for that public display of temper. She had claimed Arliss had provoked her too many times and he had purposely made her look bad to the passersby on the street.

Wasn't this just perfect? Rafe thought irritably. He had planned to send a telegraph to his parents this very afternoon, informing them that he wasn't marrying Vanessa because of his romantic interest in someone else. *Oh, and by the way, Father and Mother, the lady in*

*question is going to stand trial for a double murder. I
plan to court her—if they don't hang her first.*

That should go over well with the Hunter family.

"Any thoughts?" Micah prompted, while Rafe stared
into the distance.

"Yes, several of them," Rafe muttered bitterly.
"None of them good."

"You can't possibly believe this nonsense about Karissa," Micah said, outraged. "True, she's got a temper,
but she wouldn't do something like this."

"*You* know that and *I* know that, but convincing Jake
Horton might be another matter entirely."

"Well, the least you can do is insist that she's imprisoned in the stockade at the fort," Micah suggested.
"You can't leave her in that chain gang with those hooligans. They're a rough-looking bunch, Rafe. It'll be a
month before the court system is up and functioning
around here. I don't even want to think about what
might happen to Karissa before she's allowed to defend
herself at a trial!"

Rafe didn't want to think about that, either. Damn it,
he couldn't name one other instance in his life when he
was tempted to lie through his teeth to provide someone
with an alibi. He had been with Karissa later that evening in question, but he *hadn't* been with her at dusk.

True, he could use the power of his position and
throw his military weight around. In his attempt to save
Rissa from legal proceedings, he would ruin her reputation by announcing that he had slept with her. He
could provide false testimony and announce that he
could personally account for her whereabouts from *dusk*
to well past midnight.

And it would be an outright lie.

Scowling, Rafe nudged Sergeant into a trot. Outright

lying went against the grain. Plus, the night he had spent with Karissa had been incredibly special and satisfying. He didn't want to spoil that magical moment by twisting the truth. And at the same time, he wanted to do whatever was necessary to have the charges against her dismissed.

Damn, talk about being stuck between the devil and the deep, he thought in dismay.

"Oh hell, things have gotten progressively worse since I left town," Micah muttered when he noticed a dozen men and women toting homemade signs that demanded immediate justice and an unprecedented hanging in the new territory.

"A vigilante mob, for chrissake?" Rafe scowled as he dismounted then led his horse toward the marshal's office.

He felt the urge to shove bodies out of his way to reach the makeshift jail, but he managed to show some self-restraint. He had to at least *appear* unbiased. But it was damn near impossible when feelings of protectiveness and outrage were spurting through him.

"Hang that female outlaw high!" someone shouted.

"Don't matter if it's a man or woman," someone else hooted. "A murderer is a murderer. We demand justice!"

Rafe tethered his horse then ducked into the tent that served as the marshal's office. Jake was half sprawled in his chair, drumming his fingers on the improvised table made of wooden planks and sawhorses.

"Damn glad to see you, Commander," Jake said wearily. "I'm going to need military assistance to keep this town from blowing sky-high. These folks want that woman's head." He hitched his thumb over his broad shoulder to indicate Karissa, who was hunched over on the ground, hands lashed to her ankles.

Rafe felt as if he had been gut-punched when he saw her huddled in the middle of several scraggly-looking men. The stench in the tent was almost enough to make his eyes water. When she finally raised her head to look at him, his heart shriveled in his chest.

Never in all their encounters and confrontations had he seen Karissa look quite so defeated. It was all he could do not to rush back to where she sat, hoist her to her feet and wrap her in his arms. But if he showed her preferential treatment, his credibility would be shot to hell and gossip would be flying around town—the same way it had sizzled at the fort when he had abandoned his own quarters to house his female prisoner.

Well, flying gossip at the garrison be damned. He couldn't leave Karissa here. That crazed mob would likely get liquored up and come to fetch her. Jake Horton would be overpowered and Karissa would be swinging from the tallest tree in Reno City before Rafe could ride back to town to rescue her from calamity.

"I think it's best if we hold your female prisoner at the fort," Rafe announced authoritatively. "We are better equipped to forestall a riot than you are." He inclined his head toward the canvas walls that flapped in the breeze. "All that needs to happen is for a few trigger-happy drunks to decide to blast holes in this tent. Everyone in here, you included, could be dead."

"You'll hear no objection from me," Jake said as he came to his feet. He walked back to the chain gang to untie Karissa from the rest of the prisoners. With her hands and feet still shackled with rope, he ushered her forward. "But I don't know how we're going to get her out of here without inciting a riot."

Micah cast Rafe a wry glance. "Old Indian trick."

Rafe had been with Micah for so long that he could practically read his mind. He smiled for the first time in hours. "I'll be back as soon as I can."

Micah nodded. "I'll stall for a while."

Rafe reached for his dagger to cut the rope that shackled Karissa's ankles.

"What are you—?" Jake nodded in understanding when Rafe led his prisoner to the back of the tent then slithered under the canvas. "Let me guess, friend," he said to Micah. "You're going to saunter outside, pretending to wait for your fellow officer, who is supposedly having a lengthy conversation with me. When Rafe returns the same way he left and then walks out through the tent flap, no one will be the wiser."

"You've got it, Horton." Micah nodded as Rafe and Karissa disappeared from sight. "No one will know unless your prisoners decide to spill the beans."

Jake glanced over his shoulder to stare down the prisoners. "Anyone who opens his mouth will become that vigilante mob's consolation prize. They want blood. The drunker they get the less they'll care whose blood is shed."

The prisoners didn't say a word. Micah was pretty sure that none of them thought this was a good day for a hanging. Especially if it turned out to be their own.

"You should have left me where I was," Karissa whispered as she and Rafe belly-crawled through the tall grass behind the tent. "Any association with me is bound to be bad for your reputation."

"Just keep quiet and let me worry about my reputation," he muttered in her ear.

Karissa kept her mouth shut as they moved stealthily

away from the hustle and bustle of town. She got the impression this wasn't the first time Rafe had slithered across the ground like a snake. Given his profession, he likely knew dozens of sly tricks to avoid detection while on patrol.

Although her arms and legs felt as if they were about to give out, having been hog-tied for more than a day, she refused to give up. Rafe seemed to prefer to err on the side of caution, because he didn't come to his feet until they were surrounded in the thick underbrush that lined the North Canadian River.

The moment he pulled her up beside him, Karissa tilted her head back and stared him dead in the eye. "I know you probably don't believe me, especially since Marshal Horton says the evidence is stacked heavily against me, but I didn't kill either of those men. I *did* defend myself when Chester Gentry tried to steal my claim. And I did want to pound Arliss into the ground when he threatened to use my family to force me into selling out to him."

Rafe studied her with such piercing scrutiny that she shifted uneasily from one foot to the other. Ordinarily she didn't care what folks thought of her, but this was Rafe and she desperately wanted him to believe she wasn't involved in the killings.

"I swear to you, Rafe, I wasn't on Arliss's property that night when the shooting took place. I was down by the stream. I fell asleep from exhaustion because I had been plowing our field all day because Clint isn't able to do it. When I woke up I walked into the water to take a bath." Her gaze faltered momentarily before she added, "And you know the rest."

"Who are the two witnesses who claim to have seen you take the shots?" Rafe asked urgently.

"Marshal Horton didn't say. I suspect it's Chester Gentry and Delmer Cravens, the two other men who worked for Arliss. I saw them watching me from a distance several times the past week. I kept Clint's rifle handy in case they tried to approach my family or me. You can question Clint and Amanda if you don't believe me," she offered. "They spotted them a time or two."

"I believe you," Rafe murmured.

Karissa slumped with relief and tears welled up in her eyes. Never in her life had she needed anyone's acceptance as much as she needed his. Because *he* mattered to her the way no one else ever had.

"Well, at least when they hang me," she said on a shaky breath, "I'll rest easier knowing you don't believe that I'm capable of taking someone's life for the money in their pockets."

"Not even in self-defense?" he asked as he stared solemnly into the distance. "They didn't drag you off and force you to defend yourself?"

Karissa reared back as if he had slapped her. "Is that what you think? You believe I *might have* killed them in self-defense? You think I lied to you when I said I wasn't there?"

"I didn't say that, damn it," Rafe grumbled.

Karissa was so hurt and outraged that she couldn't prevent the tears from streaming down her cheeks. Damn him, he had been patronizing her, just to have her cooperation! He really didn't believe her at all.

Obviously Rafe didn't know her or understand what made her tick, what motivated her, what mattered to her. Oh, he had come to know her in the most intimate physical sense, but he still didn't trust her completely. And it wasn't as if their intimate night together was as sublimely special for him as it was for her.

After all, *she* hadn't been the first woman *he* had slept with. How could she have forgotten that men—even Rafe—were ruled by their lusts, when it came to their association with women? Imbecile that she was, she had let herself believe that their night of passion was a turning point in their relationship. She had wanted to think that Rafe had called off his engagement because of his affection for *her*. But it was only physical, she realized, heartbroken. She had been a challenge to him. He had come to her, thinking she had been intimate with other men. He had only discovered the truth when she surrendered to her overwhelming desire for him.

"Damn it, stop looking at me as if I just sliced you open," he muttered as he tried to reach out to her.

"You might as well have," she sputtered as she shrank away from his touch. "So much for innocent until proved guilty. I was framed, damn it, just like I was framed for clubbing my own brother over the head and stealing the money *I* gave to *him*."

"I am only trying to get all the facts straight," Rafe defended. "Do you honestly think I want to see you punished for this horrific crime?"

"I honestly think that Í can't trust you any more than you trust me. And I might not be the brightest star in the galaxy, but I'm not so dense that I can't tell this whole affair stinks to high heaven."

She swiped at the infuriating tears then poked him in the chest with her forefinger. "Answer me this, General. If I *had* stolen the money, after I killed those men outright, or in self-defense, as you seem to think, why didn't I bury the money? Do you think I would be stupid enough to leave the evidence in the saddlebag, along with that pistol that I have never seen before in my life? I told you that I no longer *own* a pistol and I didn't borrow Amanda's, either. I didn't shoot anyone, but I'm certainly contemplating taking a few shots at you!''

''Karissa, calm down. I—''

''*Me?* Calm down?'' she cried in frustration. ''*You* can just hush up! I've heard quite enough out of you!''

''You haven't allowed me to say much of anything yet,'' he growled at her, his eyes billowing like a thunderstorm.

''You have said plenty, thank you very much.'' She glared at him angrily. ''Your belief in me has its limitations, doesn't it? It will always have limitations. I know I'm outranked and outclassed and you know it, too. I'm just a nobody who would do anything to get by in life.''

She upheld her hands, which were still tied in front of her, and lifted a challenging brow. ''Are you going to untie me, General? Or do you prefer to tether me to the nearest tree because you don't trust me to be here when you get back?''

His momentary hesitation was like the last nail pounded into her coffin. He really *didn't* trust her, really didn't believe she was a woman of her word. Now there was no doubt in her mind that she had been only time he was killing, the place he had come for one night of physical satisfaction. He *didn't* think she was his social equal and, therefore, she *couldn't* be trusted completely.

To her surprise, he grabbed his dagger and slashed the rope between her wrists. ''I expect you to be exactly where I left you when Micah and I get back. Do not make me regret doing this, Rissa.''

She stared at him uncertainly. Was this supposed to be his show of faith—though it was too late in coming? He had cut her loose, but she could tell by the way he was looking at her that he was still wondering if he had made the right decision.

Well, she wasn't going to cry foul again and blubber more humiliating tears to convince him of her integrity. He either believed her because he knew, deep down in his soul, that she did have character and honor, or he didn't believe. And by damned, she wasn't going to make it easy for him. He deserved to sweat it out, she thought resentfully. Let him stew in his own juice and wonder if she would be here when he returned.

Karissa struck a cocky pose and tilted her head to a sassy angle. "Now be a daisy and run along, General," she drawled and batted her eyelashes for effect. "I'll just sit here and hold my breath till y'all get back."

"Woman, swear to God, you do not know when to quit," Rafe muttered irritably. "Don't make this more difficult for me than it already is."

She stared him down for a long, poignant moment. "You *never* quit if you hope to survive, General. I know I can depend and rely on no one but myself. I obviously suffered a momentary lapse of sanity when I let myself think that a man like *you* would honestly believe a woman like *me*."

"Rissa, you've gotten the wrong impression here," he protested heatedly.

She glared pitchforks at him. "You're right about that, and it all started the night you bought that fancy gown as payment for bedding me. What you really think is that you found me bathing in the stream because I had blood on my hands from killing my neighbors."

"That is *not* why I gave you the dress, damn it, and that is *not* what I thought when I found you in the creek," he muttered in frustration. "I have to leave and you need to stay put until I get back." After casting her one last skeptical glance, he left. "We'll get this straightened out...somehow."

"Sure we will," she whispered brokenly.

He might be able to prove her innocence and save her from a hanging, but what was between them could never be the same again. His lack of faith had broken her heart and shattered her pride all to hell.

Karissa plopped down in the grass, dropped her face into her hands and bawled her head off. Being accused of murder was bad enough, but discovering that Rafe didn't believe her beyond a shadow of a doubt was simply more than she could bear. Roiling emotions bombarded her, crumbling her composure.

She cried, then she cried some more. She cried for all the times she and Clint had been teased and ridiculed. She cried for all the years she had scratched and clawed and worked every demeaning job imaginable to keep a roof over their heads and food in their bellies.

But mostly she cried because she had discovered— the hard way—that love was the biggest illusion of all. She had lost faith and hope. For years that's all she'd had going for her.

Now she had nothing.

Well, Karissa, that's all you had when you came into this world. Absolutely nothing, she reminded herself sullenly.

It looked as if she would be going out of this world the very same way.

Rafe dropped to his hands and knees then scrunched down in the prairie grass to make the long crawl back to the marshal's makeshift office. He cursed himself soundly for displaying the slightest doubt and interjecting comments when he heard Karissa's plea of innocence and lack of involvement in a crime that had left two men dead and a mob of drunken settlers itching to throw a necktie party—with her as the guest of honor.

As long as he lived, Rafe swore he would never forget the look of hurt and disappointment that settled on Karissa's features when he questioned whether she might have acted in self-defense. And then she had gone sassy and defiant on him, leaving him to decide if he believed she was capable of taking two men's lives.

The answer to that question was yes—if she was defending herself against assault. Rafe knew Karissa was a survivor and she had fought for everything she had in life.

"Oh, hell," Rafe muttered when a memory suddenly flashed through his mind. He vividly recalled the day of the Land Run when he had ridden over the hill to see Karissa and Chester Gentry battling over the claim of the homestead. He also remembered that for a moment—when she had gained the upper hand against Chester—she hadn't shot him, not even to discourage or maim him. She had used the pistol Rafe had loaned to her to club the claim-jumper over the head.

Outright shooting to kill would have been Karissa's absolute last resort, Rafe decided.

After Rafe gave the unsettling incident second thought, he honestly wondered if she was capable of shooting a man down, even to save her own life. Certainly, she used that hard-nosed, tough-as-nails act as a means of protection and a shield of defense. But he could also cite evidence of her kindness and unfaltering devotion to her family. There was more to Karissa Baxter than met the eye—a hell of a lot more.

He never should have expressed even one iota of doubt, Rafe chastised himself. What she had needed at that crucial moment, when the world had caved in on her, was encouragement and support. He had behaved like a judge who was appraising the situation from all angles, in hopes of arriving at the truth.

She had needed a loyal friend.

He had failed her completely.

Worse, he had disillusioned her and he would really like to kick himself all the way into next week for being the cause of that devastated look on her face.

If it wasn't critically important for him to crawl back to Marshal Horton's tent—quickly—he would have turned around and scrambled back to the spot where he had left Karissa so he could apologize all over himself. Well, he would do that as soon as he and Micah rode back to the river to fetch her.

It wasn't going to be easy to return to Karissa's good graces, either, he predicted. Proud and fiery as she was, it would require considerable groveling on his part to reassure her that he had a great deal of faith and respect for her.

Rafe buried himself in the tall grass, the way Micah had taught him to do the first year they had served together as scouts in the Army of the West. It was an Indian tactic that had allowed them to reconnoiter hostile tribes without being spotted. At the moment, the technique served to prevent Rafe from being seen by the wagon driver who passed ten feet from his hiding place.

When the wagon rumbled away, Rafe slithered through the grass to enter the marshal's tent the same way he had exited—and cursed himself a thousand times over for letting Karissa think he didn't believe she was innocent.

Chapter Fourteen

When Rafe burrowed beneath the canvas and hurriedly came to his feet to dust off his uniform, Jake Horton heaved a gusty sigh of relief. "Glad you're back, Commander. The natives outside are getting restless. They wanna know why you and I are having such a long powwow in here."

"What did you tell them?" Rafe questioned.

Jake smiled wryly. "Told 'em we were trying to decide whose jurisdiction the double murders fell under, and where'd be the proper place to keep our prime suspect jailed."

The marshal inclined his head toward the tent flap. "Micah is out there, feeding the mob a bunch of mumbo jumbo from the army's rules and regulations manual and spouting about the right to a fair trial. Most of the mob got tired of listening and wandered off to the saloons to have a few more drinks. I don't think the surly crowd will know Miss Baxter is gone until long after the fact."

"Thanks, Jake, I owe you one," Rafe said as he offered the deputy marshal his hand.

"Do you think she did it?" he asked earnestly.

"No, absolutely not. I think she was set up, but I haven't figured out why or by whom."

Rafe wished he had sounded this convincing when he spoke with Karissa. No doubt, he was going to pay dearly for not beating his chest and shouting to high heaven that she was innocent and he believed every word she said.

"I also think we should move all your prisoners to the garrison under the cover of darkness." Rafe gestured toward the flimsy canvas walls. "I'm not concerned about your ability to keep these prisoners in captivity, but I don't think you stand a chance of keeping that mob of vigilantes out."

Jake nodded agreeably. "Send me some of your most reliable men after dark," he requested. "The longer we wait to make the move the more risk we take."

Rafe ducked beneath the tent flap and bit back an amused grin while he watched Micah, looking as regal as a king, pacing in front of his throne. He was citing the regulations of the army manual in a droning voice. Members of the mob who had stayed to listen looked cross-eyed, confused and befuddled. They had no idea whether the regulations Micah was quoting pertained to this infamous double murder or not.

When the mob noticed Rafe, all attention shifted to him.

"Well, who's in charge of this situation?" one of the vigilantes demanded impatiently.

"As Captain Whitfield has been trying to explain to you—" Rafe began, only to be cut off by scowls and snorts.

"Give it to us in plain English, Commander," someone else demanded sharply. "We can't figure out what the captain is talking about."

"The long and short of it is that we have a conflict of military and civil jurisdiction," Rafe said as he walked over to his horse. "The final decision will be left to my superiors, and the marshal's superiors, in Washington. I'm on my way back to the fort to send off a telegram. All the prisoners will remain here until we receive the necessary information."

Rafe halted to stare down the grumbling men. "Anyone who obstructs justice will find themselves chained to the other prisoners. The marshal and I have agreed to join forces in that instance to quell further disturbances. Go about your business and let us resolve this situation lawfully."

Still muttering, the crowd dispersed. Unfortunately, most of the men headed straight for the dance halls and saloons. Rafe decided he would send a company of soldiers to move the prisoners *immediately* after sunset—and not a moment later. He wasn't sure this rowdy crowd would be content to wait very long before they reappeared in full force. The situation had disaster written all over it.

"About time you got back," Micah muttered as he swung into the saddle. "I was running out of regulations to quote and I had to start devising a few of my own."

"It was a long crawl to the river," Rafe murmured as he trotted down the street.

"I'm sure, and I sure as hell wouldn't want to be in Karissa's shoes right now. She must think the whole world has turned against her." Micah frowned warily when he saw Rafe wince. "What's wrong now? Is she okay?"

"Not particularly," Rafe replied then glanced sideways to insure no one was watching before veering off the beaten path. "I wasn't as supportive as I should have been when I questioned her about the incident. She got a little indignant." And that was putting it mildly!

"I can understand if she had to act in self-defense."

Rafe flung up his hand. "That's where I made *my* mistake," he interrupted. "I thought she might have been dragged off by the men who wanted her homestead and she was forced to protect herself. But she claims she was nowhere near the crime scene and that someone set her up then stashed the stolen money and murder weapon in her saddlebags."

"Why would someone do that?" Micah mused aloud.

"That's what we're going to have to find out. Once we have Karissa tucked safely away, we're going to question those supposed witnesses."

Rafe looked into the distance to locate the place he had left Karissa. The tree-choked river had looked pretty much the same while he was belly-crawling to avoid detection. Now, from atop his horse, it was difficult to tell which meandering river bend was the right one.

"What are you doing?" Micah demanded when Rafe veered right then retraced his steps.

"I'm trying to figure out exactly where we are," he muttered in frustration.

"It's pretty obvious where *we* are. The question is, where is Karissa?"

A moment later Rafe noticed the flattened grass where he'd crawled and then took up the trail. "Rissa!" he called out impatiently. He waited a beat then called her name again. When she didn't emerge from the underbrush, Rafe swore ripely and bounded from the saddle.

"Just how mad *was* she when she realized you weren't totally convinced of her innocence?" Micah asked as he dismounted. "Mad enough to break and run?"

"That's the same question I'm asking myself," Rafe scowled as squatted down to brush his hand over the slight indentation of footprints.

Micah moved ahead of him, following the single set of tracks that led to the riverbank. "You know what's going to happen if she took off, don't you? That mob is going to see this escape as a confirmation of guilt."

"I know," Rafe said sourly. "Then my credibility is going to be questioned because of the rumor floating around the fort that suggested I was keeping her as my mistress."

"Oh, hell, I forgot about that." Micah scowled. "We'll probably both get demoted because of this. We had better find Karissa and we'd better be quick about it."

"This is all my fault." Rafe mentally kicked himself for leaving Karissa while she was so angry and upset. Even if time had been of the essence he should have said *something! Anything* to reassure her that he trusted her, that he believed in her character and honor. But he'd been angry and upset by the entire turn of events and he hadn't handled the situation properly.

Now he was paying for his mistake and he had alienated Karissa in the process.

Damn it to hell! He could rely on his logic and experience in all things military, but when it came to Karissa, his emotions always got tangled up. And his emotions couldn't possibly be in more turmoil than they were at this very moment.

Micah and Rafe followed the tracks that ended in the river. Rafe's shoulders slumped when he had to face the exasperating realization that she'd taken to the water so she couldn't be tracked. She'd had no intention of being here when he got back. He might as well have given her an engraved invitation to run as fast and far away as she could.

Rafe stared morosely at the river that shimmered in the sunlight. He was thoroughly disgusted with himself and annoyed that Karissa didn't have enough faith in *him* to let him straighten out this mess. He could only hope that when she got over being furious with him and came to her senses she would contact him through her brother and sister-in-law.

"Do you think Karissa will circle back to the homestead?" Micah asked as he stared downstream.

Rafe pondered that for a moment and decided it was wishful thinking. "Considering the lengths to which she's gone to stake a claim for Clint and Amanda, I doubt she'll risk having them accused of harboring a fugitive. I have the uneasy feeling that in this, like all else, she's going to bear the burden of responsibility alone."

"Dealing with a strong, independent-minded female does have its disadvantages," Micah commented. "Feisty as the devil. Sassy as the day is long and accustomed to fighting all her battles alone." He glanced surreptitiously at his friend. "It takes a special kind of man to deal with a woman like Karissa."

Affronted, Rafe jerked up his head and glared at Micah. "Are you implying that you would be better at it than I am?"

"Don't get yourself worked up more than you already are," Micah replied. "I'm just saying that you and Karissa have different backgrounds and you are accustomed to dealing with socialites like Vanessa Payton. As for me, I grew up scratching and clawing, just like Karissa. We have a hell of a lot in common, especially when it comes to feeling like an outcast of proper society. I've dealt with prejudice all my life and I think she's had to deal with it, too. I'm telling you that it makes a person sensitive and defensive. I understand her better than you do, so you should back off and let me handle her.''

Rafe did something he had never even considered doing in his long association with Micah. He reared back, socked Micah in the jaw and left him sprawled on his backside. ''You have nothing in common with her, damn it!'' he shouted. ''I *can* and *will* handle her!''

Micah propped himself up on one elbow and rubbed his throbbing jaw. A smile quirked his lips while Rafe towered over him in thunderous frustration. ''I was testing you and it's just as I thought. You're so crazy about Karissa that you don't know which way is up. The very idea that *I* might be interested in her set you off like a grenade.'' He stretched out his hand for assistance. ''Now that we have that settled and out of the way, help me up, friend. We've got a disillusioned fugitive to chase down.''

Rafe stared at Micah's extended hand then at his crafty expression. ''If you wanted to know if I have feelings for her all you had to do was ask.''

Micah chuckled. ''You nearly knocked my teeth down my throat because you have *feelings* for her? Face it, my friend, that doubled fist of yours packed more than *feelings.* You have recently discovered that there's more to life than the military. And it's about damn time, too.''

When Rafe reached out to clasp Micah's hand, something shiny caught his eye. He helped Micah to his feet then scooped up the button that he had spotted on the riverbank. That sixth sense that he had developed after years of service to the army niggled him. It was just a button, but it looked familiar and it could have come from Karissa's shirt.

He opened his hand and held the button up for Micah's inspection. Micah's eyes widened as he plucked up the button.

"Are you thinking what I'm thinking?" Micah murmured as he stared downstream once again.

"If you're thinking Karissa might not have left on her own accord I am," Rafe replied. "I'm going to scout this area to see if I can find more tracks. You need to return to the fort to gather a company of men to escort Jake Horton's prisoners to our stockade the moment it gets dark. It's best if no one in town knows they've been transported until we have them secured."

Micah nodded in understanding. "Guerilla tactics. Got it, Commander. And if you happen to find Karissa and it turns out that she broke and ran, tell her that *I* never doubted her innocence for a minute."

Rafe glared at Micah's teasing grin. He knew his friend was trying to ease the tension, but it didn't help. Rafe was worried—to the extreme.

Frantic to locate Karissa, Rafe strode one direction and then the other along the river. He cursed when he came upon two settlers who had tramped in the mud to fill barrels with water. Hell and damnation, it was going to be impossible to determine which sets of footprints that led in and out of the river belonged to whom.

After an hour Rafe was forced to give up his search and ride back to town to inform Jake Horton of Karissa's unexplained disappearance. It was going to make Rafe look like a fool for not tying up Karissa. But the label *did* fit, he reminded himself. He had bungled this situation—badly—and he had only himself to blame for it.

*   *   *

Rafe arrived in town, relieved to note the vigilantes were still in the saloons, drinking their fill. At least he hoped that's where they were. If one of them had captured Karissa, the whole lot of them might have marched off to carry out their own brand of justice. Rafe quickened his step to reach Jake's office.

Jake arched a curious brow when Rafe entered the tent. "What are you doing back here already?"

"Complications," Rafe muttered as he took the marshal aside. "Miss Baxter wasn't where I left her."

"What!" Jake hooted, incredulous. "She managed to wiggle from the ropes and escape?"

Rafe shifted uncomfortably from one booted foot to the other. "Not exactly."

Jake's gaze narrowed suspiciously. "Then *how* exactly?"

"I didn't leave her tethered to a tree because I don't think she's guilty of the crimes. It was a show of faith." When Jake scowled, Rafe continued, "I don't think she broke and ran. I think she was abducted." He fished the button from his pocket.

Jake snorted sarcastically. "You're basing this deduction on a damn button?"

"The more pressing question is whether Miss Baxter was captured by the mob and frog-marched off to be hanged."

Jake shook his head. "I would have heard the ruckus if that mob had captured their suspect. But things have been reasonably quiet since you left." He raked his hand through his hair and sighed audibly. "We've got ourselves a problem, Commander. Miss Baxter could have escaped or she could have been abducted and she could be in danger as we speak. We don't have much time to find out for certain before this mob demands action. We can't stall indefinitely and I still have a stack of complaints on my desk to investigate. I can't focus all my time on this one case.''

Rafe understood completely. He was going to have to divide his time between his duties at the fort and his own investigation. But he was definitely going to probe into this case and determine if Karissa had been set up to take the fall.

Hurriedly, Rafe presented Karissa's side of the story to Jake, then said insistently, ''I need a description of the two supposed witnesses. This case seems a little too open and shut, considering Miss Baxter's previous conflicts with Arliss Frazier and Chester Gentry. I witnessed, firsthand, Chester's illegal attempt to steal her claim. I intervened when Chester tried to shoot her. I also broke up an argument between her and Arliss. I'm inclined to believe there is more to this case than meets the eye.''

Jake stared at him for a long pensive moment then nodded agreeably. ''The two men who allegedly witnessed the shootings are Chester Gentry and Delmer Cravens. If you've encountered Chester then you'll recall that he's a thin, wiry man who stands about five feet nine inches. Last time I saw him he was wearing a floppy-brimmed straw hat, brown breeches and a long-tailed brown jacket.''

''I remember him well,'' Rafe said.

''Delmer Cravens is short and stocky and he was dressed in black clothing and a black high-crowned hat. He had two pistols riding low on his hips and he's missing a front tooth. Granted, neither of them look like your model citizens, but they relayed the same story, even when I questioned them separately.''

''Which means they could have gotten their state-

ments down pat before they approached you,'' Rafe
commented.

Well, it didn't matter how well those scoundrels had
rehearsed—Rafe was going to get to the bottom of this.
But he had to find Karissa first. She could be in grave
danger—or worse. The dismal thought prompted Rafe
to pivot on his heel.

''Once the prisoners are moved to the fort, I'll see if
I can track down the two witnesses for you,'' Jake offered. ''But like I said, I have more complaints to process than I can shake a stick at. And if we don't resolve
this case and locate Miss Baxter, both of our reputations
are going to suffer. Find that female and find her fast—
for her own good…and ours.''

Nodding resolutely, Rafe exited the tent and mounted
Sergeant. He kept his steed at a walk until he reached
the edge of town. With a sense of urgency and frustration that tempted him to pull out his hair and curse a
couple of blue streaks, Rafe hightailed it back to the fort.

His imagination was running wild, picturing Karissa
captured, molested and…Rafe gritted his teeth and
gouged Sergeant in the flanks. Karissa better not have
gotten herself killed. He hadn't apologized for not show-
ing absolute faith in her—or told her what she meant to
him.

Worrying about the woman was making him crazy.
She'd always made him crazy, but he couldn't imagine
his life without her in it. Micah was right. What he felt
was more than sexual attraction. It didn't matter that
they didn't travel in the same social circles. Hell, there
weren't any social circles in this newly formed territory,
so what difference did that make?

None whatsoever because none of that mattered, Rafe
reminded himself. He cared about Karissa. She appealed

to the wild and reckless side of his nature that he'd buried deep inside while he had advanced rapidly through the military ranks. He had become disciplined and methodical. She, on the other hand, was fiery and impulsive. Always would be, he predicted.

A rueful smile pursed his lips as he thundered toward the garrison. Wasn't it ironic that a man never realized what was truly important to him, what made him happy, until he lost it? Even if Karissa refused to speak to him again, he'd settle for knowing that she was alive. And somehow he was going to clear her name of these trumped-up charges.

Karissa awoke from what felt like a decade-long nap. The throbbing pain in her skull prevented her from noticing she had been bound—until she tried to move. A moment later it dawned on her that she had also been blindfolded. She had no idea where she was. All she could remember was walking into the river to cleanse herself—clothes and all—after being chained to the foul-smelling prisoners for more than twenty-four hours and crying her eyes out after seeing that shadow of doubt in Rafe's silvery eyes.

Then, after she had waded into the river to slop water on her face and try to reassemble her shattered composure, she had headed to shore. Caught totally unawares, she had been yanked backward and shoved underwater before she could catch her breath. The next thing she knew, pain was exploding through her skull and she had asked herself why she should keep fighting to survive when she was wanted for a double murder and robbery.

That was the last thing she remembered before the world turned black and she lost consciousness.

Now she was bound up like a roll of barbed wire and

lying who knew where. The smell of dirt was the only scent that penetrated her senses. The way her luck had been going, she'd probably been buried alive and left to await a hanging.

She tensed when she heard approaching footsteps then felt a presence hovering over her. "What do you expect to accomplish?" she spat. "Who are you?"

Oh damn, there went that mouth again, she realized a moment too late. The curse of her life was that she had never learned when to shut up.

Karissa gulped instinctively when water trickled on her lips. Her captor said not one word, just continued to dribble water on her face and into her mouth. A few moments later she realized the water had a strange aftertaste and that she'd ingested something unrecognizable. Poison?

That was Karissa's last coherent thought before a feeling of lethargy overcame her. Poison or sedative, she couldn't be sure, but it deprived her of her will to fight its effects. She heard a quiet chuckle whispering to her, as if it was gliding through a long, winding tunnel.

And then there was nothing but dark silence.

It was almost dark when Rafe skidded his horse to a halt in front of his office and inwardly groaned when Vanessa appeared on the covered porch. Obviously she had been waiting for him to return. There was a gloating smile on her lips, he noticed. Rafe had the unshakable feeling that she had heard about Karissa's arrest and was exceptionally pleased with the news.

"I heard about Miss Baxter," she said, without preamble, when he joined her on the porch. "I think it would be best for your reputation if you disassociated yourself with that—" she wrinkled her nose distastefully and shuddered "—that *woman*. To save you from public and professional disgrace, we should forge ahead with our wedding arrangements. My father and yours have clout in the military. They will have no trouble getting you reassigned back East, away from the humiliating gossip."

"I'm not going anywhere," Rafe said as he surged into his office. "I have responsibilities here. Some of them are extremely pressing. So if you'll excuse me, Vanessa, I have a lot to do."

Behind him, Vanessa stamped her foot to gain his attention. "I have been overly patient and incredibly tolerant of your indiscretions for two weeks!" she erupted indignantly. "Have you no respect for *my* feelings in all this? If nothing else, you should be begging me to marry you to compensate for the humiliation I have suffered. When you ride out of here after dark, I know perfectly well you are going to see that trollop. Well, I think you should realize by now that she is nothing but trouble. Worse, she's a murderer!"

Rafe wheeled on her so quickly that she backed up a step. Well, so much for the dignified debutante who had been teeming with sophisticated charm and engaging smiles since her unexpected arrival. Rafe was beginning to think Vanessa's true character had come pouring out. Worse, she was trying to twist the situation to her advantage—all the while claiming that she was trying to protect *his* reputation, as well as hers.

"You are deluding yourself if you think we'll be married now or six months from now. Do yourself a favor and climb aboard the stage. You don't belong out here."

"Neither do you!" she railed at him. "Your family name can open any door you please and yet you seem determined to prove some point by taking this assignment in the middle of nowhere.'' She flung her arms expansively and the jewels at her wrists winked in the lantern light. ''I'm willing to admit that I can partially understand why you were drawn to that devious trollop. Heavens, it's not as if there are women of quality in this area to associate with.''

Now she was *excusing* his supposed slumming? Was this yet another tactic to coerce him into a wedding? ''But of course, what else was I to do when basic urges overwhelmed me, correct?'' he said, and smirked.

''Exactly.'' Vanessa inclined her head regally, as if to wipe his transgression off the slate. ''And now that you realize how treacherous and dangerous that woman is, you must also realize that *like* should commit itself to *like* in life.''

She favored Rafe with an overly sweet smile. ''You and I are very much alike, Rafe. This is what our parents have arranged. This is what is best for both of us. And I must say that I'm tired of being the only one who is trying to do the right thing and honor our obligations.''

''Sorry to interrupt,'' Micah said as he hurried into the office, not looking or sounding the least bit sorry. ''Commander, we have a situation that demands immediate attention.'' He offered Vanessa a halfhearted bow. ''You'll have to excuse us.''

''Go home,'' Rafe said to Vanessa. ''The next stage heading east will be here tomorrow afternoon.''

''Whether you realize it yet or not, you need me.'' She picked up her trailing skirts and flounced from the office.

''Sure am sorry to see her go,'' Micah said, his tone nowhere near apologetic.

Rafe half collapsed in his chair and huffed out a

weary breath. "Can this day get any worse?" he muttered.

Micah braced his hands on the desk to meet Rafe face to face. "As a matter of fact, it can. Lieutenant Johnson informed me a few minutes ago that one of our men was found dead."

"Cause of death?" Rafe asked bleakly.

"Shot in the face," Micah reported. "His emptied pockets were left inside out."

Rafe braced his elbows on the desk. "Where was he found?"

"Floating in the river about an hour ago. The patrol noticed him when they stopped to water their horses."

"Who was it?" Rafe asked somberly.

Micah straightened then blew out a frustrated breath. "Corporal Harlan Billings. He was beaten, shot and robbed. His identification was all that was left behind."

Chapter Fifteen

Rafe's fist hit the desk. "Damn it to hell!"

"You don't think Karissa was so angry and desperate, not to mention vindictive toward Harlan, after he tried to take advantage of her in your quarters, that she—?"

"No!" Rafe practically bellowed in denial as he bounded to his feet then veered around his desk. "Everything that has happened around here the past few days seems as choreographed as a theatrical production."

"Well, I don't know about that since I've never actually seen one, but I'll admit that this path of destruction seems to fall neatly into place," Micah mused aloud, while Rafe paced from wall to wall. "Someone has gone to great lengths to see that Karissa is blamed for every crime committed the past few days. A few days ago Karissa confided in me that Vanessa wasn't what she seemed. She was afraid that if you married Vanessa you would regret it when the unpleasant side of her personality came pouring out."

Micah glanced pointedly at Rafe. "*Who* has something to gain from Karissa taking the heat? *Who* has seen her fair share of plays and theatrical productions back

East? Gee, let me guess.'' He struck an effeminate pose and batted his eyes coyly. ''Your ex-fiancée perhaps?''

''The thought already crossed my mind,'' Rafe muttered as he reversed direction and paced west to east. ''But how could Vanessa make contact with Arliss Frazier or his henchman? *Why* would she? I don't think she's left the garrison but a few times. And always in the company of officers' wives.'' He frowned then amended, ''At least to my knowledge. But then I haven't kept close track of Vanessa since she arrived.''

Rafe wheeled toward the door. ''While you are discreetly transferring Jake's prisoners to the stockade, I want to take a closer look at the pistol found in Karissa's saddlebags and interrogate the two witnesses. We also need to send out a search party to track down Karissa. We can't afford to let the trail get cold. Damn,'' Rafe muttered. ''I would like to be in three places at once right now.''

''I'll organize the search party before I retrieve Jake's prisoners,'' Micah volunteered. ''I'll start the patrol tracking from the spot you left Karissa by the river.''

''The trail was contaminated by settlers prancing into the water to fill their barrels,'' Rafe reported sourly. ''But if someone did abduct Karissa then we can't make it easy for him to transport her. We need a patrol breathing down his neck. Tell Lieutenant Johnson that Karissa was kidnapped.''

Micah snorted. ''Everyone around this fort knows she was being held prisoner for the crime. How am I supposed to explain how—?''

Rafe silenced him with a slashing gesture of his arm. ''Make up something, damn it. You managed to bore that vigilante mob to death by spewing army regulations. I don't care what you tell the lieutenant, other than that

Karissa's life is in danger and we believe she's being used as a pawn.''

"Got it. I'll think of something," Micah replied as he followed Rafe out the door.

"The ropes!" Rafe burst out suddenly.

"What ropes?" Micah demanded, bemused.

"I cut Karissa's hands loose when we reached the river," Rafe said quickly. "I was trying to reassure her that I trusted her, *after* I had made the critical mistake of questioning her version of the story. The frayed ropes were still dangling from her wrists. Why wouldn't she untie them and cast them aside?"

"Because someone overpowered her and used the rope to manacle her hands," Micah guessed as he veered around Rafe. "I'll go form the search party and tell them to look for two discarded lengths of rope. That should tell us whether she was abducted or left on her own accord."

"I'm betting she didn't have time to remove them before someone pounced on her."

Rafe climbed back on his horse and reined toward the gate. He glanced up to see Vanessa hovering beside the window in her upstairs quarters. If he thought for one minute that she was capable of machinating these trumped-up charges against Karissa, he would introduce her to the strong-arm tactics he had occasionally used as last resorts to wheedle information. He was beginning to think Vanessa was capable of many things—deception and pretense to name only two—but he didn't perceive her as being capable of murder.

Rafe met Vanessa's gaze—grimly—from a distance. She was going to be very sorry indeed if it turned out that Rafe was wrong about her.

* * *

Karissa regained consciousness and decided that she had been sedated rather than poisoned. She was being kept alive for some reason. That was good. But she doubted she would enjoy a long-term existence. That was bad.

When the fog in her brain cleared up, she realized she was being jostled about and transported in the back of a wagon. She could smell the mildewed tarp that was draped over her and hear the creak and clatter of wheels and the jangle of harnesses.

While she had been unconscious, her unidentified captor had stuffed a gag in her mouth to keep her quiet. Although her hands and feet were tied together, she wiggled and squirmed to dislodge whatever objects were stacked beside her legs. She heard a dull thud that indicated something had fallen from the wagon bed. When the driver didn't stop, she nudged another object toward the edge of the bed.

If nothing else, Karissa vowed to have the satisfaction of disposing of whatever supplies her captor was hauling. It wasn't precisely a trail of flags and banners that pointed a rescuer in her direction, but Karissa had learned to be resourceful and inventive.

While she was being secretly hauled away from wherever she had been stashed for safekeeping, she wondered if Rafe would bother looking for her. Of course, he would assume the worst about her. He would presume that she had escaped and he would see the act as a confirmation of guilt.

When tears filled her eyes, she determinedly blinked them back. She didn't have time to dwell on the emotion she'd wasted on Rafe Hunter. She had vowed already that she was never going to speak to him again. Her immediate concern was finding a way to escape her captor—and it wasn't going to be easy when she didn't have a weapon of defense. All she had was her wits—which were still suffering the aftereffects of the sedative.

Come on, Rissa, pay attention here, she chided herself.

She nudged another object off the back of the wagon and waited to see if the driver had noticed. Squirming sideways, now that she had more room to move, she inched across the wagon bed. If she could roll away, there was a chance her captor wouldn't notice she had dropped to the ground until long after she was gone.

Karissa hit the ground with a thud and bit back a pained shriek when she landed on her shoulder and hip. The smelly tarp remained on the wagon and she drew in a refreshing breath of cool evening air. She rolled to her knees then plunked down on her backside. She still had no idea where she was, but she wasn't going to risk sitting here until her captor realized she wasn't in the wagon.

Sinking back to the ground, Karissa rolled sideways, grimacing each time a rock or the sharp blades of weeds poked into her skin. When she paused to catch her breath, she rubbed her face against the ground until she had worked the blindfold over her head. She looked around, trying to orient herself to her surroundings, but nothing looked familiar in the darkness.

Wherever she was, she needed to put more distance between herself and the silhouette of the wagon that was rumbling southward. She chose a path perpendicular to the boxes and sacks that she had strung behind her, hoping to take cover before her captor came looking for her.

When Rafe reached Reno City, he was relieved to see the mob hadn't regathered and that the likeness of a red-haired female wasn't being burned in effigy. Although dozens of wagons and horses lined the main street, most members of the rowdy crowd were in the saloons and dance halls that took up more space in the boomtown than respectable businesses.

Rafe made a beeline for the marshal's tent and found a weary-looking Jake draped in his chair, squinting in the lantern light to study the papers on his desk.

"You're wearing a path from town to the fort," Jake remarked as he rubbed his eyes. "Bother to eat?"

Rafe shook his head. "Couldn't spare the time."

"Me either. I did send a kid to one of the restaurants to fetch some food. You can share it with me when he returns."

As if on cue, a young, mop-headed boy ducked beneath the tent flap. Rafe smiled gratefully when Jake handed him a slice of fresh bread and a slab of beef. He hadn't realized he was famished until the first bite. He wondered if Karissa's captor was offering her nourishment. Probably not. Keeping captives weak from starvation was an easy way to control them. Rafe felt guilty for devouring the meal when he knew Karissa wasn't enjoying the same comforts.

"I would like to have a look at the evidence in the murder cases," Rafe said abruptly.

Jake twisted sideways to open the trunk that sat beside his makeshift desk. "Here you go. Looking for something in particular?"

"No, just some hint of a clue, something that might lead me to Karissa," Rafe murmured as he unfastened the buckle on the saddlebag.

While Jake peered over his shoulder and munched on his meal, Rafe withdrew the pistol and checked the cylinder.

"Four shots were fired," Jake informed him. "Which matches the number of bullet holes in the victims."

"Would you leave the weapon, just as it was, if you had committed the dastardly crime?" Rafe asked as he dropped the two remaining bullets in his palm.

Jake frowned and shifted uncomfortably. "No, that would be pretty obvious."

"Sure would. I'd reload the pistol." Rafe tossed the marshal a meaningful glance. "I probably wouldn't leave the weapon in plain sight, either, not until the hubbub died down."

Jake rolled his stiff shoulders. "Okay, what else have you got in your efforts to prove Miss Baxter's innocence?"

Rafe fished into the leather bag to retrieve the cloth coin purse. When he dumped the contents on the table, a frown clouded his brow. Several shiny silver dollars stared back at him. He bent down to take a closer look.

"What's wrong?" Jake asked curiously.

Rafe picked up one of the coins and held it up to the lantern. "These look like the coins the paymaster passed out last week at the fort. The army always pays in cash."

True, he had given Karissa a handful of silver dollars before the Run, but he knew she'd spent what he'd given her to purchase supplies in town and pay the fee to register her claim. So where had the shiny coins come from? The small roll of bank notes could have been stolen from Arliss or Sam, but the shiny silver dollars drew Rafe's suspicion.

"Mind if I take two of these with me to match them with some of my men's at the garrison?" Rafe requested.

"Be my guest, Commander. Oh, and I did manage to track down one of the witnesses. Last time I checked,

Delmer Cravens was bellied up to the bar at the Pink Elephant Saloon. He said he hasn't seen Chester Gentry all day.''

Rafe tucked the coins in his pocket then stuffed the evidence in the saddlebag. ''Did Delmer or Chester identify the pistol?''

Jake nodded tiredly. ''Said it belonged to Arliss Frazier. Knew it because they had seen it in his possession several times.''

Rafe snorted. ''And they expect us to believe that a pint-size female wrestled that overweight male to the ground, while fending off Sam, then turned the pistol on both men? Sorry, Jake, but the more I hear about this crime the less believable it sounds.''

''You're right, Commander,'' Jake admitted. ''In my haste to wrap up one case and get on to the next I think I might have asked the wrong individuals the wrong questions. But then, I don't think I have the same vested interest in solving this case that you do. Sure hope she's worth all the time and effort you're putting into this investigation.''

''She is,'' Rafe confirmed as he pivoted on his heel to track down Delmer Cravens.

Rafe hurried across the street then walked into the smoke-filled saloon. He surveyed the men who leaned leisurely against the planked bar. Relying on Jake's description, it didn't take long to single out the pudgy man who had worked for Arliss Frazier. Without preamble Rafe walked up to grab the man by the nape of his shirt.

''I want to talk privately with you, Delmer,'' he demanded authoritatively.

''Hey, git yer hands off me,'' Delmer said in a slurred voice. ''I ain't done nothin' wrong.''

Despite the drunken objection, Rafe towed the man

outside and shoved him against the hitching post. "You gave false witness to that double murder," he accused gruffly. "I want to know who's responsible for setting up the Baxter woman."

The man's eyes flared momentarily before a shuttered expression crossed his whiskered face. "Don't know what you're talkin' about. I saw what I saw. Told the marshal, too."

Rafe wasn't wasting another minute with the scraggly cretin. "Where's your horse? You're coming to the fort for more questioning."

Although Delmer set his feet, Rafe uprooted him from the spot and frog-marched him across the street. "I can drag you behind my horse or you can ride your own mount. Your choice, Delmer, but you're coming with me."

When Delmer tried to break and run, Rafe hauled him backward, hooked an arm around his neck and applied pressure to his throat. "That's my horse," Delmer choked out as he gestured to the black gelding. "But I'm not tellin' ya nothin' different."

"Why not? Afraid someone might leave you in the same shape as Arliss and Sam?" Rafe muttered as he shoved Delmer toward his horse then grabbed the reins. "What happened to Chester? Is he the one who helped you plan this setup?"

Alarm registered on Delmer's face as he settled in the saddle, but he thrust out his square chin and glared down at Rafe. "I toldja I ain't sayin' nothin' about nothin'."

Rafe led Delmer toward the hitching post where he had tethered Sergeant. With practiced ease he swung into the saddle then headed out of town. "As of right now you and Chester Gentry are the prime suspects in the murders,'' Rafe insisted. ''You will be held for questioning while I round up Chester.''

''I didn't do it!'' Delmer muttered.

''So you're saying Chester did the crime and got you to corroborate the story he fed the marshal?''

''I dunno what corroborate means, but if you're sayin' he talked me into givin' my statement, then the answer's no. I dunno know where Chester went, either. He was supposed to meet me in town for supper, but he never showed up.''

Chester Gentry, the ruffian who had originally tried to steal Karissa's claim, was looking more like the guilty party by the minute, Rafe mused as he thundered toward the fort. When he spotted the search brigade carrying torches, he halted to wait for the lieutenant to join him.

''Any sign of Miss Baxter?'' Rafe asked anxiously.

Lieutenant Johnson reined to a stop. ''No, sir. We came across several sets of tracks on the riverbank, but we encountered no one except the settlers replenishing their water supplies.''

''What's that over there?'' one of the soldiers questioned as he held his torch higher in the air.

Rafe twisted in the saddle to determine what had caught the man's attention. He frowned, befuddled, when he recognized the wooden box that had U.S. Army stamped on it. Taking the lieutenant's torch, Rafe trotted forward for a better look. In the flickering light he noticed the imprints in the grass that indicated a wagon had recently crossed the area, headed south.

''Lieutenant, please detain this witness at the fort until I return. I'll see if I can find out why a box of flour from our mess hall has been dumped out here. We never send out a wagonload of supplies to Fort Sill after dark.''

"Yes, sir," the lieutenant said, giving his superior a quick salute.

"When Captain Whitfield returns with the prisoners to hold in our stockade, tell him what we have found and ask him to come join me."

As the entourage trotted off, taking Delmer Cravens with them, Rafe walked his horse forward. He'd only gone fifty yards before he spotted a sack of cornmeal, compliments of the army, lying on the ground. The sack sat directly between the tracks from the wagon wheels.

Anticipation sizzled through him when he realized that someone might have purposely left a trail to follow. Considering Karissa's resourcefulness, she could have been the one pushing objects from the wagon. Hope swelled inside Rafe as he nudged Sergeant into a faster clip.

He raced forward, noting the broken crate of canned peaches and tomatoes. Someone had obviously confiscated a wagon from the fort and stolen the goods from the mess hall, while most of the soldiers were on patrol or off duty. What Karissa was doing in the back of the wagon—at least he prayed it was Karissa—he didn't know, but if her unconventional trail markings led him to her, Rafe didn't care if a month's supply of army rations ended up on the prairie.

Karissa tensed when she heard the rumble of a wagon and the pounding of hooves. Damn it! Her captor had realized she was gone and had doubled back to locate her. She searched around wildly, trying to figure out where she could hide. She'd been rolling across the prairie, but it was at least a hundred yards to the tree-lined creek. If she could make it to cover before her captor arrived, she might have a sporting chance of avoiding his notice.

Teeth clamped into the gag in her mouth, Karissa rolled across the ground. She muttered a curse when she saw the wagon speeding toward her. She wasn't going to make it to cover. Although there wasn't a full moon blazing in the sky, there was far too much light to conceal her if the wagon rolled right past her.

She couldn't wriggle down in the grass the way Rafe had shown her how to do as they crawled from the marshal's tent. She was bound up like a mummy, making it impossible to stretch out her arms and legs to lie under the grass rather than on top of it.

Karissa angled her head to peer up at the dark silhouette on the wagon seat. Recognition dawned in her eyes immediately. Chester Gentry, that weasely scoundrel! She couldn't see his face clearly, but she remembered the floppy-brimmed hat and the long jacket he'd worn every time she had encountered him. First he had tried to steal her claim, then he had framed her for murder. Now he had abducted her—for who knows what purpose!

"Damn it, you are a royal pain in the backside. This time I'll anchor you to the wagon to make sure you don't escape again."

Karissa frowned, bemused. Those were Chester's clothes and that was Chester's hat, but that voice didn't belong to Chester.

Her bewildered thoughts scattered and her survival instincts exploded to life when she was jerked upright. Karissa threw herself backward then lifted her bound legs and struck out like a kicking mule.

A pained wail erupted in the darkness as her attacker doubled over. Karissa struck again, aiming for the knees.

She received satisfaction in hearing another agonized howl as her assailant's legs folded up. She might not be able to escape, but she wasn't going anywhere without a fight.

Or so she thought. The butt of a pistol thumped against her temple and fuzzy light exploded in her eyes. A sickening sensation settled in the pit of her stomach. She found herself being dragged toward the back of the wagon by the rope that bound her ankles. It took all the energy she could muster to resist, and she was on the verge of accepting defeat—for the moment, at least— until she heard the pounding of hooves and a snarling growl in the distance.

Her head was still swimming when her captor crouched beside her and stuffed the barrel of a pistol under her chin. Through blurred eyes, she squinted at her rescuer, who held a flaming torch in one hand and a Winchester in the other.

Even if she was so mad at Rafe that she could spit nails, she had never been so glad to see anyone in her life. He looked like the dark angel of vengeance, guiding his muscular steed with the touch of his knees.

If the expression on his face was any indication of his disposition he could have spit a few nails himself.

Chapter Sixteen

"Back off!" Rafe bellowed furiously.

"You are in no position to spout orders," came the taunting reply.

"Rissa, are you all right?" Rafe questioned anxiously.

"I'd be a lot better if I could return the favor by kicking this jackass upside the head!" she shouted, even though Rafe couldn't understand a word she said because the gag was still crammed in her mouth.

"I didn't catch any of that," Rafe said as he walked his horse forward, his attention focused on the man who was using Karissa as a shield of protection. "But she sounds mad as hell." He lifted the torch, trying to get a better look at her captor's face.

When the man finally tipped back his head, Rafe blinked in stunned amazement. "Harlan? I thought you were dead."

Harlan snickered. "I switched identities with Chester Gentry. I decided the army life wasn't for me."

"Clever," Rafe acknowledged as he nudged Sergeant sideways in hopes of getting a better shot at the murdering bastard. "So you made it difficult for us to identify Chester by distorting his face with a pistol blast then dressed him in your uniform.''

"Stay where you are, Commander,'' Harlan growled as he clutched Karissa tightly against his chest. "You try to shoot me and I'll shoot her, guaran-damn-teed. Simple as that.''

"So you left Chester floating in the river in your uniform and latched onto Karissa,'' Rafe prompted, trying to keep Harlan talking and biding his time until he could catch the man off guard.

"Easy enough to do,'' Harlan said. "I knocked Chester unconscious after he tried to blackmail me for money. Then this little spitfire walked into the river not ten yards from where I'd exchanged clothes with Chester. With her unconscious it was no trouble to dispose of Chester, leave him in the river, and stash her in Chester's dugout. It couldn't have worked out better if I had planned it. At the time I was trying to figure out how to break her out of the marshal's makeshift jail and make her look guilty as hell by escaping.''

"Why did you want to do that?'' Rafe questioned. "You knew that she was serving time for your crime. What did you have against Arliss Frazier and Sam Pickens anyway?''

"I made sure Arliss could stake the property he wanted by giving him precise directions before the Run,'' Harlan explained impatiently. "He refused to pay me what he owed me so I got rid of him and Sam, took most of their money and left a little cash in Karissa's saddlebag. But it wasn't my idea to set her up for the fall. It just worked out perfectly, and it didn't take much of a threat to convince Chester and Delmer to feed the marshal the story I concocted.''

"You assured Chester and Delmer that they would

end up like Arliss and Sam,'' Rafe assumed. ''Whose idea was it to frame Karissa?''

''You figure it out, Commander,'' he said, mocking Rafe's rank. ''You're the man with the lofty position who thinks he has more brains than the rest of us peons in the army. You'll excuse me if I'm in a hurry to be on my way. I might let your trollop live, after I take my turn with her, but if you're breathing down my neck, I'll find someone else to use as a shield of defense. Now back off. We're leaving.''

''Sorry, Harlan, but you know I'm a man who believes in following the rules and regulations.'' Rafe aimed his Winchester at Harlan and wished Karissa would move her red head just enough for him to get off a clear shot. ''You're under arrest for murder, robbery and kidnapping.''

''You always were an arrogant bastard,'' Harlan snorted. ''I'm not letting her go.''

''And I'm not letting *you* go,'' Rafe assured him. ''This standoff might last all night, but someone will come along eventually. I'm predicting the next passerby will side with me, not with you.''

''Like I said,'' Harlan jeered. ''You're an arrogant bastard—''

Rafe hurled the torch at Harlan's head. Harlan reflexively shrank away. When the pistol that had been pressed to Karissa's neck swerved toward Rafe, he snapped his Winchester into position, fired off a shot then nudged Sergeant sideways.

Harlan's bullet whizzed past Rafe's head, taking his hat with it. In the torchlight that flickered in the dew-covered grass beside Harlan's bloody leg, Rafe could see Karissa rolling to her back to kick her feet at Harlan's gun hand. She didn't dislodge the weapon, but she made Harlan furious. Rafe stopped breathing when Harlan swung his attention, and his pistol, back to Karissa.

Hands not as steady as he would have preferred, Rafe fired off another shot. Harlan yowled in outrage as the pistol cartwheeled over his injured hand and dropped between him and Karissa.

While Rafe bounded from his horse, Karissa rolled on top of the pistol. Cursing the air blue, Harlan shoved her aside and grabbed the weapon. Rafe charged forward, swinging his rifle like a club. He knocked Harlan upside the head before he could take a shot. When Harlan slumped on the ground Rafe snatched up the fallen pistol and torch then breathed a long-suffering sigh of relief.

"Damn it, woman," he scolded Karissa. "You practically asked him to blow your head off when you tried to kick the pistol from his hand."

She muttered something at him in reply. Rafe decided he was glad he couldn't translate. She still sounded mad as hell. Hesitantly, he reached down to untie her gag.

"You idiot!" she spouted off. "You all but invited Harlan to blow *your* head off before he got around to *mine!* And don't just stand there. Untie me. I lost feeling in my arms and legs an hour ago."

A smile pursed Rafe's lips as he knelt to slice away the confining ropes. "You're welcome."

She didn't say he was welcome. She just glowered at him as if he were the villain rather than her white knight, come to save her while she was in distress.

"What'd I miss?" came a voice from the darkness.

Rafe swiveled around on his haunches to see Micah jogging forward.

Micah took the torch Rafe extended to him and glanced down at the unconscious man. "Harlan? I thought he was dead."

"So did everyone else," Rafe replied as he used the rope he'd cut away from Karissa to bind up his prisoner. "I got the impression that Harlan planned to have a new life and identity with the money he had stolen from Arliss and Sam. Karissa was his hostage and the army's supplies were to be his sustenance until he got to wherever he was going to make his new start."

Micah lifted the torch to inspect Karissa, who sluggishly pulled herself into a sitting position. "You okay?"

"I've been better, but thanks for asking." She smiled gratefully at Micah then glared daggers at Rafe again.

"A hot bath, hearty meal and a good night's sleep should cure that," Micah insisted as he leaned over to help her to her feet. "I was worried about you."

Karissa brushed the grass from her breeches. "Nice to know *someone* was." She shot Rafe a scathing look.

Micah glanced back and forth between Rafe and Karissa then grinned. "I didn't interrupt an argument, did I?"

"No," she said as she tested her wobbly legs. "I'm not speaking to the general for the rest of my life. Or *his* life. Whichever comes first—"

When her voice evaporated and she teetered sideways, Rafe lunged toward her. He caught her the moment before she collapsed on the ground. When her head lolled against his arm and she slumped against him, he noticed blood streaming down her cheek.

"Oh, God, she must have been hit!" he said frantically.

Micah held the torch close to her waxen face then traced his forefinger over her hairline. "King-size knot. Two of them actually," he reported. "I think she just passed out."

Rafe glared murderously at Harlan's unconscious body. "After we find out who else is involved in this conspiracy against Karissa, and I don't need Harlan's cooperation, I'm going to take that son of a bitch apart with my bare hands for abusing her." He brushed his lips over Karissa's forehead as he lifted her limp body into his arms.

Micah chuckled. "Fine, you do that, but don't expect this hellion to thank you for beating Harlan to a pulp for her. She's never talking to you again, you recall."

"I'm just glad she's alive," Rafe murmured as he stared into her expressionless face. "At least she's going to survive so she can never speak to me."

Carefully he settled Karissa in the wagon bed. "We'll throw Harlan over Sergeant's back. "No way am I going to let that slimy bastard sprawl out next to Karissa."

"Good idea," Micah commented. "I expect she's spent more time with Harlan than she prefers already." He swung onto his horse and grabbed Sergeant's reins. "I'll drop Harlan off at the infirmary to get patched up. Sure wouldn't want gangrene to set in before he's court-martialed and hanged for his crimes."

While Micah trotted on ahead, Rafe drove the wagon at a slower pace and sent a prayer of thanks winging heavenward. At least Karissa had survived her horrendous ordeal. He'd hoped that her appreciative gratitude would negate her irritation with him. But considering how feisty and contrary she was, he supposed that really was too much to ask.

Karissa awoke to find herself in Rafe's bed. Micah was hovering over her, holding a cool compress to her throbbing head. Although her vision was still blurry, she noticed that he smiled kindly at her. Blast it, why hadn't she had the good sense to fall in love with Micah rather than Rafe? Micah was ruggedly handsome, had a playful sense of humor and came from a similar background.

But no, imbecile that she was, she had lost her heart to a man who had a pedigree as long as her arm and had grown up rubbing shoulders with the socially privileged.

"Good, you're awake," Micah greeted her. "How's the head?"

"It's pounding like a drum," Karissa mumbled as she levered herself higher on the pillow.

"Do you feel like eating? Rafe sent a tray, heaping with food."

When he set the tray on her lap Karissa realized she was ravenous. The skimpy rations Marshal Horton served were barely enough to keep a gnat alive. And Harlan had stuffed nothing but sedatives down her throat.

"Where's what's-his-name?" she asked after she took a bite of the army's version of slumgullion stew.

Micah arched a dark brow. "Who? Harlan or Rafe?"

"The latter," she mumbled between bites.

Micah nodded. "I see. Not only are you refusing to speak *to* Rafe, but you also refuse to speak of him. I guess those two thumps on the noggin left you with amnesia. You seem to forget that he saved your life."

She shrugged noncommittally, still mad at him for doubting her and mad at herself for caring that he had.

Micah chuckled in amusement. "You're every bit as stubborn as Rafe says you are. In answer to your question, Rafe is interrogating Harlan. He refuses to rest until he discovers who is involved in this conspiracy against you. He's a very dedicated officer, you know."

Karissa knew that. The army was his life. Any interest

in a female would never be anything except second priority at best. Not that she cared anymore, of course. She intended to be over her affection for Rafe about the same time she recovered from this hellish headache.

All she wanted to do was to return to the homestead. She was *needed* there. Rafe would never need her. He had the army and all his rules and regulations to keep him company.

Karissa glanced up when the door banged against the wall. Harlan Billings—a bandage wrapped around his leg and his hand and his hair standing on end—was forcefully nudged into the room. Rafe loomed behind him, looking as vicious and threatening as she'd ever seen him. In supreme satisfaction Karissa watched Harlan wince and grimace as Rafe hustled him across the room and shoved him into the chair.

"Harlan insists that he'll confide who was involved in this conspiracy if we reduce the punishment against him," Rafe growled. "Micah, as second in command, you will bear witness to the statement." He jabbed Harlan in the shoulder. "Please repeat your offer, Corporal."

Harlan jerked up his head and glanced at Micah. "I'll tell you exactly what happened if I can get off with a lighter sentence."

"Statement acknowledged," Rafe rapped out. "Captain Whitfield?"

Micah stared distastefully at the prisoner. "Acknowledged, Major Hunter."

A gloating grin twisted Harlan's lips. "Vanessa Payton paid me to make Karissa look bad by accosting a cripple in the settlers' encampment and making sure she was blamed for it. Vanessa thought that, if Karissa's reputation was further ruined, our high-and-mighty commander would finally cast her aside and pay more attention to his betrothed.''

Karissa would have come up off the bed and gone for Harlan's throat if Micah hadn't pushed her back into a prone position. "You idiot!" she railed at Harlan. "That cripple is my *brother* and you stole all the money I gave him!"

"Go on," Rafe muttered. He was outraged that the pain, misfortune and trauma Karissa had suffered were indirectly his fault. The fact that he had been betrothed to a woman who was capable of dispensing such devious cruelty on anyone, even her rival, disgusted him. "What other instructions did Vanessa convey to you to insure Karissa was publicly disgraced and imprisoned?"

"When her first scheme didn't produce the results she expected, she demanded that I try to frame Karissa for a more serious crime. She also wanted Karissa to escape—to make her look guilty. I was to take the rest of the money Vanessa paid me and tote Karissa as far away from the new territory as possible.''

Harlan stared mockingly at Rafe. "Your haughty fiancée was convinced that once your tramp was out of sight, a fugitive from justice, you would go through with your marriage." He jeered impudently at Rafe. "You really can pick 'em, Commander. A white-trash whore and a treacherous socialite.''

Rafe's fists knotted at his sides. It took all his self-discipline not to pounce on Harlan and beat him to within an inch of his life for the cruel remark that had drained what little color was left in Karissa's face. He had thought Karissa deserved to hear Harlan's confession, but the man was purposely insulting her.

When she recoiled in hurt and humiliation Rafe wanted to gather her in his arms and reassure her, but he needed a complete statement so he could arrest Vanessa for her part in this diabolical conspiracy.

"So you are claiming that Vanessa sought you out to discredit Karissa's name, see her imprisoned for murder and machinate her escape to make her appear guilty of the crimes you committed?" Rafe gritted out.

Harlan nodded. "Vanessa threatened to expose my part in the first robbery assault and lay all the blame at my feet if I didn't meet the rest of her demands. She was blackmailing me into doing her bidding and assured me that she wielded enough power with you to see that I was court-martialed and jailed. I wanted no part of this, but she insisted she would make my life miserable if I didn't help her rush through this marriage so she would have the financial security that came with your name."

Harlan smiled triumphantly as he stared at Rafe. "In return for my cooperation, I expect to serve my reduced sentence in the military stockade."

"What cooperation?" Rafe asked sardonically. "I don't recall offering to bargain with you in exchange for your statement." He glanced briefly at Micah. "Did you hear me agree to reducing the sentence of robbery, murder and kidnapping, Captain Whitfield?"

Micah shook his head. "No, sir, you specifically requested that I bear witness to Harlan's interrogation and *acknowledge* his statement. You did not ask me to agree to reduce his sentence in exchange for information." He smiled devilishly at Harlan. "You should have been paying closer attention, Corporal. My recommendation will be the same as Commander Hunter's. I think you should hang thrice."

Furious outrage registered on Harlan's face when he realized he'd been outsmarted. When he bounded to his feet, Rafe decided to presume the prisoner was trying to escape. He doubled his fist and delivered a blow that carried enough impact to send Harlan stumbling backward over the chair that broke to pieces beneath his weight.

Rafe glanced sideways when he heard Karissa crawling from bed. She was the picture of vindictive fury as she snatched up the broken chair leg and whacked Harlan on the head.

''That's for accosting my brother, you miserable, low-life excuse for a human being!'' she spat at him.

When she lifted the makeshift club, presumably to thump Harlan again for good measure, Rafe jerked the chair leg from her fist. Her green eyes spewed fire as she transferred her anger from Harlan to him.

''Why do you get to have all the satisfaction, General?'' she muttered bitterly.

Despite the outrage and frustration that was pulsating through Rafe, he couldn't help but smile at the wild-haired spitfire. Even when she was looking and feeling her worst she had too much spunk and spirit to stand aside and allow him to handle the situation.

''I get to have most of the fun because I'm the commander,'' he reminded her. ''Furthermore, I don't want to see you waste the strength you have regained on this miserable, lowlife excuse for a human being, as you so accurately described him. Save it for Vanessa. I would think you'd enjoy being on hand when I place her under arrest.''

Karissa wilted back to the edge of the bed and regarded him for a curious moment. ''You aren't going to slap her dainty wrist and let her off scot-free? Her father, I understand, is a close friend of your father. I thought the *privileged* were always granted special privileges.''

''Rules are rules,'' Rafe reminded her. ''Vanessa

broke the law and she'll pay for it.'' He glanced at Micah. ''See that our prisoner is crammed in the stockade with the other offenders. Karissa and I are going to have a word with Vanessa.''

Karissa sniffed resentfully. ''You can have one word with her if you like, but I have plenty of things to say to that prissy witch.''

''And you're mistaken if you think I'm going to miss *that* confrontation,'' Micah added as he hurried over to yank Harlan to his feet. ''You'll need another witness for the interrogation. Give me five minutes to lock up Harlan and throw away the key.''

After Micah had hustled Harlan from the room, Rafe walked over to run his hand through the wild tangle of hair that cascaded over Karissa's shoulders. ''I feel responsible for what has happened to you and you have my solemn promise that I will make it up to you.''

She swatted his hand away. ''You owe me nothing,'' she insisted, refusing to meet his gaze. She squared her shoulders and elevated her chin. ''All I want is to see Vanessa receive her just deserts. Then I want to return to my brother's homestead to begin my new life that had to be put on hold because of this fiasco.''

She frowned at him in annoyance. ''And will you please stop dragging me into conversation,'' she grumbled. ''With this pounding headache I keep forgetting than I'm not speaking to you ever again.''

''Karissa,'' he murmured as he squatted down in front of her. ''I'm sorry. I really wasn't doubting your word—''

She cut him off with the slashing gesture of her hand. ''Let's face the truth, General. You have never taken my word as truth and you don't think I'm in the same class as you. *My* truth isn't as credible as yours and it will never be.''

''That's not—'' The door flew open before Rafe could deny her bitter accusation.

Out of breath, Micah buzzed into the room. ''To save time I handed Harlan over to Lieutenant Johnson. Let's go talk to Vanessa. I can't wait to hear her try to explain her way out of this conspiracy.''

When Rafe reached out to help Karissa to her feet, she made a spectacular display of avoiding his touch.

Rafe noticed that she didn't object when Micah curled a supporting arm around her waist and ushered her from the room. Rafe had predicted it was going to take some doing to return to Karissa's good graces. Saving her life and seeing justice served apparently weren't enough to secure his forgiveness. Her wounded pride, apparently, was more valuable to her than her own life.

He followed the twosome from the officers' quarters, across the parade grounds and up the steps to Vanessa's room. He quickened his step to reach the landing, determined to be the one who placed Vanessa under arrest. No way did he want Karissa to think that he was granting his ex-fiancée preferential treatment because of their family connections and her social status.

Rafe barged through the door without knocking and stopped in his tracks when he realized Vanessa had packed her belongings and left.

''You didn't give Vanessa advance warning, did you?'' Karissa asked Rafe accusingly.

''And you accused *me* of doubting *your* word?'' he muttered. ''Seems the pot is calling the kettle black.''

''At least I didn't—''

Micah stepped between them. ''The two of you can

squabble later. Right now I want Vanessa apprehended. Are you coming with me or not?''

"We're coming," Rafe and Karissa said simultaneously as they reversed direction and breezed by Micah to retrieve horses and begin the search for Vanessa.

Chapter Seventeen

Vanessa had flown into instant panic when she realized Harlan had been captured. She had gathered her belongings hurriedly, crammed them haphazardly into her trunk and dragged it down the steps in her haste to leave the fort.

While Harlan was transported to the infirmary and Karissa was toted to Rafe's quarters, Vanessa had sneaked around the perimeter of the fort, clinging to the shadows.

She considered it a stroke of luck that she had been able to confiscate one of the unoccupied carriages that had been sitting outside the post trader's store. Vanessa had managed to exit through the front gate without drawing attention to herself and then headed for Reno City, hoping to reach the stage station that was north of the boomtown.

She had almost made it to town when she heard the clatter of hooves behind her and saw the silhouettes of three riders hard on her heels. Swearing colorfully, she snapped the reins over the horse's rump and increased speed. She shrieked when the carriage hit a rut that nearly catapulted her into the air.

Pulse pounding in alarm she uprighted herself on the seat and plunged through the darkness. When the carriage rattled down the steep slope toward the creek, crashing through thick underbrush, Vanessa tried to stamp on the brake. But it was too late. The horse and carriage plunged into the creek and came to an abrupt halt. Her forward momentum sent her flying from the seat. Yelping, she ricocheted off the horse's rump and landed midstream with a splat.

Clothes dripping wet, her expensive kid boots filled with mud and water, Vanessa tried to flounder ashore. She glanced around wildly, trying to find a place to hide, but the three riders descended on her before she could dive for cover.

Micah lit the torch he had brought along and held it overhead to cast light on the stolen buggy. Rafe nudged his steed forward and halted beside Vanessa, who looked the worse for wear after her unsuccessful escape attempt.

Karissa experienced a long-awaited sense of satisfaction as she appraised Vanessa's soiled, soggy gown and noted the muddy smudges on her cheeks. Her blond hair had come unwound from its sophisticated coiffeur and dangled off one side of her head. The prissy socialite, who had stared condescendingly at Karissa during their previous confrontations, didn't look so haughty and aloof at the moment.

"Vanessa, you are under arrest for the conspiracy to commit robbery, murder and abduction," Rafe told her gruffly.

Vanessa flashed him an arrogant smirk. "Don't be ridiculous. I have done nothing wrong."

"Harlan Billings says otherwise," Micah contradicted

her as he walked his mount downhill to dislodge the carriage from the mud.

"And *you,* being nothing but a half-breed bumpkin, would take the word of some no-account soldier over mine, wouldn't you?" she huffed indignantly then turned back to Rafe. "Harlan was trying to sabotage your credibility as a military officer. He also sent me a telegram in Virginia, informing me that you were involved with this trollop."

She shot Karissa a disdainful glance. "All I did was arrive here to protect my interests and see that our wedding took place. Harlan approached me when I first arrived and offered to ruin your mistress's name and reputation if I would pay him for his efforts. Naturally I was upset when I discovered you were keeping your whore in your quarters, practically flaunting her in my face!"

Rafe frowned pensively as he listened to Vanessa present her rendition of the story. He wasn't sure who was the biggest liar, Vanessa or Harlan.

"Because of my annoyance with you I reacted rashly and agreed to Harlan's scheme to force this woman from your life. But to my shock and outrage Harlan insisted upon blackmail payments. He threatened to go to you with his twisted account of the incidents if I didn't pay him for his silence. In fact, I paid him with the money you gave me after I depleted my funds," she added pointedly.

Rafe swore he saw a sardonic twist to her lips when she made that last remark. He suspected Vanessa had derived wicked pleasure in knowing that Rafe was the one who had financed this scheme against Karissa.

"I have no idea what that devious scoundrel has been doing since our first few encounters, but all *I* have been doing is trying to organize the marriage our families arranged and hope you would come to your senses and realize our wedding should take place.''

"According to Harlan, *you* paid *him* to see Karissa accused of murder and facilitate her escape so she would look guilty," Rafe muttered. "He also claims *you* blackmailed *him*. Are you denying his accusations?"

"Of course I'm denying it. That is preposterous!" Vanessa erupted. "And this is all *your* fault, Rafe. This whole affair would never have happened if you had honored your commitment to me. And don't think for one minute that I'm not going to inform my father, and yours, of the humiliating disgrace you put me through when I return home!"

"You aren't going anywhere until this matter is cleared up," Rafe insisted. He dismounted then slogged through the stream to grab her arm. Although she tried to resist, he shepherded her toward the buggy that Micah had returned to higher ground.

"I am the victim here," Vanessa sputtered as Rafe handed her into the carriage. "All I did was try to honor our parents' wishes. And you call yourself a man of honor?" she sniffed sarcastically. "You tried to cast me aside for that nobody of a female who isn't worthy to be my servant, much less my rival for your attention! How dare you choose that ill-mannered harlot over me!"

"That's enough, Vanessa," Rafe snapped. He looked sideways, expecting to see Karissa hunched dejectedly in the saddle after overhearing the insulting remarks. But she was nowhere to be seen. It was as if she had vanished into the darkness. "Micah?"

Micah shrugged as he shot Vanessa a disgruntled glance. "I'm sure Karissa heard more than enough.

Can't blame her for quitting this place to avoid bad company. I'd like to do the same thing myself.'' He walked over to grab Sergeant's reins. ''You can handle the situation from here, Rafe. I'll lead your mount back to the stables while you're transporting the prisoner.''

When Micah extinguished the torch and rode away, Rafe climbed into the carriage. ''It makes no difference that you and Harlan are accusing each other of relying on blackmail to coerce each other in this conspiracy,'' Rafe said as he pointed the buggy toward the garrison. ''You are both guilty and you are not above serving time for your part in these crimes.''

Vanessa reared back and gaped at him. ''Serve time? You cannot be serious! One word from you and I can be on my way home. That's one of the many advantages of being born and raised in our elite social class. In exchange for your leniency I won't hold you to the marriage,'' she negotiated frantically. ''I will simply find someone else who can support me in the manner to which I've grown accustomed.''

If Rafe had the slightest inclination to go easy on Vanessa, it vanished when she insisted that the upper crust of society was exempt from obeying the law. ''You won't have to worry about financial support,'' he assured her. ''You'll be taking an extended holiday, compliments of the U.S. government. I'm told the lodging and rations in prison are tolerable, though far below your customary standards. You broke the law, Vanessa. Now you'll pay the consequences. Rules, after all, are rules.''

Vanessa switched tactics by bursting into blubbering tears. In between her theatrical sobs and sniffles, she begged and pleaded with him to show mercy on her because of their fathers' long-standing friendship.

Rafe couldn't work up much sympathy for this

woman who had tried to sacrifice Karissa's life for her selfish benefit. He might never be able to compensate for the hurt and anguish Karissa endured during this ordeal, but he would see to it that Vanessa and Harlan paid to the full extent of the law for trying to ruin Karissa's life.

And because he was indirectly responsible he would see to it that Karissa didn't suffer more hardships in this new territory, Rafe vowed. Maybe he didn't deserve her forgiveness, but he damn well intended to make her life easier. It was the *very least* he could do for her.

"Oh, thank God, you're back, Kari!" Amanda erupted in relief. "Clint and I have been worried sick!"

Karissa noticed the lack of color in Amanda's face before being engulfed in her sister-in-law's loving hug and her brother's consoling embrace. They bustled her into the tent and situated her on the edge of their bed.

"Did the authorities catch the awful person who set you up for murder?" Amanda questioned as her hand moved restlessly over her swollen belly. "And why would anyone in his right mind believe you were capable of such a brutal act?"

Well, at least there were *two* people around here who had unwavering faith in her, Karissa mused. At least here she was respected, welcomed and wanted. In fact, her ordeal seemed to have been excessively stressful for Amanda. If her difficulties with Harlan and Vanessa caused complications with Amanda's pregnancy, Karissa would never forgive herself.

When Clint and Amanda demanded an explanation, Karissa presented the boiled-down version of her ordeal and finished by informing her family that the two guilty parties had been apprehended. She didn't bother to mention that she had serious doubts about whether Vanessa—being a prominent figure in Eastern society, the daughter of some highfalutin general—would serve a prison sentence. Rafe wouldn't permit his former fiancée to spend time in a penitentiary, she predicted cynically.

"I'm so grateful your commander has cleared your name," Amanda gushed.

"I keep telling you that he isn't *my* commander. He's not my anything!" Karissa snapped more gruffly than she intended.

Karissa chewed herself out royally when the last of the color drained from Amanda's face. As much as Karissa needed rest to recover from her exhausting week, she decided Amanda needed it even more. The poor woman looked as if she needed to lie down and sleep for a full day.

"Commander Hunter *did* save your life," Clint reminded her. "I hope you thanked him properly for it."

Karissa couldn't remember if she had—and didn't care if she hadn't. Rafe had offended her pride and dignity. She definitely remembered *that.*

"Did *you,* for one moment, doubt my innocence?" she asked Clint and Amanda.

"Certainly not," Amanda quickly assured her as she sank down on the side of the cot.

"How can you even ask that?" Clint said, affronted.

"Well, the commander didn't believe me," she nearly shouted in frustration.

Clint smiled wryly. "Ah, so that's why you're in a snit. The man had the audacity to question your honor, while trying to investigate the murders impartially. And you, of course, took offense, didn't you? Sometimes, big sister, you let your pride get the better of you."

"Well, it obviously runs in the family," Karissa

sniped defensively. "You have certainly done your share of brooding and sulking because Amanda and I have been handling the responsibilities while you're on the mend."

Clint winced. "Yes, well, that's Baxter pride for you. It's more hindrance than help."

"Don't you think it was Commander Hunter's place to ask the difficult questions in order to get to the truth?" Amanda asked gently. "Isn't it his responsibility to listen to all sides of the story? He is the symbol of law and justice in this new territory, isn't he?"

"Yes, he is," Karissa said begrudgingly. "But now the ordeal is over and, from this day forward, I don't plan to break any of his laws. There will be no reason whatsoever for me to have future dealings with the man. Now if you don't mind, I would like to bed down for the night." She heaved an exhausted sigh. "I've had a trying week and Amanda looks as if she could use a good night's rest, too."

Karissa surged to her feet, ignoring the head rush that assured her she hadn't fully recovered from the painful blows Harlan had delivered to her head. "I'll camp out by the creek, as usual."

"You will do no such thing," Amanda contradicted, and Clint seconded. "You will sleep on the bed and we'll make a pallet on the ground."

Karissa smiled faintly. "Believe me, considering what I've been through, sprawling out on a pallet under a canopy of stars sounds as luxurious as a feather bed. But I do appreciate your concern and, most of all, your votes of confidence in my innocence. That means more to me than you can possibly know."

Karissa stretched out on her pallet a few minutes later and heaved an exhausted sigh. She was going to have to reconstruct the barriers she'd used to protect herself from hurt and disappointment. She functioned much better when she expected nothing and relied only upon herself. She would focus on turning this homestead into a true home for Clint and Amanda and then she would bid them farewell and wish them all the happiness they rightfully deserved. She would find herself a job—somewhere—to support herself.

And *that* was the rest of her life, she told herself realistically. She had achieved her goal when she raced into Oklahoma Territory and claimed the free land for Clint and Amanda. Problem was that, in the process, she'd gotten her heart trampled by a man who was so far above her social standing that it was laughable.

But she was a survivor, always had been. She would get over Rafe and she would be her old self again.

Karissa knew she'd be doomed to disappointment if she was foolish enough to hope for anything more than to build a roof over her head and keep food on the table.

This was as good as one could expect from life, she told herself sensibly as she drifted off to sleep. Wishing otherwise would not make it so.

Karissa swore she had only been asleep for an hour when her brother jostled her awake. "Kari," Clint whispered urgently. "I know you desperately need your rest, but I think Amanda has gone into labor."

Karissa was on her feet in a single bound. "It's too soon," she muttered as she raked her tangled hair from her face and stared uphill toward the lighted tent.

"I know." Clint's fists clenched and flexed nervously. "I'm such an imbecile. I didn't think this through before I dragged Amanda down from Kansas for this Run. I should have left her with her family until we had our home built.'' His frantic gaze flew to Karissa. ''I don't know a damn thing about delivering babies, especially one that has decided to make an early arrival. Damn it, Kari, I'm scared.''

Karissa jogged uphill, with Clint hobbling along as fast as he could behind her. Guilt hounded Karissa every step of the way. She knew Amanda had been extremely worried about her after the day Jake Horton had arrived at the homestead to arrest her. Obviously the stressful fretting had sent Amanda into premature labor. The baby wasn't due for another month and if anything happened to Amanda or this child…

She shoved the grim thought aside and tried to assume Amanda's optimistic approach to life. The very last thing she wanted to do right now was alarm Amanda more than she probably was.

Out of breath, Karissa ducked inside the tent. She had to school her expression to conceal her concern when she saw Amanda lying on the cot. Pain twisted Amanda's delicate features and beads of perspiration covered her forehead and upper lip. There was no color whatsoever in her cheeks and dark circles surrounded her eyes.

''Decided to have this baby early, did you?'' Karissa said as she eased a hip onto the edge of the cot.

Teeth gritted, fists knotted, Amanda nodded jerkily. ''I guess so.''

''Well, don't you worry about a thing,'' Karissa said as cheerfully as she knew how. ''I'm going to ride to the fort and fetch the army surgeon. I shouldn't be gone too long.'' She folded her hand over Amanda's clenched fist. ''Everything is going to be fine, Amanda.'' She hoped!

When she heard Clint huffing and puffing behind her,

she twisted sideways. "Dip a cloth in water and wipe the perspiration from her face," she instructed before she focused her attention on Amanda. "Try to relax as best you can. I'll be back with help before you know it."

Amanda panted for breath as tears trickled down her cheeks. "I'm so sorry about this, Karissa. You've had a terrible week, with so little time to rest, and now I'm being a bother."

Kari grabbed both her hands and stared into her wan face. "You are no such thing. Never have been, never will be." She forced a smile for Amanda's benefit. "Just name this baby after me if she's a girl and we'll call it square. Deal?"

A faint smile pursed Amanda's ashen lips. "Deal...ow! Oh, my, Mamma didn't tell me it was going to hurt like this!"

When Amanda clutched her belly and moaned in agony, Karissa leaped to her feet. She wanted to stay here and offer Amanda all the comfort possible, but she needed to race to the fort for assistance. No doubt, she was going to worry herself sick until she returned to find Amanda and the baby were all right.

"I'll be back as soon as I can," Karissa promised. "Do not have this baby until I get back!"

Karissa dashed outside and hurriedly snatched up a bridle. She didn't waste time saddling the mount Rafe had provided for her earlier that evening. Better the sure-footed army mount than the old gray mare, she mused as she pulled herself onto the horse.

Despite the dull headache pounding against her skull, Karissa thundered toward the fort, pushing the horse to its limits. She shouted out her name as she rode past the guard tower and raced through the gate at full canter.

Karissa headed straight for the officers' quarters and bounded from the winded horse before it came to a full stop. She burst into Rafe's room unannounced and found him bare chested and barefoot, preparing for bed.

It suddenly dawned on her that Rafe was the first place she came when she needed help. He was the only person she had ever allowed herself to depend on when she needed support and assistance—even now, when she was still irritated with him for doubting her word about the murder case.

Karissa made a mental note never to come to him for help again. If not for her concern for Amanda she wouldn't be here at all.

"Amanda is having her baby prematurely," she said hurriedly. "I think she worried so much about me while I was under arrest that she worked herself into early labor. I need to borrow your army surgeon."

"Down three doors on the right," Rafe said quickly then grabbed his discarded shirt. "I'll saddle the horses while you're rousing Doc Winston. And I'm sorry, Rissa. I'm sorry about everything."

She nodded without looking back at Rafe on her way out the door. This was no time to become distracted, she told herself firmly. Time was of the essence and she was dreadfully concerned about Amanda.

She pounded on the door three times then poked her head inside the darkened room. "Doc Winston? I need your assistance. My sister-in-law is having her baby prematurely. Please come quickly."

"I'll meet you outside as soon as I dress," said the raspy voice from the darkness.

Karissa walked outside, inhaled a steadying breath and paced back and forth until Rafe arrived with the horses. She barely acknowledged his presence, because her emotions were in so much turmoil that she feared she would throw herself into his arms and burst into tears if she let her guard down for even an instant.

"You take Sergeant," Rafe said as he swung from the saddle. "I'll ride bareback."

"No, I—"

"Don't argue with me," Rafe insisted as he placed the reins in her hand. "Just this once."

She sighed heavily, nodded then mounted Sergeant. Rafe could see the lines of worry and exhaustion that claimed Karissa's features. He wanted to pull her into his arms and hold her close, but he doubted she would be receptive.

Now was not the time to try to make amends. Karissa was wrapped up in concern for her sister-in-law. But later, he would compensate, Rafe promised himself resolutely.

Doc Winston scurried outside to mount the horse Rafe had saddled for him. "I'm going to alert Micah," Rafe said. "I'll have him bring a wagon to transport mother and child back to the infirmary. The facilities will be better while Amanda is recovering from birthing and you can keep a close watch on her progress."

"Good idea," Doc Winston replied as he reined away.

When Karissa and the surgeon trotted off, Rafe hurried back into the officers' quarters to alert Micah. He was back outside in two minutes. Riding bareback, Rafe thundered toward the Baxter homestead, praying Amanda and her child would have the opportunity to recuperate with a solid roof over their heads at the fort.

Rafe wasn't sure what he would encounter when he thundered uphill to reach the Baxter homestead. He could see the silhouettes hovering inside the lighted tent as he brought his horse to a halt. Behind him, the clatter of the wagon indicated that Micah was fast approaching.

When Rafe saw Karissa step outside he hurried forward. "Is everything all right with Amanda and the baby?" He winced when he saw the stream of tears that glittered on Karissa's cheeks.

"Oh, God!" she wailed.

To his concern and amazement Karissa flung herself at him and he reflexively wrapped her up in his arms. "Oh, God, what?" he demanded worriedly as he held her close to his heart at long last.

"Everything is okay," she blubbered in relief. "I have a niece and she's beautiful and perfect, even if she's just a tiny little thing. Doc says mother and baby are going to be all right. But, Lord, I was so worried!"

Rafe hugged her close while she vented her concern and frustration and cried more tears on his shirt. He rested his chin on the top of her head and thanked the powers that be that this long, harrowing day had turned out much better than he had anticipated.

"What's the baby's name?" Rafe murmured.

"Lily Karissa Baxter," she said on a hitched breath. "She has red-gold hair and she came squawking into the world, mad as the dickens."

"Sounds as if she's done her aunt proud. Red hair and a big mouth," Rafe teased. "I'm sure Clint and Amanda are bursting with pride over their daughter."

He felt Karissa nod her head against his chest and heard her sniffle before she pulled herself together and stepped away from him. Rafe instantly felt the defensive wall rise. Karissa had leaned on him momentarily for support. But once she had recovered she was distant and remote, assuring Rafe she still hadn't forgiven him.

"This is where we say our last goodbye," she told him flatly. "I will always be immensely grateful for all your assistance. Have a good life, General."

Rafe sighed heavily as Karissa turned around and walked back into the tent to pack a bag for Clint and Amanda's stay at the post infirmary.

Well, he thought, even if Karissa was still perturbed, he could ease her concern for her family by providing comfortable accommodations at the fort.

When Micah arrived, Rafe walked over to check that the wagon bed had been filled with enough soft padding for a smooth ride to the fort. Then he and Micah carried Amanda and her baby outside to situate them in the wagon. Karissa, he noted, didn't come near him again.

As he rode away with the entourage, he saw Karissa standing alone outside the tent. Naturally, she had refused his offer of accommodations at the post. She insisted that she needed to remain behind to protect their new homestead.

Rafe breathed a tired sigh and told himself that this was *not* their last goodbye. The mere thought of not having that feisty female in his life was pure hell. He was going to out-stubborn her, he decided resolutely.

Rafe dragged himself through the paces of military routine the following morning. Although he was dead on his feet, he reported for roll call at ten minutes after five then immediately attended stable call to groom and care for Sergeant. After breakfast at six o'clock he placed Micah in charge of fatigue call and mounting of the guard. He made a beeline to his office to write up his investigative reports. At noon he tucked his reports inside the jacket of his uniform and went in search of Micah.

"I'm leaving the garrison in your capable hands for the rest of the day," Rafe said when he intercepted Micah on his way to the mess hall. "I'm going to report the results of our investigation to Jake Horton. I'm also placing him in charge of transporting all of our prisoners to the U.S. Court for the Western District in Fort Smith. The law states that the accused have a right to a speedy trial and we can't provide one here, not until the territorial government is organized."

Micah nodded agreeably then said, "*All* of the prisoners? No favoritism to the one in skirts?"

"No," Rafe insisted. "Before I leave the garrison I'll be sending off several telegrams. One of them will be addressed to Vanessa's father. He can provide an attorney for her upcoming trial. My errands and duties in town will take most of the day."

Micah arched a curious brow. "What, no visit to a certain homestead southeast of the fort?"

Rafe snorted. "You witnessed the mood Karissa was in yesterday. Do you think a visit from me will be well received?" When Micah grimaced, Rafe nodded. "I didn't think so either. At this point, all I can do is insure that news of her exoneration is passed around town and the vigilante mob understands that the guilty parties will be transferred to Fort Smith to stand trial in court. Damage control is the best I can offer until Karissa recovers from her exhausting ordeal. That and making her life easier while she's doing it," he added.

"What are you implying?" Micah questioned. "Don't tell me you plan to wave that magic wand you've refused to take in hand during your long stint in the army."

Rafe shrugged. "It's at my disposal and I can't think of a better place to use it."

The magic wand Micah referred to was Rafe's trust fund that had been accruing interest for years on end. He could well afford to provide financial compensation for his indirect—and direct—contribution to Karissa's misery.

Micah's expression sobered as he stared meaningfully at Rafe. "Don't go to all this trouble, and *expense,* unless you intend to alter your priorities. You, my friend, have a choice to make. The most important one of your life."

Rafe turned and walked away, mulling over what Micah had said. Dealing with Karissa Baxter had definitely demanded a reevaluation of his priorities. And even if his perspectives had changed drastically there was no guarantee that Karissa would forgive him completely. Nevertheless, he was going to make it his mission to soften her up, he mused as he mounted up and rode into town.

Sometimes a man just had to stick his neck out and hope like hell that the woman who held his heart wouldn't grab an ax and chop it into bite-size pieces.

In his best estimation, it could go either way at the moment.

Chapter Eighteen

There days after Clint and Amanda returned to the homestead a crew of carpenters and two wagonloads of lumber stopped near the corral. Obviously the men had taken a wrong turn and had gotten lost.

Karissa paused from her chore of crawling around on her hands and knees to plant seeds in their vegetable garden. "Whose homestead are you looking for?" she questioned as she approached the man who appeared to be in charge.

"Yours." The man smiled as he reached out to pump her hand. "I'm John Saxton." He gestured toward the crew behind him. "We signed on to make extra money for improvements on our own homestead by building your home for you."

Karissa blinked, bemused. "There must be some mistake. I didn't purchase all this lumber and hire your crew."

"No, ma'am," John agreed. "Commander Hunter hired us and said to build you a house three times the size you originally planned."

"Three times larger?" Amanda chirped as she strode

up beside Karissa. She cuddled little Lily in her arms and beamed in delight.

Karissa surveyed her brother and sister-in-law's pleased expressions. "I'm sorry, but we can't accept charity from Commander Hunter."

John chuckled. "The commander told me you would probably say something to that effect. He also told us to ignore your objections and get right to work." He motioned for the crew to unload the lumber. "We're being well paid to build a fine house. We can use the money to build our own improvements on our homesteads, so we're going to set right to work."

Karissa silently fumed while Clint and Amanda chattered excitedly and discussed the design of their dream house with John Saxton. She and her family could make their own way, thank you very much. She did not need Rafe Hunter trying to compensate for his lack of faith in her by hiring a workforce to erect a mansion when a modest cabin would suit well enough.

Annoyed, Karissa returned to the garden to cram corn seed into the ground.

The very next day, another wagon arrived with a tent that was three times the size of the one Clint and Amanda occupied. The deliveryman announced that he had been sent to set up the new tent and that he was instructed not to take no for an answer.

The day after that Karissa hadn't even made it through her skimpy breakfast before another crew and wagon arrived. This time it was fence posts and barbed wire that magically appeared, compliments of her generous benefactor. She was told to stake out the location for a pasture because the herd of cows that would be delivered at the end of the week needed to be contained.

Although Clint and Amanda were practically floating

on air, shouting praises to Rafe's name, Karissa was outraged. First off, acts of kindness and generosity had always made her suspicious of ulterior motives. She had no doubt that Rafe was trying to buy her forgiveness because he felt partially responsible for the calamity that had befallen her and contributed to the premature birth of her brother's daughter.

Secondly, the only thing she really wanted from Rafe was the very thing she would never have. These expensive improvements to the Baxter homestead had to stop—even if she was secretly delighted that Clint's family would have a grand new home to begin their new life.

Filled with purpose, she saddled the gray mare and made a beeline to the fort. She encountered Micah who was overseeing fatigue call. Some of the soldiers were making repairs to the barracks while others were chopping weeds and tending the post garden.

"Where is he?" she demanded without preamble.

Micah appraised the agitated frown on her face and said, "Got a bee in your bonnet, do you, Karissa?"

"I don't own a bonnet," she said impatiently. "Where is he?"

Micah gestured to the west. "He's conducting target practice with the new recruits. But don't go charging out there, because you might get shot. Some of those new recruits who showed up a couple of days ago don't know one end of a rifle from the other."

Karissa reined her horse around and trotted through the gate. In the distance she could see the new recruits firing at their targets. Rafe was moving from one soldier to the next, offering instruction. Approaching from the rear, so as not to get her head blown off, she halted beside Rafe.

"I want to talk to you," she demanded brusquely.

"The answer is no," Rafe replied as he glanced up at her momentarily.

"I didn't come here to ask questions, but rather to make a demand. Stop sending me lumber, barbed wire and work crews. I'll have you know that I can take care of myself."

"No one implied that you couldn't," Rafe said calmly.

"Don't think that I'm so dense that I don't realize you are trying to purchase my forgiveness," she snapped. "Fine, you are forgiven for questioning my honor and integrity. Do not send more extravagant gifts."

He smiled at her ramrod-stiff position on the back of the gray nag. "You don't sound all that forgiving," he remarked. "I was only trying to do my job, as an unbiased law official, to the best of my ability."

Karissa refused to melt beneath his charming smile. If she let her guard down for one moment she'd start wishing for the impossible again. "This is your first and last warning," she told him crisply. "No more manna from heaven, Major God."

"Duly noted, but I don't consider myself God, just one of his humble servants," he said before he turned his attention back to the incompetent recruits.

Having been dismissed by his highness of the military, Karissa nudged the mare into a jolting trot. She arrived home immediately after a wagonload of food supplies were delivered, compliments of Rafe Hunter.

"This has gone too far," Karissa muttered grouchily.

Clint propped himself on his crutch and chuckled at her sour frown. "I don't know why you can't accept the fact that Commander Hunter cares enough about you to see that you have a fresh new start.''

"It's the principle of the matter," Karissa grumbled. "We've worked for everything we have and I don't intend to keep accepting charity, just because Rafe Hunter happens to have more money than the Lord above."

"I think the man is in love with you and he's just trying to show it through his generosity," Clint commented.

"And I think you've been out in the sun too long," Karissa countered. "You are starting to hallucinate."

"Fine, be stubborn and hardheaded, sis," he said with a shrug. "Why don't you get back on your high horse and charge back to the fort and just shoot him. That should bring his generosity to a screeching halt," he teased. "You were acquitted of the last murder so maybe you can get off on this one, too."

She glared at her brother's mocking grin. "Why don't I just shoot you for practice before I go gunning for him?"

"Because you love me and I think you love him, too, but heaven forbid that you admit to any such thing. That might put you in a vulnerable position and you've spent your entire life avoiding that."

Karissa inwardly winced. Damn, her kid brother could see right through her. When had he gotten so perceptive? When he had grown up from the undernourished child she had protected and provided for to become an adult?

Obviously she had been so busy taking care of Clint that she hadn't noticed how much he had matured these past ten years. Even when he had married Amanda, Karissa had still viewed her brother and sister-in-law as her responsibility. But her brother really had grown up and didn't need her the way he used to.

"And answer me this, sis," Clint continued. "Hasn't Rafe been there for you during every hair-raising crisis? If he didn't care about you, why would he make so much effort in your behalf?" He rushed on before she could reply. "And do you know what else I think?"

"I'm afraid to ask," she mumbled.

"I think you're afraid to trust what's in your heart, because you don't think you measure up to Commander Hunter," he said with brotherly candor. "Plus, I think you're afraid you might get hurt, the same way we were both hurt when Pops left us to fend for ourselves while he gambled away everything we had."

Karissa grimaced, remembering all the disillusionment and disappointments she had suffered because of her father's lack of responsibility and concern for his family.

"But loving Amanda the way I do, I can tell you that it *is* worth the risk to your heart. You have focused your efforts on seeing that we're happy, but you aren't comfortable with allowing yourself to be happy."

"I'm happy. In fact, I'm ecstatic," she insisted, flashing him an overly cheerful smile. "I'm exactly where I want to be, with the people I love most."

Clint hobbled over to press a kiss to her cheek. "There's more, Kari. Don't sell yourself short. You don't have to center your life around me anymore. In case you haven't noticed, I'm all grown up."

She nodded and murmured, "Yes, I'm beginning to realize that."

"I also think Rafe Hunter is having just as much trouble admitting that he wants more from life than a bunch of soldiers to command, Indian tribal lands to protect from would-be settlers who failed to stake free homesteads and this new territory to bring under law and order. You two are stubborn fools if you don't realize you belong together, despite your different backgrounds. It seems to me that the only thing either of you is really afraid of is how you feel about each other.''

When Clint limped away to rejoin his wife and daughter, Karissa stood there, watching the construction crew frame the second story of the new house. Then she turned her attention to the men who were digging holes for fence posts.

Was Clint right? Did Rafe care enough to give her what he thought she wanted, just to make her happy?

Well, Clint was right about one thing, she mused. She was afraid to come right out and tell Rafe that, hard as she tried, she couldn't get past the hurdle of loving him. And she had tried, damn it. She had worked harder at it than anything she had ever done in her life.

But there it was, still staring her right in the face and whispering in her soul. She loved him and all the consoling platitudes and sensible lectures hadn't changed her feelings for him.

Her troubled thoughts trailed off when she saw Jake Horton—the deputy marshal who had arrested her—riding toward her. He halted his horse a few feet away and tipped his hat politely.

''Miss Baxter, I've come to apologize for any discomfort or humiliation you might have suffered when you were wrongfully jailed for crimes you didn't commit.''

''I suppose Rafe, the good fairy, sent you, just like he's sent the rest of his elves,'' she replied.

''No, I'm here on my own accord, but since I was headed this direction after I swung by the fort, Rafe asked me to give you this.'' Jake reached into his pocket to retrieve a folded paper then leaned down to place it in her hand.

Befuddled, Karissa unfolded the document then gaped at Jake in disbelief.

''The two adjoining properties to the east and south were claimed by Arliss Frazier and his henchmen. Now they belong to you,'' he announced. ''These deeds have been legally registered in your name, Miss Baxter.''

Karissa stood there like a tongue-tied idiot while the marshal reversed direction and headed back to town. Oh, now Rafe had really gone and done it, she thought as the dam of tears broke loose and flooded down her cheeks. He'd given her the one thing she'd thought she wanted most of all. Her name on the deed to her own land—two deeds, in fact. She had given up her own long-held dream so that Clint had a place to call his own. Now, thanks to Rafe, she had acquired the rights to *two* adjacent homesteads.

But even while she stood there, clutching the deeds to her chest, all she felt was hollow satisfaction. Having her own land to build her own home and put down solid roots suddenly wasn't enough.

Now there was irony for you, she mused as she swiped at the tears with the back of her hand. Give a woman what she *thought* she wanted and she wasn't appeased. Oh no, she had to get greedy. She started wishing for the moon instead of settling for a handful of stars.

Her own brother had called her a coward for running from her feelings for Rafe rather than confronting them. Rather than confronting *Rafe* face-to-face with her affection for him.

''For someone with your spit-in-the-eye determination, you've turned into a cowardly sissy,'' Karissa chided herself, in between sniffles. ''If you could face

down the men who tried to dispose of you then surely
you can face Rafe.''

Resolved to go for broke—the way her father had
done for the better part of his life—and usually *went*
broke—Karissa drew herself up, turned herself around
and hiked down to the creek. She was going to bathe
and get herself all gussied up in the one nice dress she
owned. Then she was going to march herself over to the
fort and tell Rafe that she loved him like crazy. Loved
him so much that she was willing to settle for being
second priority in his life.

She would swallow her damnable pride and become
his mistress since he was already married to the military.
A man couldn't have more than one wife, after all. It
was against the law in this new territory and she knew
Rafe was a stickler for following the rules and regulations.

When Karissa walked uphill to fetch her horse, Clint
didn't ask where she was going. He simply smiled approvingly as he hugged his wife and child affectionately
against him.

Rafe was hunched over his desk in profound concentration when Micah rapped on the opened door and
poked his head around the corner. He was grinning from
ear to ear as he stepped inside.

''You have a visitor,'' Micah announced.

''God, not another one. This place has been a mad-
house all day,'' Rafe bemoaned.

''Yup, we've been as busy as bumblebees in a bucket
of tar,'' Micah agreed, lips twitching.

''Now who's here to complain about what?'' Rafe
grumbled sourly.

Micah didn't reply, just stepped aside to motion the visitor inside.

When Karissa stepped into view, looking good enough to gobble alive in her sunflower-yellow gown, Rafe bounded to his feet. His chair teetered backward and crashed to the floor.

She stood before him, *not* looking peeved and defensive, as he expected. She looked...well, besides looking like a radiant burst of sunlight in his shadowy office, she looked nervous. She shifted from one foot to the other, stared at the air over his right shoulder and knotted her fists in the folds of her gown.

"I would like a private word with you, General," she requested then glanced over at Micah, silently requesting that he make himself scarce.

Micah snickered playfully. "You aren't planning to shoot him, are you? If so, I really must object because I would be left to fill out all that paperwork on his desk. I dislike all those administrative duties." His blue eyes twinkled down on her when he added, "Maim him if you feel you must, just don't kill him outright. For my sake?"

An answering smile pursed her lips. "I'll leave him in one piece, more or less," she agreed.

When Micah exited, Rafe watched Karissa draw herself up to full stature and moisten her lips. He inwardly groaned when his body clenched and his attention settled on the tempting curve of her mouth. He was starving to death for a taste of her. He felt as if it had been months rather than weeks since he had been able to hold her, since he had been deep inside her and discovered what heaven was like without actually dying first.

Another wave of unfulfilled desire rippled through him. He tensed when she drew in a deep breath, calling his attention to the rising swell of her breasts. Damn, he wanted to rip away those garments that hid what he had discovered to be absolute feminine perfection and fill his hands with her soft flesh.

Good gad, would you listen to him? She was here, obviously with something important but difficult to say and all he could think about was getting her naked and appeasing this craving that had sunk its teeth into him and wouldn't let go.

"General…er…Rafe," she blurted out nervously. She shifted on her feet again, cleared her throat and stared over his left shoulder.

"Yes?" he prodded. He would have chuckled in amusement in response to her miserable expression, but that would likely set her off. She would slice him into bite-size pieces with the sharp side of her tongue.

She blew out her breath, wrung her hands in front of her, and then said, "I'm in love with you, in case you don't know it, and I want to be your mistress."

Rafe wasn't sure what he expected her to say, but the abrupt declaration caught him so far off guard that he wilted back into his chair. Only his chair was still sitting upside down on the floor and he tumbled sideways in a graceless sprawl. He banged his chin on the floor, snapping his teeth together so fast that he bit his tongue. Swearing, he clambered onto his hands and knees and looked up to see Karissa, her hands braced on his desk, staring down at him in concern.

"Are you all right?"

"Um…yes…fine." He came inelegantly to his feet to dust off his uniform. "Would you mind saying that again. I'm not sure I heard you right."

Her gaze narrowed on him. "You heard me loud and

clear, General. Don't make me repeat myself. Are you interested in the offer or not?''

Well, *he* sure as hell was going to repeat it, because *he* couldn't believe she had stood right there in his office and said it. ''You love me and you want to be my mistress?'' he croaked in amazement.

She scowled at him. Now *that* looked like the Karissa he knew. That other woman, who had seemed so nervous and unsure of herself, he did *not* know.

''Well?'' she prompted impatiently. ''It's not as if I intend to twist your arm a dozen different ways. Either you want to have an affair with me or you don't. Which is it?''

''Oh, I most definitely do,'' Rafe assured her. ''Just what prompted you to come here with this offer that no man in his right mind could possibly refuse?''

She flashed him a look that indicated that, if asked, she wouldn't testify that he was in his right mind. He ignored that expressive stare and asked, ''Was it the lumber and carpenters? The fencing and farmhands?'' He nodded speculatively. ''No, I'll bet it was the deeds to your new properties. Am I right?''

''None of the above,'' she informed him. ''You can't *buy* my affection or forgiveness. But nice try, General.'' Her confidence faltered once again and she nervously stacked the papers that were scattered across his desk. ''Clint and Amanda were thrilled with your generosity, of course. They are very grateful.''

''They are very welcome,'' Rafe replied. ''Now about this affair we're going to have. Were you planning to move into my quarters or are we going to set a schedule so you can expect me to visit the homestead on certain days of the week?''

She shot him a dark look as she moved the inkwell

from the left side of his desk to the right side. Rafe was thoroughly enjoying this encounter with Karissa. It compensated for all those times she'd driven him nuts with that sassy mouth and those defensive airs. Lord, she was so adorable standing there, trying to discuss an affair, as if she were hammering out the details of a serious business arrangement.

"Visitations to my tent down by the creek would be best, I think. Three days a week should suffice."

Rafe eased a hip on the edge of the desk, crossed his arms over his chest and battled like the devil to keep from bursting out in riotous laughter. "I beg to differ. Seven days a week is more to my liking."

Her green eyes bugged out and her jaw scraped her chest. He reached over to close her gaping mouth. "Don't look so surprised, Rissa. Loving you the way I do, I'm not about to settle for three measly days a week. And you can forget about having an affair because I'm not settling for anything less than marriage."

"You love me?" she bleated, bewildered. "You are kidding."

His silvery eyes glittered like mercury as he shook his dark head and smiled the devastating smile that threatened to knock her knees right out from under her—and they weren't all that steady to begin with. She had been so nervous and self-conscious that it was all she could do to stand still to make her heartfelt confession and suggest the affair.

He reached over to draw her between his legs then cupped her face in his hands. "I couldn't be more serious, Rissa. How can I not love you, considering all the flattery and glowing compliments you have bestowed on me since we first met?" he added with a playful grin.

She looped her arms around his neck, feeling relieved

and giddy and hopelessly infatuated. "I never once complimented your dashing good looks or your sharp mind," she teased impishly. "Though you are definitely handsome and intelligent. And I may be many things, General, but I am *not* a liar."

Rafe chuckled. "No, you aren't and I never meant to imply that you are." His smiled faded as he stared deeply into her eyes. "You are my heart, Rissa. I suffered nine kinds of hell when I realized you had been kidnapped and I was racing around, trying to figure out where you were and who had taken you away from me.

"I have learned to conquer fear for my own safety, in the line of duty. But I tell you truly, Rissa, I was terrified every blasted time I found you face-to-face with disaster," he confided huskily.

She toyed with the lock of raven hair that dangled on his forehead. "Truly? And here I thought you had applauded all those men who tried to send me on a one-way trip to hell and get me out of your life for good."

"Hardly that," he said. "I have never been in love before and I wasn't quite sure what to do about it. I had my life all mapped out, my priorities in perfect order, as precise as the army's regimental routine. And then here you came, like a red-haired cyclone, disrupting all my plans, challenging my rules, defying my commands. How was I supposed to maintain order at this garrison when I couldn't even control a mere wisp of a woman during our constant clash of wills?"

Karissa laughed mischievously as she leaned forward to deliver a smacking kiss to his sensuous lips. "I'm going to let you in on a little secret, General. You're never going to control me and I'm probably not going to march to the beat of your drum. I have run wild and free for too many years. I'm afraid I have developed a strong independent streak.''

He shrugged his broad shoulders. ''Ah, well, I suppose I can deal with that, so long as I have you with me. I discovered this past two weeks that my life wasn't a bit of fun without you in it. I was going to come crawling on my hands and knees to you this evening, as soon as I battled my way through this heap of papers.''

''Really?'' When she smiled, Rafe's heart caved in on itself. ''A general crawling on his hands and knees? Damn, I shouldn't have been so impatient. I would've liked to see that.'' She grinned saucily as she unfastened the buttons on his jacket. ''But better yet, I'd like to see you out of uniform.''

Desire barreled into him like a freight train. His breath stuck in his throat when her hand slid inside his jacket then delved beneath his shirt to make stimulating contact with his flesh. Rafe swept his arm across his cluttered desk, sending papers fluttering to the floor and upending the inkwell. He pulled Karissa down on top of him and kissed her urgently.

''God, I love you, woman. Sass me all you want, but please don't ever leave me, because I need you. You make me happy.''

''How could I leave when you've become the very breath I take, every dream I've ever dreamed?'' she whispered as she held on to him for dear life. ''I thought I could be satisfied if I had a place of my own for the first time in forever. But even that wasn't enough.''

Pulling her closer, Rafe focused his undivided attention on divesting Karissa of her dress and getting his greedy hands all over her luscious body. ''One of these days,'' he said huskily. ''We really should try making love on a bed. This desk isn't going to offer much in the way of comfort.''

She grinned impishly as she peeled off his jacket and shirt. "I've discovered that I'm most *comfortable* when I'm wearing nothing but you."

The thought sent Rafe's self-control flying out the window. He wanted Karissa out of that confining dress and he wanted her out of it *now*. Whatever gentlemanly reserve he was supposed to possess went the same direction as his self-restraint. He sent buttons popping in his haste to have her naked in his arms. He could replace his uniform and her gown, but he couldn't replace or duplicate the sensations that surrendering to his love for her sent crashing down upon him.

His hands and lips were all over her curvaceous body and her hands swept over him. They were urgent and impatient for each other. Downright desperate, in fact. There would be time later for gentle loving and whispered endearments that reaffirmed their commitment to each other. But right now, in the heat of the moment, he needed to be as close to Karissa as a man could get to the woman he loved.

He was too breathless and frantic to bother with finesse. He rolled onto his back and lifted her exactly above him. He held her gaze, mesmerized by the fiery desire in her emerald eyes. When she wrapped her hand around his aroused flesh and guided him to her moist, welcoming heat, immeasurable pleasure burned through him until it melted his soul.

This was what he loved best about Karissa, he thought as he arched into her and she met his driving thrusts with the same mindless impatience. She was as wild and unrestrained as the wind sweeping across the plains. She did nothing halfway. Her passion for life, her feisty tem-

perament, her tenacity and resilience captivated him, bewitched him. She was the sum composite of what a
woman should be—lovely beyond description, lively beyond a man's wildest dreams and generous of heart and
soul.

He had met his match in Karissa, no doubt about that.
She could be the general in their household, as long as
he had her loyalty and devotion, as long as she filled
his nights with incredible lovemaking and his days with
fiery spirit.

When she threw back her head, sending the curly tendrils of living flames cascading around her, and rode him
until she shimmered around him and cried out his name
on a shattered breath, Rafe shuddered in helpless release.
He grabbed a handful of that glorious red hair and drew
her head down to his. He sealed their all-consuming passion for each other with a searing kiss that expressed
what he couldn't find the words—or the breath—to say.

He held her in his arms for the longest time, buried
deep inside her, and realized he'd been a fool for thinking he could settle for the kind of arranged marriage his
parents and grandparents had accepted.

Micah was right. Love made all the difference and
Rafe couldn't be content with anything less than being
hopelessly in love and being loved wholeheartedly in
return.

"What are you thinking?" Karissa murmured as she
nuzzled her face against his neck.

He absently stroked her back. "I was thinking how
much I love you and that I'm never going to be able to
sit down behind this desk without thinking that I would
rather be doing *this* with you instead of signing and
filing a bunch of bureaucratic papers. The sooner I finish
my duties the sooner I can order more lumber and con-

tract the laborers to build a home on your new property.''

Karissa blinked at him in surprise. ''A home?'' she chirped, wide-eyed.

Rafe speared his hands into her hair, letting the flaming tendrils glide through his fingers. ''I'm meeting with John Saxton tomorrow to contract the construction project. I thought we might divide our time between our quarters at the garrison and our new home. After all, I will be able to retire from the military in five years and I was thinking of raising cattle to sell to the army posts in the territory.''

Karissa opened and shut her mouth, but no words came out. Rafe was pleased that he had the honor and distinction of leaving her speechless. It didn't happen often.

Karissa levered up on one elbow to trace the smiling curve of his lips. ''You're doing all this for me?'' she asked, her voice wobbly.

''For us,'' he assured her softly.

''But I thought your goal in life was to attain the rank of general, like your father and grandfather.''

''I've found something intensely more inspiring and satisfying in you. I'm crazy in love with you, Rissa,'' he whispered earnestly. ''And I will be until long past forever. Marry me.''

''I was counting on you to say that, General,'' she murmured. ''I love you like crazy, too, Rafe, and I always will.''

When she kissed him hungrily, the world spiraled into erotic oblivion. This, he knew, was what had been missing in his regimented life—and he hadn't even realized it until he fell deeply, completely in love with this lively green-eyed, red-haired firebrand who challenged him, defied him…and loved him with every beat of her wild heart.

* * * * *

PICK UP THESE HARLEQUIN HISTORICALS AND IMMERSE YOURSELF IN THRILLING AND EMOTIONAL LOVE STORIES SET IN THE AMERICAN FRONTIER

On sale January 2004

CHEYENNE WIFE by Judith Stacy
(Colorado, 1844)

Will opposites attract when a handsome
half-Cheyenne horse trader comes to the rescue
of a proper young lady from back east?

WHIRLWIND BRIDE by Debra Cowan
(Texas, 1883)

A widowed rancher unexpectedly falls in love with
a beautiful and pregnant young woman.

On sale February 2004

COLORADO COURTSHIP by Carolyn Davidson
(Colorado, 1862)

A young widow finds a father for her unborn child—
and a man for her heart—in a loving wagon train scout.

THE LIGHTKEEPER'S WOMAN by Mary Burton
(North Carolina, 1879)

When an heiress reunites with her former fiancée,
will they rekindle their romance or say goodbye
once and for all?

Visit us at www.eHarlequin.com

HARLEQUIN HISTORICALS®

HHWEST29

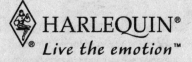

COMING NEXT MONTH FROM

HARLEQUIN HISTORICALS®

- **CHEYENNE WIFE**
  by **Judith Stacy,** the first of three historicals in the *Colorado Confidential* series
  Alone and broke after her father died on a wagon train out west, Lily St. Claire knew her future was bleak. Until North Walker, a half-Cheyenne horse trader, arrived with a bargain for Lily: if she would tutor his sister, North would escort her back to Virginia… unless she lost her heart to him first!
  HH #687 ISBN# 29287-2 $5.25 U.S./$6.25 CAN.

- **THE KNAVE AND THE MAIDEN**
  by **Blythe Gifford,** Harlequin Historical debut
  Sir Garren was a mercenary knight with faith in nothing. Dominica was a would-be nun with nothing but her faith. Though two people could never be more different, as Garren and Dominica traveled across England on a pilgrimage, would they discover that love is the greatest miracle of all?
  HH #688 ISBN# 29288-0 $5.25 U.S./$6.25 CAN.

- **MARRYING THE MAJOR**
  by **Joanna Maitland,** Mills & Boon reprint
  Back from the Peninsular War, Major Hugo Stratton was scarred and embittered, much altered from the young man Emma Fitzwilliam had fantasized about over the years. Now the toast of London society, Emma inflamed Hugo's blood like no other woman. But could this beautiful woman see beyond his scars to the man hidden beneath?
  HH #689 ISBN# 29289-9 $5.25 U.S./$6.25 CAN.

- **WHIRLWIND BRIDE**
  by **Debra Cowan,** Harlequin Historical debut
  Pregnant and abandoned, Susannah Phelps arrived on Riley Holt's doorstep under the assumption that the widowed rancher planned to marry her and make her child legitimate. Problem was, Riley knew nothing of the plan and had no intention of marrying again—especially not a pampered beauty like Susannah!
  HH #690 ISBN# 29290-2 $5.25 U.S./$6.25 CAN.

KEEP AN EYE OUT FOR ALL FOUR OF THESE TERRIFIC NEW TITLES

HHCNM1203